Sanctuary Cove

ROCHELLE ALERS

Sanctuary Cove

A
CAVANAUGH ISLAND
NOVEL

FOREVER

NEW YORK   BOSTON

Copyright © 2012 by Rochelle Alers
Preview of *Cherry Lane* copyright © 2015 by Rochelle Alers
Excerpt from *Angels Landing* copyright © 2012 by Rochelle Alers

Forever
Hachette Book Group
1290 Avenue of the Americas
New York, NY 10104
www.HachetteBookGroup.com

Forever is an imprint of Grand Central Publishing.
The Forever name and logo are trademarks of Hachette Book Group, Inc.

The Hachette Speakers Bureau provides a wide range of authors for speaking events. To find out more, go to www.hachettespeakersbureau.com or call (866) 376-6591.

The publisher is not responsible for websites (or their content) that are not owned by the publisher.

Printed in the United States of America

First printing: January 2012
Reissued: May 2015

10 9 8 7 6 5 4 3 2 1
OPM

A time to weep, and a time to laugh; a time to mourn and a time to dance.

Ecclesiastes 3:4

Sanctuary Cove

Chapter One

◦

Barbara, are you sure you don't mind looking after Whitney and Crystal for the week? You know I can always take them with me."

"Deborah Robinson! Do you realize how many times you've asked the same question and I've given you the same answer? No, I don't mind at all. Now go before you miss your ferry. And no cell phone calls from the car."

"Thanks for everything," Deborah whispered, hugging her friend. "I'll call you from the island."

Deborah ran across the front lawn, jumped into her car, fastened the seatbelt and pulled away from the curb. Smiling at years of happy memories as she drove through the back streets of Charleston, Deborah made it to the pier before sailing time. She drove onto the ferry, turned off the car, and got out to stand at the rail, instantly refreshed by the cool breeze. This time her return to the small community of Sanctuary Cove wouldn't be for a weekend or mini-vacation, but to air out the house she'd inherited from her grandparents in order to make it her home and to look at a vacant store she'd rented where she'd open her bookstore.

Two blasts from the ferry's horn echoed it was time to sail; a man on the pier tossed the thick coil of hemp to another worker on the ferry, freeing it; below deck engines belched, coughed, and rumbled. There came another horn blast and the ferryman deftly steered the boat through the narrow inlet until he reached open water.

Resting her elbows on the rail, Deborah watched as steeples and spires of the many churches rising above the landscape disappeared from view. As the boat headed in a southeast direction she stared at the island shorelines of Kiawah, Seabrook and Edisto Islands before the ferry-boat slowed, chugging slowly and docking at Cavanaugh Island. She was the last one off the boat, and waved to the captain as he tipped his hat.

Driving off the ferry, she felt herself blinking back tears, remembering the last time she'd come here. It had been Thanksgiving and she, Louis and their kids had decided to celebrate the holiday at the Cove rather than in Charleston. Louis never could have imagined as he'd carved turkey that a week later he would become embroiled in a scandal. That he would be seen in a compromising position with one of his female students.

Despite declaring that he was simply comforting her, and there was nothing improper going on between him and the student, Louis Robinson was suspended pending a school board hearing. Tensions and emotions were fever-pitched as Charlestonians formed opposing factions while Louis awaited his fate. Deborah blamed those who were quick to judge her husband for his death, and all of their condolences fell on deaf ears when the truth was finally revealed. The truth had come too late. She'd lost her husband of eighteen years and Whitney and Crystal their father.

Slowing and coming to a complete stop, she reached for a tissue and blotted the tears, praying for a time when the tears wouldn't come without warning, or so easily. It took several minutes, but after taking a few deep breaths, she was back in control.

Stepping on the accelerator, Deborah drove slowly along the paved road, bordered on both sides by palmetto trees and ancient oaks draped with Spanish moss.

She maneuvered onto the quaint Main Street and suddenly felt another rush of sadness, but this one was not personal. Like so many small towns across the United States she realized the Cove was slowly dying. She noticed more boarded-up storefronts; the sidewalks were cracked and even the Cove Inn, a boardinghouse and one of the grandest houses on the island, needed a new coat of white paint.

Deborah drove into the small parking lot behind Jack's Fish House. After only a cup of coffee earlier that morning she needed to eat before throwing herself into the chore of cleaning the house. There were more than a dozen cars in the lot; some she recognized as belonging to local fishermen.

The winter temperature on Cavanaugh was at least ten degrees warmer than in Charleston, so she left her wool jacket in the car. Reaching for her purse she walked up from the lot to the entrance of the restaurant, an establishment that was known for serving some of the best seafood in the Lowcountry.

The familiar interior of Jack's Fish House hadn't

changed in decades. Tables hewn from tree trunks bore the names and initials of countless lovers, ex-lovers, and those who wanted to achieve immortality by carving their names into a piece of wood. Only the light fixtures had changed, from bulbs covered by frosted globes to hanging lamps with Tiffany-style shades. A trio of ceiling fans turned at the lowest speed to offset the buildup of heat coming from the kitchen each time the café doors swung open. The year before the Jacksons had added a quartet of flat screen televisions, primarily for the fishermen who went out at dawn and returned midday with their nets laden with crabs, oysters, and shrimp.

Deborah walked past restaurant regulars and a few strange faces to sit at a round table for two in a far corner. The mouthwatering aromas coming from dishes carried by the waitstaff triggered a hunger she hadn't felt in weeks. She knew she'd lost too much weight, and although she had cooked for Whitney and Crystal, she would take only a few forkfuls of food before feeling full.

Suddenly, a shadow fell over the table and her head popped up. Luvina Jackson, wearing a pair of overalls and a bibbed apron, arms crossed under her ample bosom, gave Deborah a sad smile. Her gray hair was covered with a hairnet. "Stand up, baby, and let Vina hold you. I'm so sorry about Louis."

Deborah couldn't hold back tears as she sank into the comforting softness of Luvina's well-rounded figure. The smell of yeast and lily of the valley wafted in her nostrils, a fragrance Luvina had worn for as long as Deborah remembered.

"Thank you, Miss Vina."

Luvina rocked her back and forth. "You know the

Cove would have turned out for you if you hadn't had a private service."

"I know that, Miss Vina. But I would've lost it if the hypocrites who were so quick to judge Louis would've shown up to pay their so-called respects."

"All you had to do was say the word and we would've been there for you with bells on. Ain't no way we gonna let dem two-face, egg-suckin' vultures hurt one of our own. We would have turned it out."

"Then we all would've been on the front page of *The State* or *The Post and Courier*, not to mention footage on the local television news," Deborah murmured.

"I just want you to know we would have been there for you, baby. How are your kids doing?"

Easing out of her embrace, Deborah met Luvina's eyes. "They're coping as well as they can. But kids are kids and they are much more resilient than grown folks. They're spending the week with friends until school begins again."

"Thank goodness for that. Enough talk. I know you came in here to git somethin' to eat. Whatcha want?"

Deborah smiled. Even though she'd been born and raised in Charleston, coming back to the Cove and listening to the different inflections interspersed with the Gullah dialect made her feel as if she had come home. "Do you have any okra gumbo?"

Luvina's broad dark face, with features that bore her Gullah ancestry, softened as she smiled. "I jest put up a long pot earlier dis mornin'."

Deborah returned Luvina's smile. She liked Jack's okra gumbo because they fried the okra with oil to reduce the slime and added corn to the savory dish. "I'll have a bowl with a couple of buttered biscuits."

"Do you want rice?"

"No, thank you. But I'm going to order something to take home for dinner."

"Whatcha want fo' dinner?"

"Anything that's good, Miss Vina."

Eyes wide, Luvina stared at Deborah. "Now you got to know that everything we makes at Jack's is good. Have you been gone so long that you forgot that?"

"No, ma'am."

"Let me put somethin' together for you. You like oxtails?"

"I love them."

"Good. Then I'll fix you some oxtails with ham hocks. I'll also give you some rice, because you need some meat on your bones. Collards and a slice of my coconut cake should fill you right up."

"That sounds good, Miss Vina."

"Rest yourself and I'll be right back."

When Deborah sat down, closed her eyes and pressed the back of her head to the wall behind her, she realized she was hungry and unbelievably tired. Tired from stress that had worn her down like a steady rush of water over a pile of rocks.

Her parents had come up from Florida for the funeral and had all but begged her to move down there, but Deborah told them she couldn't uproot Whitney and Crystal. Whitney was in his last year of high school, and fifteen-year-old Crystal would have problems adjusting and making friends at a new school. Crystal had taken her father's death much harder than Whitney, who'd grieved in private.

Her musings were interrupted when Luvina's grand-daughter walked over to the table with a large glass of sweet tea and a plate with two biscuits. "Sorry about Mr. Robinson, Miss Deborah. All the kids cried for days when we heard he'd drowned. He was the best math teacher in the whole high school."

Deborah smiled at the girl, who lived on the island but went to high school with her children. "Thank you, Johnetta. How are you?"

"I'm good, Miss Deborah. Right now I'm applying to nursing schools up north, but my momma and daddy don't want me to leave the state, so I have to apply to one here."

"Charleston Southern University has a school of nursing. You can live here while you're taking classes. That would save you a lot of money."

Johnetta smiled, displaying the braces on her teeth. "You're right. I could take the ferry or get my father to drop me off when he goes to work."

"That sounds like a plan."

"Thank you, Miss Deborah. I'm going to go and bring out your food."

Deborah stared at the tall girl, who'd at one time admitted she liked Whitney, but he'd acted as if she didn't exist. She'd wanted to tell Johnetta that Whitney was more interested in sports than he was in a relationship with a girl. It wasn't as if he didn't like girls, but sports and academics were his priority.

Johnetta returned with a bowl of okra gumbo and after the first spoonful Deborah felt as if she'd been revived. The soup was delicious, the biscuits light and buttery and the sweet tea brewed to perfection. She'd tried over and over, but whenever she brewed tea it was either too strong or too weak. Too strong meant adding copious amounts of sugar and too weak made it taste like sugar water.

She finished her lunch and paid the check, reminding Johnetta she'd come back to pick up her takeout order. Leaving Jack's, Deborah strolled along Main Street, stopping to stare through the windows of stores and shops. Grass had sprouted up through the cracks in the sidewalk. There had been a time when there were no cracks and the only thing that had littered the sidewalks or curbs was sand and palmetto leaves. The sand-littered streets added to the charm of the town, but dead leaves and debris were swept away by shopkeepers every morning.

She continued her stroll, turning onto Moss Alley, and then came to a complete stop. Moss Alley was appropriately named because of the large oak draped in Spanish moss on the corner. Shading her eyes, Deborah peered through the glass window of a store that had once been a gift shop. The space wasn't particularly wide, but deep enough for her bookstore. And what made it even more attractive was it had a second floor—space where she could store her inventory.

A flutter of excitement raced through her. It was perfect for The Parlor. It was off the main street, but on the corner where anyone walking or driving by would notice it. With hand-painted letters on the plate-glass, a colorful awning, and furniture resembling a parlor, it would generate enough curiosity to draw in customers.

She walked down the street, stopping at the opposite end of the block. Smiling, she waved through the window of the Muffin Corner at the woman behind the counter, who beckoned her.

She opened the screen door and was met with tantalizing aromas of fruit and freshly made cakes, pies, and donuts. Lester and Mabel Kelly had opened the shop the year before. Both had worked as pastry chefs for a hotel chain, but had tired of the frantic pace of baking for catered parties and returned to the Cove to open the Muffin Corner.

Mabel Kelly flashed a gap-tooth smile when Deborah walked in. Coming from behind the counter, she hugged her. "How's it going, girl?"

Deborah returned the hug. "I'm good."

Pulling back, Mabel narrowed her eyes. She and Deborah were the same age, thirty-eight, but there was sadness in Deborah's eyes that made her appear older. "I'm sorry about Louis, Debs. It's a damn shame folks accused him of something he didn't do, and would never think of doing. I can tell you that folks here were ready to get in their cars and start some mess Charleston hasn't seen in a while."

"I know that, Mabel."

"Is that why you decided to have a private funeral?"

"It was one of the reasons."

"You know I called your house but some woman named Barbara answered. Damn, you thought I was trying to set up a lunch date with President Obama the way she interrogated me. In the end, I told her to let you know I'd called."

"She did, Mabel. And, I do appreciate you calling."

"Can I get you something?"

"No thanks. I just came from Jack's."

Physically Deborah and Mabel were complete opposites. Mabel was barely five foot and had what people call birthing hips, yet she'd never had any children. She said she didn't want any because she'd helped her father raise six younger siblings after her mother got hooked on drugs.

The year she'd turned fourteen her mother had taken the ferry to Charleston to score and never came back. There were reports that someone had seen her in Savannah, strung-out, but it was never confirmed.

The wind chime over the door tinkled musically. "Excuse me, Debs," Mabel whispered. "Let me take care of this customer, then we'll sit and talk." Her smile grew wider. "Afternoon, Asa. Can I get you to sample today's special along with your black coffee with a shot of espresso?"

"No thank you, Mabel. I'll just have coffee," she heard the man reply.

Deborah sat, enjoying the aromas of the shop before her gaze lingered on Mabel's customer. He was a tall, slender, middle-aged black man. Though he was dressed casually in khakis, long-sleeved light-blue button-down shirt, and black leather slip-ons, Deborah couldn't take her eyes off the handsome stranger. He didn't look familiar, so either he was a newcomer, visitor, or tourist. Cavanaugh Island didn't get many tourists during the winter months, but the balmy seventy-degree temperatures attracted a few snow-birds from the northeast and Midwest.

Without warning, he turned and caught her staring. Their gazes met and fused, and they shared a smile. He continued to stare and Deborah couldn't control the rush of heat in her face; she lowered her eyes and didn't glance up again until the wind chime tinkled when the door closed behind the very attractive man.

"I like what you've done with the shop," Deborah said to Mabel when she joined her at the table.

"We don't have a Starbucks here in the Cove, so Lester and I decided to offer something other than regular coffee to go along with the muffins. Business has really picked up since we put in the tables. We mostly get retirees who order their favorite muffin, coffee, and read the newspaper whenever it gets too hot to sit in the square, or during rainy weather. It's a big hit, especially with the snowbirds." Mabel bit her lip. "If it wasn't for the snowbirds businesses in the Cove would really have a hard time staying open."

"It's that bad?" Deborah asked.

"Just say it could be better. Most of us are hanging on by the skin of our teeth, waiting for the summer season. Take Asa Monroe, the man who just left."

"What about him?" she asked. For a reason she couldn't fathom, Deborah wanted to know more about the stranger who unknowingly intrigued her.

"He rents a suite at the Cove Inn, been here about six weeks. He eats lunch at Jack's, sends his laundry out and comes in every day for his black coffee with a shot of espresso. Multiply that by twenty or thirty snowbirds and it's enough revenue to keep small shopkeepers afloat until the summer season."

Deborah nodded. "I noticed a few more vacant stores since the last time I was here."

"The gift shop closed up last month."

"I just rented it."

A beat passed before Mabel said, "You're kidding?"

"No I'm not. I'm moving to the Cove and—"

"Permanently?"

Deborah nodded again. "Yes. I'm also moving my bookstore. I called the chamber and they gave me a listing of the vacant stores. Once I found out the gift shop had closed, I realized it would be perfect. It has more square footage than my Charleston store and having a second floor is a bonus."

Mabel leaned closer. "What about your kids?"

"Nothing's going to change, Mabel, except that they'll live here instead of in Charleston. They'll still go to the same high school and hang out with their same friends."

"What are you going to do with your house on the mainland?"

"I'm putting it up for sale. I know the real estate market is soft," Deborah said quickly when Mabel opened her mouth, "but I'm willing to accept a reasonable offer because I don't want to rent it." She glanced at her watch, then stood up, Mabel rising with her. "I have to get back to the house. I'll drop by again in a couple of days."

"How long are you staying?"

"I'm leaving New Year's Eve. I promised the kids I'd be back in time to bring in the new year with them." Extending her arms, Deborah hugged Mabel.

She left the Muffin Corner, stopping again at the vacant store on Moss Alley that was soon to be the new home of The Parlor bookstore.

Chapter Two

~

Asa Monroe was sitting at a bistro table outside of the Muffin Corner sipping his coffee when he saw the woman with the infectious smile walk out and head in the opposite direction. Her smile was like a ray of sunshine, spreading over her face and lighting up her eyes. And that body...Asa couldn't take his gaze off of her. She was the first woman to intrigue him since his arrival in Sanctuary Cove. As soon as she disappeared from his line of vision, he got up and walked back into the pastry shop, curiosity getting the best of him.

"Can I help you with something else?" Mabel Kelly asked when he dropped the empty cup into a plastic-lined wastebasket, a puzzled expression on her face.

"The lady that was just in here...I—"

"You must be talking about Mrs. Robinson?"

Asa nodded. Mabel referring to her as Mrs. Robinson meant that she was married, even though he'd noticed she hadn't worn a ring. "This is the first time I've seen her. I was wondering if she lives here."

"Deborah," she paused, amusement crossing her features, "just told me that she's moving to the Cove permanently come the first of the year. She and I were what kids nowadays call BFFs. I used to count down the days when school was out for her to come from Charleston to stay on the Cove with her grandmother. And once the summer was over and school started we would cry like we were never going to see each other again."

"Did you ever stop crying?" Asa joked.

Throwing back her head, Mabel laughed. "The year we turned twelve we decided we were too old to cry and stopped."

"Did you stay in touch after summer vacation ended?" Asa didn't know why he continued to question Mabel about Deborah Robinson, because after all she was a married woman.

Mabel nodded. "We designed our own greeting cards with peel-off stickers and mailed them to each other."

"Why didn't you call?"

"I'm one of seven, so with six other kids in the house the phone was always busy, unlike today when kids have their own cell phones."

The tinkling of the wind chime preempted Asa from asking another question. He smiled at Mabel. "Thanks, I'll see you tomorrow." Turning on his heel, he nodded to Eddie Wilkes, editor of the *Sanctuary Chronicle*, the island's biweekly newspaper.

Rather than return to the bench outside, he headed in the direction of the beach. His routine since his arrival on the island had become predictable. After lunch he came to the Muffin Corner for coffee, then spent the next hour strolling along the beach. This was nothing like his demanding lifestyle in Dover, Delaware. Sanctuary Cove had no fast food restaurants, malls, department stores, traffic jams, or even street lights. Life was slow, laid-back and stress-free.

When he'd come to Cavanaugh Island nearly two months ago, Asa wasn't certain what he'd been looking for until he'd checked into the Cove Inn. What he needed was peace. Staring out the window of his suite he saw palmetto trees, a stretch of beach, and the ocean—a landscape so different from the one in the Dover suburb where he'd lived and practiced medicine. Even the air smelled different.

The hardest thing for Asa to get used to was the quiet. As soon as the sun set it was as if Sanctuary Cove went to sleep. Even those who sat on the benches at the town square talked quietly to each other, as if they didn't want disturb the stillness of the evening. He'd heard sounds that were completely foreign to his ears, and when he'd asked someone about roaring noises he was told they came from the alligators in a nearby swamp.

A friend had accused him of running away when he'd closed his medical practice and sold his house. What his friend didn't understand was that he couldn't stay there any longer, not with the memories of his family haunting him relentlessly. It was as if he could still hear his son's childish laughter through the halls, or his wife's knocking on his home office door to tell him dinner was ready. The only time they hadn't sat down to eat as a family was the one night a week when he offered evening hours. A shudder worked its way through Asa, and he shook his head trying to cleanse his mind of the past.

November made it a year since he'd lost his wife and

son in a horrific automobile accident, when the car she'd
been driving skidded off an icy road. A year in which he'd
become a widower and a nomad, traveling from state to
state, city to city while awaiting approval of his application to Doctors Without Borders.

Sanctuary Cove had become just that—a sanctuary—
because it was here that he'd discovered the peace that
had eluded him since that fateful day when he'd lost the
two people he loved most.

Reaching into her handbag, Deborah took out the key
to the vacant storefront that had been mailed to her along
with the executed lease. She unlocked the front door,
leaving it open, and flipped a wall switch. Track lighting
cast a warm glow over the empty space with walls painted
a soft, calming pistachio green.

She had lost track of the number of times she'd been
inside the gift shop, and when she'd spoken to the agent
handling the property she knew unequivocally that she
wanted to rent the store. She'd met with the agent in
Charleston, signed the necessary documents, and written
checks to cover the rent for the first and last month of a
two-year lease. She figured she'd know within two years
if the bookstore would be a success. If not, she would go
out of business and apply for a teaching position at the
local school.

Deborah felt a shiver of excitement as she envisioned
shelves stacked with books, tables, chairs, loveseats, and
floor and table lamps that would reflect the bookstore's
name. There was enough space for the concert piano that
had once belonged to her maternal grandmother, and for
cozy reading corners.

A door at the back led to a staircase. Deborah counted nine steps before she stood on a landing that opened out to a studio-type apartment. An antique iron bed, sans mattress, occupied one corner, a sofa and matching chair filled another; there was an efficiency kitchen with a refrigerator, stove, and sink. A table with two chairs made up the dining area, and when she opened a door she discovered a small bathroom. She touched a wall switch and light from a floor lamp cast a soft glow over the dust-covered floor. Two grimy windows faced Main Street and another two overlooked Moss Alley. The walls were off-white and like those on the first floor appeared as if they had been recently painted.

She opened one more door to a flight of stairs that led down to the rear of the store. The apartment needed a good cleaning, but with a new mattress for the bed and a wardrobe to store clothes it would be in move-in condition should she decide to rent out the space. Closing that door, she walked to the other entrance, leaving the imprint of her shoes in the dust as she descended the staircase to the first floor. Stepping outside, she locked *her* new bookstore and walked back to Jack's Fish House.

About twenty minutes later, Deborah unlocked the door to her house, shouldering it open as she cradled a large paper sack to her chest. Something told her that Luvina had added to her takeout order. The buildup of heat inside the two-story, three-bedroom house was overwhelming. Placing the bags on a table in the narrow entryway, she began opening the windows on the first floor. One window in the dining room resisted her efforts before she remembered it was the one Louis had promised to repair.

She raced up the staircase and opened windows in the bedrooms. An ocean breeze filtered through the screens, gently lifting the sheers; within minutes the scent of salt water had dispelled the slightly musty smell. Five weeks. It'd been five weeks since she'd prepared a meal in the kitchen or slept in the queen-sized bed, but so much had changed in that time that it could have been five years.

Blowing out her breath, she retraced her steps to put away the food she'd ordered from Jack's. She was right. Luvina had added containers of shrimp, nut and apple, and potato salads.

There was also a Styrofoam container with fried chicken and Jack's celebrated poppin' fried shrimp.

"Thank you, Miss Vina," she whispered. It was obvious Luvina wasn't going to let her go hungry.

Deborah opened the refrigerator, storing the containers. Boxes of baking soda had kept it fresh smelling, although she'd also emptied it of all foodstuffs before leaving after the Thanksgiving weekend. The refrigerator had been left running because they'd planned to return to spend Christmas and the school recess on the island.

She mentally outlined what she needed to do, but first things first. She called Barbara to check on her children, and was told they had gone bowling with Barbara's son and daughter. Deborah hung up, not wanting to appear an anxious, clinging mother.

As soon as she ended the call, her cell phone rang. Deborah smiled when she recognized the number on the display. It was the real-estate broker handling the sale of her home. "Hi, Sherilee. Please give me some good news."

"I have very good news. A young couple with twin

boys met your asking price. Believe it or not, I'm sitting here staring at a bank check for the full amount."

"What!"

"You heard me."

"What did they do? Rob a bank?"

"Close," Sherilee crooned. "Her father owns a bank. He wanted her to buy some monstrosity with double-digit rooms, but she'd grown up in what amounts to a mansion and she didn't want that for her children."

Deborah's smile was dazzling. "Good for her *and* good for me." Her house hadn't been on the market two weeks and she had a buyer. That also meant she had to pack up eighteen years of memories. She also had to pack up her store and make arrangements to have the books and shelves transported to Sanctuary Cove. "When do you think we'll close?"

"I'm hoping it will happen within two weeks."

"Whether it happens or not, I'm still moving."

"I understand why you're doing it, Deborah," Sherilee said sadly before continuing. "On a happier note, I also have some more good news. I just handled the sale of a house that belonged to an eighty-eight-year-old woman. Her great-grandchildren found a couple of boxes of old books in a closet, some dating back to the thirties and forties. I immediately thought of you. They were going to throw them out, but I managed to salvage them. They're here in my cubicle if you want them."

Deborah could hardly contain her excitement. "Sherilee, I love you for looking out for me."

"Come on, Deborah. We go way back, and I know you'd do the same for me."

"You know I would," she said with complete sincerity.

Deborah and Sherilee had been roommates at Bennington College. Both were southern girls away from home for the first time, and during their second year they began a friendship that had lasted two decades.

"When are you coming back to Charleston?"

"I'd planned to return New Year's Eve, but it looks like I'm coming back sooner. I have to arrange to have the house and bookstore packed up."

"What are you going to do with your furniture?" Sherilee asked.

"I'm going to take mostly personal items like china, silver, crystal, and a few chairs for the bookstore, and donate the rest. I'll red tag everything I'm taking to the Cove, so if there is something you want feel free to take it."

"I have a former client who lost practically everything in a house fire. Would you mind if I picked up some things for her?" Sherilee asked. "What makes things so difficult is that she just went through a very nasty divorce and her ex won't give her one penny above what he pays for child support."

The house on the Cove was fully furnished; she'd had the plumbing and wiring updated and had replaced all the floors two years ago. The refrigerator, washer, and dryer were less than a year old and only one window in the dining room needed repair.

"As soon as I get back and inventory the house she can come over and pick out what she needs."

"God bless you, Deborah."

Again a rush of tears filled her eyes. She wiped them away with the back of her hand. "He has, Sherilee. I'll call you when I get back to Charleston." She ended the call before breaking down completely.

During the moments when she didn't wallow in self-pity, Deborah realized although she'd lost her husband she was grateful she still had her children. Her own mother had miscarried three times before she was able to carry to term, resulting in Deborah's birth. Pearl Williams had tried again to have another child, but when she miscarried a fourth time she opted for a hysterectomy.

Bringing her legs up, Deborah rested her feet on the edge of the chair, buried her head on her knees, and cried. She cried for what was and would never be again. She cried until she was spent, then got up and went into the half-bath off the kitchen to splash cold water on her face. No more crying, no more self-pity. She had to be strong for herself and her children. They were depending on her to take care of them and she would. It was something she'd promised the first time she'd held her son and daughter in her arms.

Later, lying in bed, Deborah's mind continued to wander, making her restless. Rolling over onto her belly she closed her eyes, willing sleep to claim her tired mind and exhausted body. She counted slowly, reaching one hundred sixty-three, and she was still wide awake. After tossing and turning restlessly, she got out of bed and went downstairs to make a cup of hot chocolate. The warm liquid managed to relax her enough that when she got back into bed she fell asleep within minutes of her head touching the pillow.

"What are you doing, Barbara?" Deborah asked when she was practically pushed out the door. She'd gotten up early to make the trip to Charleston and pick up the kids from Barbara's house, but barely had a chance to ring the bell before Barbara's front door flew open.

"Keep your voice down. We have to talk—at your house. Please."

She'd never known her friend to plead for anything, and there was a look in her eyes that indicated something was wrong. "Okay."

Moments later, Deborah sat opposite Barbara on matching loveseats in her family room. "You want *me* to tell *your* husband that I'm inviting you and your children to Sanctuary Cove for New Year's Eve?"

Barbara nodded, a wealth of salt-and-pepper twists moving around her round face with the motion. The registered nurse had begun graying at nineteen and now at forty was almost completely gray. "My numbskull of a husband is talking about hosting an open house get-together at our place. And, you know who he wants to invite?"

Deborah rolled her eyes upward. "Don't tell me some of the high school teachers?"

"Exactly. I don't know what Terrell was thinking about. He knows I'd invited you to spend the holiday with us."

Clasping her hands between her denim-covered knees, Deborah leaned forward. Terrell Nash was a guidance counselor and assistant football coach at the same school where Louis had taught math. "It's not the end of the world, Barbara. I can stay home."

"No!"

"Yes!"

"I'm not going to let you stay home by yourself. It's too soon."

"Too soon for what? And what are you afraid of, Barbara? That I'm going to become unhinged and harm myself because this will be the first New Year's Eve in twenty years that I'll spend alone?" Biting her lip, Barbara nodded. "Don't worry about me. I'll be all right."

"There's no way I'm going to suck up to a bunch of fake-ass people because they just happen to work with my husband. I've been trying to change his mind. The only consolation is he still hasn't called anyone to invite them to drop in for drinks and hors d'oeuvres."

"Not dealing with Louis's former colleagues is my choice. It shouldn't be yours."

"I made it mine, Deborah, when some of them got in my face because I'd defended Louis. And now my husband wants to invite these hypocrites into my home. What .the hell is he thinking?" Barbara enunciated each word. "And you know how my kids love going to Sanctuary Cove."

Deborah stared at her friend. If she'd had a sister she would've wanted her to be Barbara Nash. She didn't know what she would've done if her neighbor hadn't run interference for her when members of the press camped outside her door, seeking photographs of her and her children once the girl whom Louis was allegedly involved with had revealed she was pregnant. Barbara had called her police officer brother, who had threatened the media with trespassing if they didn't leave Deborah's property. And it was Barbara who fed Whitney and Crystal when Deborah couldn't get out of bed, and Barbara who had been with her when she went to the morgue to identify Louis's body.

"Okay. I'm officially inviting you and your family to Sanctuary Cove for the New Year's weekend. We'll take my car and Whitney's. That way you won't have to pay the outrageous parking permit fee."

Barbara's light brown eyes sparkled like newly minted copper pennies, and a smile spread across her tawny brown face. "I've already shopped for food, so I'll pack up everything in cooler chests and bring it along."

"Do you think Terrell will go along with this?"

"All he has to hear is 'Sanctuary Cove' and he's in the car ready to go."

Deborah nodded. It was Wednesday and it'd been two days since she'd spoken to Sherilee. She would've spent the week on the Cove, but had decided to come back to Charleston earlier than Friday to start packing up the house. "We'll leave Friday morning after noon."

Deborah sat staring at the photos on the fireplace mantle after she heard the door close behind her neighbor. The house was eerily silent without Crystal and Whitney. Whenever they were home the refrigerator door opened and closed like an accordion, music spilled out from ear buds and clatter filled the kitchen, since they preferred doing their homework at the dining table instead of at the desks in their bedrooms. The instant Deborah announced dinner was ready the books would disappear and together they'd wash up and set the table.

She stood up when she heard a door slam, then Whitney's voice, deep and resonant. When had it changed? "Whitney. I'm in the family room."

"Aunt Barbara told me you were back. I thought you weren't coming home until Friday." Tall and broad shouldered, seventeen-year-old Whitney had grown into a fine young man. He'd inherited his mother's fine features and hair texture. Leaning down, he kissed his mother's cheek, then folded his long frame down opposite her.

"Um, Whitney, did you actually buy jeans with ripped knees?"

"Yep. They're awesome."

"Oh...well."

"Is it true we're going to the Cove for New Year's?"

"Yes, Whitney. I thought it would be nice to bring in the New Year there."

He smiled and an elusive dimple shown in his right cheek. "I think it would be nice if we moved there now."

"I'm shocked you don't want to wait until the house is sold."

"Why are you so surprised, Mom? It's not as if we have to sell this house before we can move into Grandma's."

"Go get Crystal and tell her to pack enough clothes to last the weekend and all of next week. You do the same. When we drive Aunt Barbara and her family back you can bring anything you want to use on the Cove."

Whitney stood and gave his mom a firm hug and kiss. "Thanks, Mom."

Deborah pounded his hard back. "You're very welcome, Whit. Now, go and tell Crystal to come home and pack," she repeated when he finally released her.

Pushing to her feet, she walked over to the window overlooking the flower garden she'd begun the year Crystal was born. Each year for the past fourteen she had added another variety of flowers on Crystal's birthday. She sighed, realizing the ritual would end when they moved.

Celebrations would continue, but not in Charleston.

Chapter Three

"Welcome to the new Parlor Bookstore!"

Deborah opened the door, flipped the light switch, and stood aside to allow Barbara, Crystal, and thirteen-year-old Janelle Nash to enter the space that was to become her bookstore. Terrell, his son Nate, and Whitney were on their way to Jack's to reserve a table for their pre–New Year's Eve dinner. She had decided not to head over to the Abundant Life Church for the night watch service.

"What do you think?" Deborah could barely hide her excitement.

"It smells nice, Mom," Crystal said, hugging Deborah.

Deborah gave her daughter a tender smile. "Thank you."

"Can we look around, Mom?" Crystal asked.

Deborah shared a glance with Barbara, who nodded. "Yes. But be careful when you go upstairs. There's a light switch on the right wall. Make certain you turn it on before you go up."

"So, it's real," Barbara stated in a quiet tone.

Deborah nodded. "It's very real. I didn't tell you, but I have a buyer for the house. A young married couple with twin boys and they're paying cash."

"Damn! What are they into? Drugs?"

"Be nice, though I have to admit I thought they robbed a bank at first," she chided. "Her father just happens to own one."

Looping her arm through her soon-to-be ex-neighbor's arm, Deborah steered Barbara to the door that led to the upstairs apartment. Crystal and Janelle were already there peering through the windows she'd spent time cleaning.

"Oh, how charming," Barbara intoned. "Once the kids are off to college, you could certainly live up here."

"Or it could be my first apartment if I decide to go to college in Charleston," Crystal announced.

Janelle gave Crystal an incredulous stare. "Why would you need your own apartment if you already live in a house?"

Crystal returned the stare. "Once you go to college you need your own place."

"Hello!" shouted a man from the first floor.

"Wait here," Deborah told the others as she headed for the stairs. "Who is it?" she called out, walking down the staircase as quickly as she could without falling.

"Is that you, Deborah?"

Standing in the middle of the store was Jeffrey Hamilton, sheriff of Cavanaugh Island. Tall, dark, and handsome, the ex-Marine captain had managed to evade the advances of every single woman on the island since he'd returned to the Cove. He'd moved in with his grandmother, assuming the duties of sheriff after his predecessor retired.

Resting her hands at her waist, Deborah gave him a warm smile. "Hey, Jeff."

Taking a step and extending his arms, he pulled her close. "Hey yourself, beautiful." He sobered and kissed her forehead. "I'm sorry to hear about Louis. He was an incredible human being."

Deborah kissed Jeffrey's smooth cheek. "Thanks."

"How are your kids doing?"

"Coping." The single word spoke volumes.

Jeffrey released her, his dark eyes meeting hers. "I was just patrolling the area when I saw the light and open door. I thought some kids who couldn't get off the island decided to raise a little hell and break in and leave their tags."

Her eyebrows lifted a fraction. "We have a graffiti problem?"

"No. Not yet. What we're trying to do is stop it before it becomes a problem. A few of the fisherman have found tags scrawled on their boats. As soon as they paint over them the vandals strike again, then move to another location. I had the town council install cameras here on the Cove, but the folks in Angels Landing and Haven Creek claim they don't want the law monitoring their every move."

"They've always been a strange lot."

Jeffrey smiled, lines fanning out around his large, deep-set eyes. "Don't you mean *breed*?"

"Don't even go there, Jeff," Deborah admonished. "My grandmother used to give me the *look* whenever I mentioned wanting to visit the other parts of the island to see if they were the same as the Cove. I guess she got tired of me asking when she told me that some of the people who lived there had tails and cloven hooves like goats. I had nightmares for years until I saw someone from Angels Landing and the only thing I found strange was the contrast of his light-gray eyes and his very dark skin."

"What are you doing in here?" Jeffrey asked, deftly changing the topic.

"I'm renting this space. It's going to be the new location for my bookstore. And before you ask I'm going to tell you that I'm moving to the Cove!"

Jeffrey's expression was sincere as he gently patted Deborah on the back. "Good for you. How about your son and daughter? How do they feel about leaving Charleston?"

"Let's just say they're not crying about leaving."

"Good for them. I'll leave..." His words trailed off as a woman followed by two giggling teenage girls joined them. Deborah made the introductions, Jeffrey shaking each hand and wishing them health, peace, and happiness for the coming year. He touched the bill of his baseball cap, turned on his heel, and continued his patrol of the downtown district.

"We'll meet you at Jack's!" Crystal called as she and Janelle took off running.

Barbara raised her hand. "Don't—"

"It's all right," Deborah interrupted, turning off the lights and locking the front door. "Nothing's going to happen. Jeff's going that way, so I'm certain he'll keep an eye on them."

As they headed toward Jack's, Deborah nodded to longtime residents as they strolled leisurely along Main Street. They'd reached the town square with its huge fountain and statue of patriot militia General Francis Marion atop a stallion, standing more than thirty feet high. It was the tallest structure on the island. The fountain was empty, but during the summer months people threw coins into the flowing water with the hope their wishes would come true. Stone and wrought-iron benches were crowded with revelers and those taking advantage of the comfortable nighttime temperatures. There was enough space on one of the wrought-iron benches for them to sit together.

Deborah stared at the line outside of Jack's, waving to Crystal and Janelle when they turned in their direction. Janelle tugged on her father's arm, pointing. It appeared as if half of the Cove had turned out to eat at Jack's before attending the night watch service.

Barbara also waved to the girls and her husband when he raised his arm. "How long will it be before we can get a table?"

"Probably about twenty minutes, judging from the length of the line."

Deborah saw the man who had been in the Muffin Corner the first day she'd returned to the Cove. He sat a short distance away on a stone bench. Their eyes met and again they shared a smile. "Happy New Year, Mr. Monroe."

He nodded. "Happy New Year to you, too."

"Who is *that*?" Barbara asked sotto voce.

Deborah leaned closer to Barbara, while shifting her gaze to an elderly couple. "His name is Asa Monroe, and he's a snowbird."

"He's delicious," Barbara whispered again.

Deborah chanced a surreptitious glance at the man, who was sitting with one leg crossed gracefully over the other. He appeared totally relaxed, his right arm stretched out over the back of the bench he shared with a trio of teenagers.

"He is handsome," she agreed. And he was. Asa's smooth skin, even features, salt-and-pepper cropped hair made him strikingly handsome, while he possessed an elegant sophistication some men spent their entire lives striving to perfect.

"When did you meet him?" Barbara asked, continuing with her questioning.

"We were never formally introduced." Deborah told Barbara about seeing Asa when he'd walked into the Muffin Corner.

"Don't look now, but he's staring at you."

"Stop it, Babs."

Barbara smiled. "It's been a while since you've called me that."

Deborah exhaled audibly. "It's been a while since I've felt this relaxed."

"Are you relaxed enough to start over again?" Barbara asked.

"What are you talking about?"

Barbara covered Deborah's hand with hers, gently squeezing her fingers. "I know you just lost your husband, but that doesn't mean you have to stop living and loving. You're only thirty-eight and your son is seventeen. In eight months he'll be off to college. And in another three years it will be Crystal. You'll be what—forty-one or two—still a young woman who has the other half of her life in front of her. Do you plan to live it alone?"

"How can you talk about me hooking up with a man when I buried my husband exactly four weeks ago today?"

"I'm not talking about you hooking up with a man, Debs. I just want you to keep your options open. If a man shows an interest in you, I don't want you to give him a screw face. Be nice," she continued, her voice lower, softer. "There's nothing wrong with going to dinner with him or even inviting him over for coffee."

Deborah knew Barbara was right. In another three years she would be in her early forties and alone. Both her children would be in college and she would encounter the empty-nest syndrome for the first time. "I'll think about it. But there is something I need to tell you about myself, but that will have to wait until we're alone."

Barbara nodded, then stood up. "Terrell is signaling us it's time to go in."

She also rose to her feet, and when she turned she saw that Asa was no longer there. They were ushered inside Jack's Fish House. To say the place was humming and jumping was an understatement. Every table was occupied and the noise level was ear-shattering. The muted televisions were turned to different stations, showing pre-holiday entertainment, and the platters of fried catfish, buttery, sweet cornbread, black-eyed peas, and rice made her mouth water.

Deborah did get to see Asa again, this time inside Jack's when he was seated at a table for six. She didn't recognize any of the other four men or the one woman at his table. The Cove was only three square miles with a permanent resident population of eight hundred, and that translated into everyone knew everyone—if not by name then by sight.

She thought about Mabel's statement about the monies snowbirds spent that helped to sustain the mom-and-pop businesses throughout the winter season until the horde of tourists swelled the population to more than two thousand throughout the summer. Deborah knew it was risky opening a business in the Cove when so many were closing, but she had a slight advantage. The Parlor would be the only bookstore on Cavanaugh Island.

What she didn't want to think about was *not* making a go of her bookstore, and also of Asa Monroe—a stranger who had managed to intrigue her. She knew nothing about him other than his name, but there was something in the way he stared that made Deborah feel slightly off-balance. The last time that had happened was twenty years ago when she'd met Louis Robinson.

Asa Monroe half-listened to the conversations floating around the table as he pretended to concentrate on the food on his plate. He sat with guests who were also living at the Cove Inn for the winter. He hadn't wanted to join them, but it was either share their table or wait hours until a table for one was available.

As the diners chattered around him, Asa stole surreptitious glances at the woman he'd first seen at the Muffin Corner, now seated a few tables away. He didn't know anything else about her other than what Mabel had told him, but there was something about this mystery woman he mentally referred to as Sunshine that drew him to her like a powerful magnet. Her smile was mesmerizing, her sultry drawl hypnotic. Deborah Robinson was also the first woman in the two months since he'd come to Cavanaugh Island that piqued his interest. And in a town as small as Sanctuary Cove, Asa loathed asking too many questions about her. After all, he was a snowbird, a transient, and although he'd been warmly welcomed by everyone he didn't want to raise a red flag when he made it known he was interested in a woman who could be married. The first thing Asa had noticed was she wasn't wearing a ring, but neither had he when he'd been married.

Asa speared another forkful of seafood rice, enjoying the piquant blend of bacon, onion, pepper, garlic, crabmeat, oysters, and shrimp. His expression softened noticeably when Sunshine draped an arm over a teenage girl's shoulders and then pressed a kiss to her hair.

She has to be her daughter, he mused. Asa knew the boy sitting opposite Sunshine was her son, because of their striking resemblance. He'd inherited her golden-brown coloring, the expressive black arching eyebrows, and even the shape of her eyes. He had usually never been one to engage in people-watching. But observing Sunshine was something Asa enjoyed and looked forward to doing again and again.

Reaching for his mug of beer, he held it aloft when Sunshine glanced in his direction. Holding her gaze, he winked at her then took a deep swallow. A smile crinkled the skin around Asa's eyes when Sunshine's jaw dropped. He was hard-pressed not to laugh when he noticed she had raised her glass of tea in a silent toast. He mouthed *Happy New Year*, and he wasn't disappointed when Sunshine inclined her head in acknowledgment.

Chapter Four

"Why aren't you asleep, Mom?"

"Why aren't you asleep, Whit?" Deborah asked, answering her son's question with one of her own. "It's after three."

Whitney stood by the doorway to the screened-in back porch in a tank top and pajama pants, staring at the flickering black-and-white images on the television. She'd muted the sound and closed captions appeared on the large flat-screen that sat on a stand on an oaken pedestal table.

Deborah had continued a tradition begun after her parents had introduced her to the fantasy/science fiction television show made popular in the late fifties; she'd watched six half-hour episodes of the New Year's all-day marathon of *The Twilight Zone.*

"I got up to get some water and saw that Janelle and Crystal weren't in their room."

Deborah had given Terrell and Barbara her bedroom, while Janelle shared Crystal's bedroom and she'd paired

Nate with Whitney. She'd bedded down on the queen-size convertible sofa on the back porch.

"They're under the covers." She smiled, gesturing to the bumps on the far side of the sofa bed. "They claim this episode is too scary to watch."

When Whitney entered the porch he saw what his mother was talking about. "Oh, this is the one with the talking doll." He flopped down on a cushioned rocker. One of the bumps moved under the quilt. "I loved this one, especially when Talky Tina tells the little girl's stepfather, 'My name is Talky Tina and I don't think I like you.'"

"Hush, Whit. The girls can hear you," Deborah chastised. "Why do you think I muted the sound?"

"I can't understand why they're freaking over a silly looking doll. Now, if they were afraid of the seed of Chucky I'd see why they would hide under the covers."

"That's enough talk about demonic dolls," Deborah whispered even though she'd unmuted the sound as the episode ended. "The girls don't play with dolls anymore, but they still have their collections." Placing a finger over her lips, she winked at Whitney. "Girls, it's over." Their heads emerged from under the pile of quilts. "I think it's time you go back to your bedroom."

Crystal gave her mother a sorrowful look. "Mom, please. Just until six o'clock."

"No, Crystal. You have to get enough rest because I want you and your brother to clean out the trunks in the crawl space. Something the two of you were supposed to have done over the Thanksgiving weekend."

"Can't it wait until next weekend?"

Deborah didn't want to get into a debate with her

daughter. Each and every time she asked Crystal to do something there was always a squabble because Crystal's mantra was *what you don't want to do today can be done tomorrow*. "No, it can't. You know this house is smaller than the one in Charleston, and if there is something you want and it doesn't fit in your bedroom, then it can be stored in the crawl space. If you don't clean it out and there's no room then I will donate your things to charity. Now, please get up, go to your bedroom, and go to sleep."

Crystal went still, her gaze shifting from her mother to Janelle. "Okay, Mom."

Deborah extended her arms, kissing her daughter's cheek, then Janelle's. "Sleep tight—"

"And don't let the bedbugs bite," the two girls chorused.

"I'm going back to bed, too." Whitney pushed off the rocker. Closing the distance between them, he leaned down and dropped a kiss on Deborah's hair. "Good night. Or, should I say, good morning."

"Good morning, Whit."

Waiting until she was alone, Deborah stared at the television, thinking about her new life ahead. As a widow and a single mother she would have to balance running her business with taking care of her home, because now she wouldn't have Louis to pick up the slack. He had always left home at six-thirty to work with students who needed extra help and usually returned before the bus dropped Crystal and Whitney off from school. Her Charleston-based bookstore was open Tuesday through Saturday from ten to six. Thursday was the late night when she stayed open until eight. Most days Deborah prepared dinner, set aside in oven-proof dishes with cooking instructions, and when she didn't Louis and Crystal had concocted gourmet dinners that rivaled those served in upscale restaurants.

When she opened the bookstore on Sanctuary Cove, Deborah realized she would have to hire an assistant. She was certain she would be able to get a retiree or a college student to cover the store when she had to take care of things at home. Her children didn't need a babysitter, but they did require supervision. Although she hadn't had a problem with Whitney and Crystal becoming involved with drug use or underage drinking, she didn't want to present them with the opportunity to experiment if they were left unsupervised. Deborah was a firm believer in little children, little problems. Big children, big problems. And she was firm and uncompromising when it came to no kids in the house without a parent present, and no entertaining in their bedrooms.

Her children weren't perfect, but at least she hadn't had to bail them out of jail or send them to rehab. What they hadn't known was she'd worn out her knees praying they would reach adulthood without making mistakes that would impact negatively on their futures.

She had not known when she recorded Whitney's birth in her journal that seventeen years later she and Louis would not attend his high school graduation together, or see him off to college. Over the years Deborah had recorded entries in her journal: chronicling births, deaths, earning her graduate degree, opening the bookstore, Whitney getting his driver's license, and Crystal making the cheerleading squad.

When Barbara had suggested she join her children in their grief counseling sessions, Deborah's response was she didn't need a counselor when she had her journals in which to record her innermost thoughts. However, she'd told her friend a half-truth. The last entry she'd written was on the day Louis died.

> December 4th—The police came to the house today to tell me Louis had drowned. They haven't recovered his body, so there is still hope that he will be found alive.

Her journal was in the drawer of the bedside table at the house in Charleston. She made a mental note to bring it to Sanctuary Cove to record all that had happened since that tragic day in early December. She watched two more episodes of the marathon, then turned off the television and settled down on the pile of pillows cradling her shoulders. It was a new year and she'd made only one resolution, and that was to make the transition of relocating from Charleston to Sanctuary Cove as uneventful as humanly possible.

"Mom, look what we found in the last trunk!"

Crystal's strident tone shattered the quiet in the kitchen. Deborah, who'd spent the past half hour sitting at the kitchen table, drinking coffee, and flipping through the pages of magazines, stared at her daughter. The household hadn't begun to stir until noontime. Deborah had awakened as slivers of sunlight pierced the fabric of the woven blinds that covered the porch's windows and French door. Somehow she forced herself to remain in bed until ten, then showered in the half-bath off the kitchen. As she was cleaning up the family room Barbara came to tell her she was planning to prepare brunch.

Deborah hadn't wanted to think about food—not after all she'd consumed the night before. She had made certain to sample every dish, unable to believe the quality of the food hadn't diminished in all the years she'd eaten at Jack's. This morning, while everyone ate slices of sweet smoked ham, grits, eggs, and biscuits, she'd drunk two cups of coffee with a serving of soft-scrambled eggs. Another one of her resolutions should be to cut back on her coffee consumption. Lately, she'd been drinking at least four cups a day when normally one or two would suffice.

After brunch Barbara and Terrell had taken Whitney's car for a tour of Cavanaugh Island, leaving Deborah to savor a few moments of solitude. Although the island was only eight square miles, with a total population of approximately twenty-three hundred, there were unpaved roads with no markers and people had been known to get lost for hours.

"What did you find, sweetheart?"

Crystal, cradling a plastic envelope filled with letters and newspaper clippings, spilled the contents on the table. "Whitney has more."

Picking up a letter, Deborah recognized her grandmother's neatly slanting writing. She smiled. The letter was addressed to James Williams, while the return address read Sallie Ann Payne. Payne had been her grandmother's maiden name. She counted more than twenty letters. "How many does Whitney have?" she asked Crystal.

"These are journals," Whitney said as he entered the kitchen with six hard-covered books. "They belonged to Grandma Sallie."

Crystal picked up an envelope. "Can we read them? We finished emptying all the trunks," she added quickly.

Deborah knew Crystal and Whitney had spent the better part of two hours going through four steamer trunks filled with old quilts, hardcover books, and sets of dishes, and another filled with sweet-grass baskets. Everything was neatly packed and stored in plastic to ward off mildew in the tropical heat. Whitney had carried the empty trunks down the ladder that led to the crawl space and placed them on the front porch to air out, while their contents were stacked in an area off the kitchen that doubled as a pantry.

"You can read the newspaper articles," Deborah said. She didn't want her children to read their great-grandmother's letters or journals until she read them. Perhaps there was something in them that wasn't appropriate.

Whitney flopped down on a chair at the table and began unfolding the clippings. "Some of these are real old." He held up a clipping that had yellowed with age.

Deborah smiled again. "Your Grandma Sallie read everything. Remember, when she grew up the radio and newspapers were her only link with the outside world."

Crystal scrunched up her nose. "Mom, how did everyone get along without a computer and texting?"

"Quite well, thank you."

"How did you talk to your friends?" she asked.

Deborah's eyebrows lifted with her daughter's query. "I picked up the telephone and called them."

"What about Grandma Pearl?"

"She, too, picked up a phone and called her friends. However, Grandma Sallie told me she didn't get a telephone until the mid-1950s, when the island was wired for telephone service. If she had to contact someone in an emergency she would go to the store that's now the pharmacy and post office, where the telegrapher would send a telegram to someone on the mainland."

"What about television?" Whitney asked.

"My grandmother always had a television. It was nothing like the thin flat-screen high-definition ones we have today, but I can remember watching soap operas with her during the summer months when she wasn't teaching."

Deborah watched Crystal tunnel her hands through her short hair, and then lift it with her fingertips. Crystal was a much softer feminine version of her late father, but Deborah wished she would let her hair grow out a little longer so she could style it differently.

Whitney stared at the article's headline. "This says that Grandma Sallie was the first Negro teacher to integrate the Cove's white school. She never mentioned anything to us about it."

Crystal stopped touching her hair. "You didn't have a problem when you came here as a young girl, did you Mom?"

Reaching across the table, Deborah rested her hand atop Crystal's. "Why are you asking questions about the Cove? Are you having second thoughts about moving here permanently?"

"No. We like it here," Whitney answered, speaking for himself and his sister. "It's just that you never told us what it was like for you to spend your summers here."

"Whenever I tried talking to you about it you claimed you didn't want to hear about what I did back in the day. All you were interested in was playing with your friends and hanging out on the beach."

Crystal affected a sheepish expression. "We want to hear about it now."

Deborah leaned back in her chair. "I can remember coming to the Cove the summer I celebrated my fourth birthday. I used to get up early, put on a pair of boots, then go to gather eggs from the chicken coop for Grandpoppa's breakfast before he went out in his boat. I'd watch my grandmother make lunch for him, and then she would make breakfast for us. After that it was working in the garden before the sun got too hot."

Crystal's eyes grew larger. "How far was the coop from the house?"

"It was far enough away from the house so we didn't have to smell it," Deborah answered with a laugh. "Grandpoppa had put up a large structure made of wire like those on the window screens to keep out unwanted critters and to keep the chickens safe when they were out in their yard. Even the bugs couldn't get through. We'd had problems with snakes stealing the eggs and foxes eating the chickens."

Deborah told them about planting, weeding, and harvesting homegrown vegetables. Then the canning process began. The best part was seeing the many labeled jars lining the pantry shelves. "We had and still have a lot of fruit trees on this property and Grandmomma would gather apples, pears, cherries, and peaches to make jellies, preserves, and marmalade."

With wide eyes, Crystal clutched her mother's hand. "Mom, can I go fruit-picking and put up a garden?"

"You may, but only after I get someone to cut back the underbrush. I don't want to think of what may be hiding under a pile of leaves."

Crystal rolled her eyes upward. "I'm not afraid of snakes."

"You don't have to be afraid of them," Deborah countered, "but I still don't want you bitten by one—especially if it is venomous. You could die before we could get you to the mainland, even if you were airlifted there. I'll ask Hannah Forsyth if she knows of anyone willing to do some yard work."

"Isn't Ms. Forsyth the librarian?" Whitney questioned.

"Yes, and she's also the island historian. She knows everyone on the island, and if you want or need something she's the one to go to. I'll also let her know I want to clear some land for a garden. Just what do you intend to plant?"

Crystal pulled her lower lip between her teeth. "I don't know yet."

"You're going to have to know," Deborah said quietly, "because if you want to put in collards or watermelon you'll need to have enough room for them to grow without choking the other veggies. My grandmother divided her garden into sections for tomatoes and peppers because they grew on stakes. Another section was for leaf vegetables: collards, green and white cabbage, kale, and lettuce. Peppers and tomatoes were together as were root vegetables like carrots, beets, and turnips. That left green and wax beans, cucumbers, and melons. And you can still find the strawberries, raspberries, and blackberry bushes right before you get to the fruit trees."

"Can I put in an herb garden?"

A beat passed before Deborah said, "If you commit to putting in a garden, then I don't want you to be so consumed with it that you neglect your schoolwork. And don't forget you have cheerleading—"

"I can do it, Mama. Please say it's okay."

The last time Crystal had called her Mama was when

she'd been told that her father had died. It was the only word she'd been able to utter as she cried herself to sleep, with Deborah lying beside her and comforting her whenever she woke to begin crying again. It was a full sixty seconds before Deborah said, "Okay, Crystal. But if your grades slip, then I'll pay someone to oversee the garden."

"They won't," she promised.

Whitney folded the newspaper clipping, placing it gently back into the plastic envelope and securing the clasp. "Did you make any friends?" He and Crystal were familiar with the high school students who lived on Cavanaugh Island, but didn't hang out with them.

"Yes. Mabel Davis, who lived down the road from here, and I were thick as thieves. You rarely saw one of us without the other. She's now Mabel Kelly and she and her husband own the Muffin Corner near Moss Alley. The Davises had several horses and Mabel and I would ride them down to the beach and race each other along the sand."

Whitney and Crystal shared a glance. "You never told us you could ride a horse," he said.

"You never asked, son. The highlight of my summers was when my grandfather took me with him when he went out before dawn to drop his nets and traps for shrimp, oysters, crabs, and lobsters. The first time I boarded the boat I nearly gagged from the lingering smell of fish, then after a while it was like the most expensive perfume. The only time I freaked out was when they caught a squid."

Resting her elbows on the table, Crystal leaned closer. "What did they do with it?"

"It was sold to a fish store in Charleston where it was tenderized and cut up for calamari. Most of grandfather's catch was sold to fish stores on the mainland, and some to Jack's Fish House. The rest Grandmomma stored in the freezer. We usually had fried chicken or baked ham for Sunday dinner, and pork on special occasions. But fish played a big part in our daily diet."

Crossing his arms over his chest, Whitney leaned back on his chair. "Didn't you get tired of eating fish?"

"Never. We had fried shrimp, garlic shrimp, fried crabs, crab cakes, broiled lobster, and shrimp and grits, Frogmore stew, shrimp and crab gumbo—and then there were the fish salads and soups. My favorite dish was jambalaya with shrimp and ham." Deborah smiled. "I have my grandmother's recipe," she said in singsong.

Crystal jumped up, nearly upsetting her chair when she raced over to a drawer under the countertop to get a pen and paper. "What ingredients do you need?" she said, her voice rising in excitement.

Deborah's expressive eyebrows lifted a fraction. "Do you intend to make it?"

"No, Mom. I want you to make it for next Sunday's dinner."

"And, what makes you think I can duplicate my grandmother's recipe?"

"Stop playing," Whitney drawled. "You know you can cook even if you don't like to."

Her son was right. She was a more than adequate cook, but had much preferred to let Louis do the cooking. "Okay. Next Sunday's dinner will be jambalaya with shrimp and ham."

Deborah didn't want to be reminded that next Sunday would be the first time since Louis's drowning they would sit down together for dinner as a family in this house. It had taken a month, and she was ready to start life anew; this time without her husband. And if she hadn't had her children Deborah knew she would've continued to wallow in a maelstrom of self-pity. She knew she had to be strong not only for herself but also for Crystal and Whitney, because they still were dependent upon her for emotional *and* physical support.

Chapter Five

"Are you certain you don't want me to drop you off?"

Deborah picked up the fob for her car. "Very certain, Whit."

"It's not going to be a problem, Mom. You can call me when the meeting is over and I'll come and pick you up."

"I'll see you later," she said over her shoulder as she walked out the front door, closing it behind her.

It had taken Deborah less than a week to figure out what her children were up to. She was certain they were attempting to keep an eye on her lest she'd undergo an emotional meltdown.

They hadn't seen her cry or get hysterical and they wouldn't. What they didn't know was that she did cry. She cried at night, in bed and in the shower, or when she locked herself in the bathroom to take a bubble bath. She cried until spent or until dry heaves made breathing difficult.

With the end of the New Year's holiday weekend, she had returned to Charleston to supervise the dismantling of her bookstore, and to confer with a moving company to pack up the contents of her household she wanted shipped to Cavanaugh Island. She'd given Sherilee a key to the house, informing her that she could take all red-tagged items and boxes.

Her grandmother's trunks yielded a treasure trove of first edition books she'd listed on The Parlor's website under rare and collectible editions and the response from various collectors was overwhelming. A new mattress, bed dressing, towels for the bathroom, and window shades were scheduled to be delivered Friday morning, and Deborah projected the bookstore would be open for business by the coming weekend.

Whitney read the many newspaper clippings and had surprised her when he announced he wanted to write articles for the *Sanctuary Chronicle*, the Cove's biweekly newspaper, about his great-grandmother's extraordinary accomplishments and contribution to the children who'd grown up on the island. He'd placed a call to the newspaper's editor to set up an appointment to meet with him to discuss his project. Deborah had no doubt the articles would be well-written because Whitney, editor of his school's newspaper, planned for a career in communications.

Touching the car's handle, she opened the door and slipped behind the wheel. Minutes later she maneuvered into a parking space behind the library. It would be the first time she would attend a monthly town council meeting. Now that she was a permanent resident and business owner she needed to know what was going on in her new hometown. There was a monthly newsletter, recapping events and activities, but Deborah wanted to see the proceedings in person.

She followed the sign directing her to the meeting room. The mayor and his town council met the second Tuesday of each month to bring residents up to date on proposed new ordinances, budget items, and reports from department heads, including but not limited to transportation, engineering, housing, fire, police, and the school board.

Walking into the brightly lit room, she took an empty chair near the front. Deborah had barely settled on the folding chair when a shadow loomed over her. Her head popped up and she stared at Asa Monroe, trying to ignore the shiver of awareness that eddied over her body. Barbara was right. Seeing him up close Deborah concluded Asa *was* truly delicious.

Her eyebrows lifted a fraction. "Are you stalking me, Mr. Monroe?"

Asa gestured to the chair beside her. "Is someone sitting here?" he asked.

"No. Please sit. You didn't answer my question," Deborah said. He sat down, looping one leg over the opposite knee. She stared at the toe of his running shoe. Tonight he wore a white cotton V-necked pullover with a pair of jeans.

"I'm not stalking you, Mrs...."

"It's Ms. Robinson."

"Does Ms. Robinson have a first name? Because it seems as if everyone in Sanctuary Cove is on a first-name basis."

Deborah stared at his distinctive profile. His strong jaw was smooth from a recent shave and the scent of his cologne was like the man—potent. "Deborah."

He extended his hand. "It's nice putting a name with a face. It's my pleasure, Deborah."

She stared at the broad palm with long, slender well-groomed fingers for several seconds before she took it. Even his hands were perfect. "Nice meeting you, Asa."

"I'm not stalking you," he said with a grin, "I was told that non-residents are welcome to attend a town council meeting and voice their opinions."

Lowering her eyes, Deborah felt properly chastised. How could she have been that self-centered? Asa had smiled at her—something men in the Cove did every day, while she'd believed he was stalking her. "I'm sorry," she apologized, withdrawing her hand from his firm grip.

"For what?"

Deborah gave him a direct stare. "For accusing you of stalking me." Asa continued to smile, attractive lines fanning out around his eyes, drawing her gaze to his straight, white teeth.

"There's no need to apologize. Sanctuary Cove is not *that* big, so there is always the possibility of running into the same people several times a day."

She nodded. "You're right. How many meetings have you attended?"

"This is my first. How many have you attended?" Asa asked.

Deborah stared straight ahead. "This is also my first."

"I thought—"

"Hey, Debs," Mabel called out as she walked into the room. "Nice seeing you, Asa," she added, giving him a friendly smile.

"Same here," Asa acknowledged.

"Was I interrupting something?" Mabel asked, her gaze shifting from Deborah to Asa.

"No," Deborah and Asa said in unison.

"Please excuse us, Asa, but I need to talk to Deborah," Mabel said, sitting on Deborah's left and patting her knee. "As soon as you're finished settling in Les and I would like to have you and your kids over for Sunday dinner."

Deborah leaned to her left, her shoulder touching Mabel's. "There's not much I have to do at the house, but it's the bookstore that's taking up most of my time."

She'd taken out a home improvement loan to make repairs, update, expand and redecorate the house, because she and Louis had planned to use it as their permanent residence after they'd retired. All of the rooms were painted, a new roof replaced the old one, and the clapboard siding was restored with white vinyl. The navy-blue shutters, a new front porch, and the expanded back porch made the near century-old structure a standout on the Cove, especially when compared to some of the smaller homes on the island. Up until thirty years ago some of them still hadn't had indoor plumbing.

Upon the advice of the contractor, she hadn't bricked up the kitchen fireplace. It added to the character of the room with its exposed brick walls. And on the occasional cool evening she would light a fire and either roast marshmallows with her children or sit and read ghost stories to them by the light of the flames.

When her great-grandfather built the house he'd designed it with two fireplaces: one in the kitchen and another in a separate outdoor structure as was the custom. The exterior building and fireplace had been destroyed when a hurricane swept the island in 1917.

"Do you want some help? After we close the Muffin Corner I could come over and help you unpack."

Deborah shook her head. "Thanks, but no thanks. The

shelves are up and the only thing left to do is to stack books. As soon as the piano and a few other pieces of furniture are delivered The Parlor will open for business. What I'm going to need from you is muffins."

Mabel ran a hand over her braided hair. "You need muffins?"

"Yes. I plan to set up a reading corner and I'd like to offer my customers something to munch on if they decide to browse or hang out for a while. I'm not going to serve coffee, because that would conflict with your business, but gourmet tea. If they want coffee, then they can get it at the Muffin Corner."

"That's great!" Mabel crooned. "It sounds as if you're going to bring a little class to the Cove and keep the parlor theme. That's what made your Charleston bookstore so different from the others. Do you realize what's going to happen?"

"No. What?" Deborah asked, staring at Mabel's gap-toothed grin.

"You're going to get folks who'll come in and sit so long they're going to leave a distinct imprint of their behinds on your chairs."

She smiled. "I don't mind as long as they're paying customers. I'm not going to be able to compete with the chain bookstores on the mainland, but if anyone wants a title I can call a distributor and get it within two to three days."

"Are you going..." Whatever Mabel was going to say died on her lips when the mayor and members of the town council filed in, taking seats at the table in the front of the room.

• • •

Lowering his leg, Asa settled back in his chair and crossed his arms over his chest, while cursing Mabel Kelly's timing. Just when his attempt to engage Deborah Robinson in conversation had begun, it was thwarted by the owner of the Muffin Corner. He'd been in Sanctuary Cove for a little more than two months, and Deborah Robinson was the first woman who'd made him sit up and take notice. Her face was flawless, with a light sprinkling of freckles over the bridge of her nose, high cheekbones, and a lush mouth. When she smiled it just wasn't with her mouth, but also her eyes. And they'd sparkled with laughter during the brief seconds they'd stared at each other in the Muffin Corner and again at Jack's. He glanced at her bare fingers. Deborah had introduced herself as Ms. Robinson, which probably meant she was either unmarried and/or divorced, and what he hadn't realized during those seconds in the little pastry shop was that she was someone he'd like to get to know better.

Mayor Spencer White rapped his gavel, calling the meeting to order. He had earned the distinction of becoming a third generation mayor of the Cove. His grandfather had been the Cove's first black mayor, serving six four-year terms. Spencer's father then ran for the vacated office and won. He hadn't completed his second term, when he resigned to care for his wife who'd been diagnosed with multiple sclerosis. Spencer served out his father's term, and then ran unopposed in the subsequent election. He had married a model-turned-actress, who'd spent more than half of their brief two-year marriage in Los Angeles. They'd parted amicably, and as a lawyer with movie star looks, he joined the ranks of a small number of single men on Cavanaugh Island who were under the age of forty.

"If I wasn't married to Lester I would definitely ask our illustrious mayor to park his slippers under my bed," Mabel whispered to Deborah through clenched teeth. "Damn! He makes Blair Underwood look ugly. And, we both know *that* man is some kinda fine!"

Deborah pressed the back of her hand to her lips to conceal the smile tilting the corners of her mouth. She could always count on Barbara and Mabel to make her laugh. There had been a time growing up that she'd laughed a lot. But that had changed once she married and became a mother. She'd married at twenty, had become a mother for the first time at twenty-one, and it had taken careful planning and budgeting to stretch her husband's paycheck. They rented movies instead of going to the theater, delegated one day a month when they went out to eat, and she'd packed home-cooked nutritional lunches for Louis to heat up in the teachers' lounge microwave.

At twenty-three, when Deborah Robinson should have been teaching, jetting off to exotic locales for vacations, socializing in clubs and dating like other young women her age, she was proficient enough to go toe-to-toe with Martha Stewart as a goddess of homemaking.

"I think Blair is better looking," she whispered.

"I think so, too," Mabel paused, glancing in Asa's direction, "but you have to admit that Asa is nice on the eyes," Mabel whispered back.

Deborah nodded. It was the second time within a week that a woman had talked about Asa being eye candy. Yes, she had to admit he was delicious-looking eye candy, but also a snowbird, and that made him a transient.

Spencer straightened his tie as he cleared his voice, garnering the attention of all in the room. He was the only one sitting at the table wearing a suit and tie. Sanctuary Cove was like its residents—laidback and unpretentious.

"I'd like to thank everyone for coming out tonight. Before we start our official meeting I'd like to acknowledge a few new faces. Those who are here for the first time should know you're always welcome." He stared directly at Deborah. "Mrs. Robinson, on behalf of those on the town council and all who live in the Cove I would like to offer my condolences for your husband's accidental drowning as he tried to rescue a young man. He truly was a hero, and if there is anything you or your children need, please do not hesitate to call my office."

Deborah swallowed to relieve the constriction in her throat as a swell of emotion made it difficult for her to draw a normal breath, because she hadn't expected Spencer to put her on the spot. But she should have known he would acknowledge everyone in town, new and old. His tone and words, along with his cropped hair, tailored suit, flawless brown skin, and even features, made him the consummate politician. She wondered if he would be content to remain mayor of Sanctuary Cove, or whether he might set his sights on a position with more visibility—something loftier.

"Thank you, Mayor White."

Spencer nodded. "For those who are unfamiliar with Deborah Robinson, she is the granddaughter of our own Sallie Ann and James Williams." He paused when there was a spatter of applause. "My office also has received official notification that the Robinsons will now make Sanctuary Cove their legal residence." He flashed a toothpaste-ad smile. "Welcome home, Deborah."

Eyelids fluttering to stem the flow of tears pricking the backs of her lids, Deborah flashed a demure smile. "Thank you again."

Spencer's eyebrows lifted a fraction as he returned her smile. "Isn't there something else you'd like to tell your fellow residents?"

All eyes were trained on Deborah as she stared straight ahead. What was he talking about? Did the mayor know something she should have known? A pregnant silence ensued until it finally came to her. "Yes, there is. I'll be opening a bookstore at the corner of Main and Moss Alley." Her announcement was followed by rousing applause. "If any of you know someone looking for a part-time position, please tell them to stop by the old gift shop off Moss Alley."

"When do you expect your grand opening?" Spencer asked, flashing a practiced smile.

"I'll call your office and let you know so we can have a ribbon-cutting ceremony." Deborah almost burst out laughing when she saw his smile fade, as if someone had stuck Spencer with a sharp object. She'd usurped him, because she knew he'd wanted to mention the ribbon-cutting that had become an important component of his administration.

"Let's hope it's soon." Shifting his attention from Deborah to another, Spencer nodded to an elderly couple sitting in the front row. "Sir, madam, do you mind telling us why you've come to Sanctuary Cove?"

"I'm Shelly Miner and this is my husband Ralph. We're from Edina, Minnesota," the wife announced proudly, "and as snowbirds we usually winter in a different place every year. This year it's Sanctuary Cove." She held up a hand. "And before you ask, Mayor White, I know I speak for Ralph as well when I say your town is wonderful." Shifting on her chair, she wagged a finger at Deborah. "And, young lady, I'll be waiting for you to open that bookstore."

Spencer laughed with the others. He gestured to Asa. "Sir, do you mind telling us what brought you to Sanctuary Cove?"

"I'm Asa Monroe. I'm a first-time snowbird, and this is my first visit to the Carolina Lowcountry and hopefully it won't be my last."

"Are you enjoying your stay, Mr. Monroe?" Spencer asked.

Asa smiled. "Most definitely."

Spencer smiled like a Cheshire cat. "Perhaps we can get you and Mr. and Mrs. Miner to consider living here year-round."

"It is something to think about," Asa said.

"Try not to think too hard, Mr. Monroe." Again, there was laughter.

There were more introductions before Spencer White rapped his gavel, officially opening the meeting. There were reports from Sheriff Jeffrey Hamilton; the commissioner of roads and transportation, who informed the assembly that Sanctuary Cove had been awarded a grant from the state to repair the sidewalks and parking lots in the business district; and a very lengthy report from the town's treasurer. Then Spencer rapped his gavel again, announcing a fifteen-minute recess.

Asa checked his watch. It was eight-fifteen. He'd come to the library to look for something to read, but when he checked the community bulletin board in the lobby and found the announcement for the open town council meeting he'd decided to stay and observe some of the proceedings.

What he hadn't expected to find was the woman who'd occupied his thoughts since the first time he saw her. Now that he knew her name and that she was opening a bookstore, there was no reason for him to stay for the remainder of the meeting.

Asa saw Deborah talking with the sheriff, the lawman tucking a curl that had escaped the elastic band on the nape of her neck behind Deborah's ear. The scene was so tender and intimate that he felt like a voyeur. Mixed feelings surged through Asa. He found himself lusting after a woman he knew nothing about, other than her name, that she was going to open a bookstore, and that she had a teenage son. He knew Jeffrey Hamilton wasn't married, so there was the remote possibility that he and Deborah were seeing each other. However, in a town as small as Sanctuary Cove it would be easy enough to find out.

He left the library and began walking back to the Cove Inn. The library was a twenty-minute brisk walk to the boardinghouse, and now he wished he'd driven. Walking allowed him time to think—something he hadn't wanted to do. At least inside his Range Rover he could turn on the radio or listen to a CD. Shoving his hands into the pockets of his jeans, Asa stared straight ahead as he made his way back to what he thought of as his temporary home.

Once he closed the door to his room, he could grieve without having to explain to anyone why he didn't want to talk. Asa knew he had to do something to keep himself busy. He was forty-six, much too young to retire, although financially he could maintain a very comfortable lifestyle well into old age. He'd closed his practice, referred his patients to another physician, put his house on the market, and submitted an application to Doctors Without Borders.

He couldn't remain in Sanctuary and continue to do the same thing every day: get up and share a buffet breakfast with the other guests, go for a walk along the beach, return to sit on the porch and read for hours, sit down to dine with the same guests, then retreat to his bedroom to watch aimless hours of television before preparing for bed.

"Mr. Monroe."

Asa turned when he heard someone call his name. Sitting on a stone bench near the fountain in the town square was Rachel Dukes's brother-in law and the boardinghouse's handyman. It was nearly impossible to pinpoint his age despite the lines and creases in his lean jaw and forehead. The man's coloring and features reminded Asa of ebony African masks he'd seen at craft shows and museums. He wore a short-sleeved white shirt with a pair of sharply creased khakis.

Asa extended his hand. "Good evening, Mr. Walker."

"That it is," Jake Walker replied. Asa shook the proffered well-groomed hand. "Nice night for walking or sitting outside." Jake gestured to several couples sitting across the square. "They think so, too."

Since he'd moved into the boardinghouse, Asa couldn't remember hearing the taciturn man say any more than *morning* or *evening*. "That it is," he said. The square was brightly lit and nighttime temperatures were in the low seventies.

"Sit down and rest yourself, Mr. Monroe." Waiting until Asa sat facing him, Jake smiled as a network of fine lines fanned out around his raven-black eyes. "You came from the meeting?"

Asa nodded, smiling. "Yes."

"How did you like it?"

"It was interesting."

"Interesting how?"

"I would have never anticipated the mayor would ask tourists to introduce themselves."

Crossing his feet at the ankles, Jake stared at the toes of his scuffed work boots. "We do things different 'round here, 'specially now with Spencer White as the new mayor. He is a little bit of a blowhard, but we think he really wants the best for the Cove."

Asa wanted to tell Jake that the man was more pompous than a blowhard, and was probably using his position as mayor as a stepping stone to advance his political career. "What about the mayors in Haven Creek and Angels Landing?"

The seconds ticked by and Jake stared at his hands sandwiched between his knees. "Folks in the Cove don't have much to do with folks in the Creek or Landing, and vice versa."

"Are you saying you don't visit the other parts of the island?"

"That's not what I'm saying. I go to Angels Landing to visit my kin, but they don't like coming here." He smiled when Asa told him about his attempt to drive to Angels Landing. "You can't drive there from here. You've got to go on foot, because it's too swampy to drive. Even with four-wheel drive you still can get stuck."

Asa gave the older man an incredulous look. "I'm not about to go walking in a swamp."

Jake grunted. "There's nothing to it, son. You just put on a pair of boots that come to the knee and head due northwest. The boots are to protect your ankles from them moccasins and copperheads. It would also help if you bring a rifle 'cause you never know what else might jump out at you."

"That's okay. The next time I'll take the causeway." Asa glanced at his watch. He wanted to return to the boardinghouse and check his e-mail on his laptop. "Are you ready to go back?"

Jake had revealed that he and his wife moved into the bungalow behind the boardinghouse after their children married and moved away. He'd wanted to ask the older man about Deborah and Jeffrey, but changed his mind. That was something he would uncover himself—tomorrow.

"Yeah, I guess so." Jake rose slowly to his feet, swaying slightly until he regained his balance. "I sit out here most nights because I can't stand the chatter of the folks setting in the parlor. When you get to my age, son, you need a little peace and quiet."

Smiling, Asa slowed his stride to accommodate the much shorter man. "I know what you mean." After the evening meal, the boarders gathered in the parlor to either play cards or board games. An open bar with cordials was available for those who wanted some liquid libation. Those who imbibed too much usually fell asleep where they sat, while others became more animated. It was only when Rachel dimmed the lights at ten that they put away their games and retreated to their suites. Both men turned when they heard two short taps from a car's horn.

Jake stopped, waving to Deborah when she maneuvered over to the curb. "Hey, Missy."

Deborah lowered the passenger-side window, leaning to her right. "Mr. Walker. Asa. Can I give you a ride back to the boardinghouse?"

"I don't mind if it won't put you out," Jake said.

"Please get in. You, too, Asa."

Asa rested a hand on Jake's shoulder. "You go. I'll walk."

The older man took a step, moving closer to Asa so Deborah couldn't overhear him. "Look, son, around here when someone offers to do you a favor you accept it. Not to is an insult. Now, please get in the car."

Knowing he'd just been chastised, Asa opened the passenger-side door, waiting until Jake was comfortably seated and belted in before he slipped onto the backseat. The subtle scent of perfume wafted in his nostrils. It was the same fragrance Deborah Robinson wore the day he saw her in the Muffin Corner.

What had shocked him was Mayor White offering his condolences on the drowning of her husband, which meant she was recently widowed. The mayor had also welcomed her home, leading Asa to surmise that she'd left Sanctuary Cove but had come back to live.

She'd lost her husband and he his wife. There were similarities yet one profound difference. He'd also lost his child, while she still had hers. Staring out the side window, Asa watched the slowly passing landscape. The bright lights from the town square disappeared, replaced by an occasional streetlight, then complete darkness as they left the downtown area.

The in-ground miniature solar lights lining the driveway

led to the sprawling two-story structure that once had been the winter residence of a Charleston-based cotton planter before the Civil War. They reminded Asa of those on an airport runway. Rachel Dukes told each of her new boarders that she'd invested her blood, sweat, and tears in restoring the mansion to its original magnificence, and prided herself on offering services comparable to those found at the finest mainland-based hotels.

He could attest to that because the décor was quintessential antebellum and the cuisine classic lowcountry. At times, the charming southern hospitality generated by Rachel left Asa feeling slightly overwhelmed. The housekeeping staff moved about the eight–thousand-square-foot, twenty-two room house silently and efficiently. At any given time a white-glove examination would not pick up a speck of dust anywhere.

He was out of the car as soon as it stopped, to assist Jake who was slower exiting. Bending lower, Asa smiled at Deborah. He extended his hand. Her bare face shimmered under the lights from the dashboard. "Thank you very much for the ride."

She returned his smile and took his hand. "It was my pleasure. Good night, Asa."

He closed the door, took a step back, and stared at the red taillights of the silver-gray sedan. Waiting until she disappeared from view, Asa turned and mounted the steps to the porch, walking around to a side door. He wanted to avoid the small crowd that had gathered in the parlor. Every time they'd asked him to join them he'd turned them down. It had reached a point where the other guests had begun avoiding him at breakfast and dinner, leaving him to sit alone while he ate in the formal dining room;

he knew they thought him strange or maybe even a little crazy. He didn't want to answer their endless questions, while at the same time regurgitating his life story to strangers.

Taking a back staircase, he made it to his room without encountering anyone. He unlocked the door, reached for the Do Not Disturb placard and slipped it on the door-knob, closing and locking the door.

Walking over to the casement windows, he opened them and stepped out onto the veranda. The chaises positioned outside the other rooms were unoccupied. It wasn't often he had the veranda to himself, but tonight had to be his lucky night. Flopping down on the thick cushion, Asa ran his hand over his face, then went completely still. The lingering scent of Deborah's perfume clung to his palm. He inhaled deeply, trying to identify what made up the notes to the fragrance. He recognized musk and vanilla but there was another component that made it distinctive, memorable like its wearer.

There was something about Deborah that stirred emotions Asa did not want to feel—at least not consciously. Her beauty, smile, and feminine smell made him feel desire, something he'd sworn off after his wife was killed.

Chapter Six

Deborah sat in bed, a pile of pillows supporting her back and shoulders. A stack of her grandmother's letters and her journal lay beside her.

After the town council meeting Eddie Wilkes had approached her with the news he wanted Whitney to come to his office Saturday morning to interview for a position as a freelance reporter. The newspaper editor told her that Whitney had e-mailed him several articles he'd written for his high school newspaper. She was aware that her son was a straight-A student, but for an award-winning journalist to endorse Whitney's reporting ability filled her with pride.

Reaching for the stack of letters Sallie Ann Payne had written to James Williams, Deborah untied the ribbon she'd used to bundle the nearly two dozen envelopes. If Whitney was going to write about his great-grandmother, then she had to glean as much information about the woman who'd spent her entire life in Sanctuary Cove. Not even her father's urging could get his parents to leave once they retired. She remembered Sallie Ann declaring emphatically that if she was buried anywhere but on the Cove her soul would wander until it found its way back home. She removed the letter with the earliest postmark from its envelope.

Deborah spent the next ninety minutes reading the letters. They were erotic love letters from Sallie to James. She smiled. If she were a writer Deborah would have turned the letters into a novel. Reaching for her journal and a pen, she opened it to a blank page.

January 11th—I met a man. His name is Asa Monroe and he is spending the winter in the Cove. I don't know what it is about him, but whenever he smiles at me, something stirs my blood. He makes me feel things I've never felt with any man. Not even with Louis.

Capping the pen, Deborah stared at what she had written. *He makes me feel things I've never felt with any man.* There. She'd whispered what she had felt and had been feeling since she and Asa exchanged their first smile. Initially Deborah had been flattered that an attractive man had smiled at her, because it had been twenty years since she had returned a man's stare with a blatant one of her own. Once she had become involved with Louis she hadn't looked at another man.

Then, there was the scene in Jack's on New Year's Eve. Although there was another woman at Asa's table, he seemed intent on staring at her. It was the subtle wink that confirmed Asa Monroe was interested in her. And Deborah wasn't so gauche that she didn't know when a man was flirting with her.

She had to ask herself whether she was willing to engage in a little harmless flirtation with a man who affected her with such intensity. Smiling, Deborah stored the journal and pen in the drawer of the bedside table, recounting her conversation with Barbara: *I know you just lost your husband, but that doesn't mean you have to stop living and loving.*

Her friend was right. She couldn't stop living or loving because of Louis's death. What Deborah had to decide was whether or not she was willing to take a chance on love again. She knew it wouldn't be with Asa, because he would leave the Cove come spring, but that didn't mean she couldn't enjoy his company in the meantime.

Slowly, methodically, Deborah stacked the letters, retied them with the ribbon and placed them in a drawer under her lingerie. Even though her grandmother hadn't left instructions, she knew the letters were for her eyes only.

Slipping back into bed, she rearranged the pillows and turned off the lamp. Within minutes of her head touching the pillow Deborah fell asleep. It was the first night since that fateful day in December that she hadn't stared at the clock waiting for sleep to overtake her, so she could forget that the man who'd lain beside her for so many years was gone and would not be coming back.

Deborah stood on the sidewalk, admiring the gold lettering on the plate-glass window: THE PARLOR BOOKSTORE. Although she hadn't yet officially opened for business just seeing the words made it all the more real. The shelves were anchored to the walls; the ladders slid easily along the rails, permitting her access to the higher rows. Half the books were stacked, and with the delivery of the piano, tables, and chairs the residents of Sanctuary Cove could avail themselves of the town's first bookstore.

Her gaze shifted to the HELP WANTED sign she'd placed in the window earlier that morning. It had taken her a while to decide on the hours of operation for the bookstore, especially now that she was solely responsible for caring for her children. She hoped that whoever filled the position would be flexible enough to allow her time to run errands and be available for meetings with her children's teachers and advisors. Deborah walked back into the store, nearly colliding with the cable technician.

"I'm going to wire upstairs, then I'll hook up your televisions. I should be out of your hair in about half an hour."

Deborah wanted to ask him if he could do it within fifteen minutes because her stomach was making gurgling noises. She'd gotten up early to make breakfast for her children, but had only drunk a cup of coffee herself. If she'd known Peter Raney was going to show up an hour later than scheduled she would've stopped at the Muffin Corner to eat something.

Picking up a box cutter off a side table, she cut through the tape on one of eight cartons labeled AFRICAN-AMERICAN. When she had dismantled her bookstore, she'd made certain the books were packed by genre. Thus far she'd shelved self-help, study guides, travel, and cookbooks. Fiction, nonfiction, mystery, teen, art, science fiction, romance, biography, literature, and African-American literature and Black Studies still needed to be dusted and alphabetized.

Deborah sat on a low stool, wiping off the covers and jackets of a carton of books featuring African-American

history and literature. She flipped through the pages of
The *Divine Nine—The History of African American Fra-*
ternities and Sororities written by Lawrence C. Ross, Jr.
The only thing she'd regretted when in college was that
she hadn't pledged a sorority. She'd written her grandmother asking her advice, and Sallie Ann had written
back advising her to concentrate on her coursework. Now
that she'd read her grandmother's letters to James Williams, Deborah regretted not saving the ones her grandmother had written to her while she'd attended college.
It wasn't what she'd written, but how she'd written them,
using a vintage fountain pen when most people used ball-
point pens. When she'd asked her why she still used such
an antiquated writing utensil that had to be manually
filled with ink, the older woman had replied that she loved
seeing the flow of ink across a blank page and then waiting for it to dry.

Deborah had managed to empty one carton when a tap
on the door garnered her attention. Turning, she saw Asa
Monroe peering through the glass. She stared at him staring back at her, the sound of her pounding heartbeat echoing in her ears. Her feelings toward him were becoming
more confusing. What, she mused, was there about Asa
that made her react like an adolescent girl with her first
crush? Her palms were sweating, her knees shaking, and
Deborah didn't have to glance down at her chest to know
her nipples were visible through her shirt.

A grin tilted the corners of her mouth, and much to
her surprise Asa winked at her. Walking to the door, she
unlocked and opened it a few inches. His gaze moved
from her face to her white tee-shirt to her cropped jeans
and ballet-type shoes.

"Good morning. We're still not open."

"I know. I came to ask you about the sign in the window."

Deborah stared up at the man, noticing for the first time he was taller than she'd expected or remembered. At five-eight, there weren't too many men who were a full head taller than she was. He looked as if he was ready to pose for an ad in a golfing magazine with his navy blue golf shirt, tan slacks, and imported slip-ons. "You...you want to work here?"

Asa smiled. "You mentioned last night that you needed a part-time employee. I just came to ask if the position has been filled."

"Oh no," she said much too quickly. "It's still available. But I just didn't expect someone like you to apply."

"May I come in?" Asa asked. He entered the shop when Deborah opened the door wider, then closed it behind him. "I don't know if you're aware of it, but it's against the law to discriminate against an employee because of age, race or gender."

Her mouth curved into an unconscious smile. Not only was Asa Monroe very attractive, but he was as equally charming. His face was the color of gold-brown autumn leaves and there was a hint of gold in his large, deep-set brown eyes. He had what Deborah thought of as balanced features: his eyes and nose making for an arresting face. She stared at his mouth, finding his lower lip a bit too sensuous for a man. But it was his voice—velvet, resonant—that unnerved her.

"I haven't discriminated against you because I haven't interviewed you."

"Will you?"

"Will I what, Asa?"

"Will you give me an interview?"

"I can't interview you now because I have someone working upstairs. As soon as he's finished we'll talk."

An expression of bewilderment crossed Asa's face when he heard the sound of Deborah's hunger. "Is that your stomach growling?"

A rush of heat that began in Deborah's chest moved upward, stinging her cheeks. "I'm afraid it is," she admitted. "I'm waiting for the technician to finish up, then I'm going to get lunch."

Crossing his arms over his chest, Asa angled his head. "Would you mind sharing lunch with me over at Jack's? You can interview me while we eat," he added quickly.

The sweep hand on Deborah's watch made a full revolution before she spoke again. "Okay. But I'm picking up the tab, because it will be a business expense."

Asa smiled again. "Okay. While you wait for the technician to finish, I'll help you shelve books."

Deborah's eyebrows lifted a fraction. Either Asa Monroe really did want a job, or he was trying to impress her. She hoped it wasn't the former reason because she could only pay him a little more than minimum wage. The woman who'd worked for her in the Charleston location was an independently wealthy, retired school librarian. Books had become her life and she couldn't bear not to be involved with them. When the discussion of a salary was broached, she'd quickly agreed to accept the lowest hourly wage mandated by law.

"Asa, I don't know what you're looking for when it comes to a salary, but I can't afford to pay much more than the minimum wage. If business is good the first three months, then I'll give you a raise."

"Are you saying I'm hired?"

Resting her hands at her hips, Deborah exhaled an audible sigh.

"I'll need someone to unpack and shelve new stock. I'll also need that person to cover the front desk when I have to run errands or look in on my children."

"How old are your children?" he asked.

"Seventeen and fifteen. They're not babies, but they still need my supervision."

"How many hours would you need me?"

"Probably between ten and fifteen hours a week."

"How many days a week?"

"No more than three or four days. The bookstore will open from Tuesday through Saturday, nine-thirty to six."

"Will you have a late night?" Asa questioned.

"Thursdays. I'll stay open until eight. May I ask you a question?"

"Of course, Deborah." She loved the way he said her name. It came out in three distinct syllables, like *De-boar-rah*, stressing the middle syllable.

"Why are you looking for work? And why a bookstore?"

Asa flashed a sheepish grin. "Becoming a snowbird isn't what I'd envisioned it to be. Most times I'm so bored I begin talking to myself just to hear my own voice. Now I know what prisoners in solitary confinement experience."

"How can it be quiet when you're staying at the boardinghouse? This time of year it's nearly filled to capacity."

"I usually keep to myself. I'm not much for board games and discussions that involve grandchildren. And, why not a bookstore? It's the perfect place to work for a bibliophile."

Deborah felt a shiver of excitement. It was apparent Asa Monroe was also an avid reader. "Who are some of your favorite authors?"

"American or across the pond?"

"Across the pond," she said in a clipped British accent.

"Is this a test?" Asa asked, smiling.

"It could be," Deborah teased.

"Coleridge, Sir Thomas More, Milton, Ben Johnson, James Joyce, E.M. Forster, and Chaucer. Did I pass?"

"Give me a few Americans and I'll let you know."

She watched as Asa seemed to search his memory for American writers. "Hannah Webster Foster—"

"You've read *Charlotte Temple*?" Deborah asked, cutting him off.

"Not the book itself, but a photocopy. Do I pass?" he asked again.

"Give me three more."

"Charles Chesnutt, Henry James, and Sinclair Lewis."

Pressing her palms together in a prayerful gesture, Deborah pressed her fingers to her mouth. It was more than apparent Asa Monroe was an intellectual and he had no interest in board games. He was also knowledgeable enough to answer questions from customers inquiring about her rare and first edition titles.

"You pass."

Crossing his hands over his heart, Asa bowed his head. "Thank you."

Amusement danced in his eyes as they met Deborah's. She realized the man standing in her store was no ordinary clerk, and she knew she had to even the odds. Her gaze lingered on his hands. They were as exquisite as the rest of Asa Monroe. Again, she thought them beautifully formed with long tapered fingers, well-groomed with square-cut nails. She closed her eyes, fantasizing about how they would feel against her skin. Her eyes flew open as a rush of heat flooded Deborah's face when she realized the direction her thoughts had taken.

"How would you like a change of residence?" she asked, much too quickly.

Asa's smile vanished, replaced by an expression mirroring confusion. "Where would I live?"

"Upstairs, there's a furnished apartment and you can live there rent-free. It's the least I can offer to offset the low salary. I've ordered a new mattress, wardrobe, and blinds, which are scheduled to be delivered on Friday. I'm also waiting for a few other pieces, so by the time we open for business your apartment should be ready." Her cell phone chimed. "Please excuse me," Deborah said, reaching into the pocket of her jeans and walking away from Asa to answer the call.

Pushing his hands into the pockets of his slacks, Asa seemed to be deep in thought about Deborah's offer.

"Do you mind if I see the apartment before I give you my answer?" he asked when she returned after finishing her call.

"Not at all." She pointed to the back of the store. "There's a staircase behind the second door on the left that leads upstairs."

Deborah went back to unpacking books. She'd managed to shelve half the titles in the African-American Literature and Black Studies section when she heard two pairs of footsteps descending the staircase. Asa and Peter

Raney, dressed in a pair of coveralls with his name and company's logo stitched over his heart, were talking about football.

"Mrs. Robinson, where is the other television, and where do you want it hooked up?"

Deborah had had the moving company bring the thirty-six-inch flat-screen television she had mounted on the wall of her Charleston store to the one at the Cove. "It's in a box against the wall. I'd appreciate it if you would also connect the DVD and tuner." She'd placed a call to a local electrician to mount the TV on the wall once the cable connection was installed.

"Do you have your audio speakers?" Peter asked.

"They are also in the box." Peter had done all the electrical work on her house when she'd had it renovated.

Asa moved closer to Deborah. "It looks as if he's going to be a while. Tell me what you want from Jack's and I'll go pick it up."

Deborah was so grateful for his suggestion that she wanted to kiss Asa. "I'd like an order of shrimp and grits."

"You want grits for lunch?"

"What's wrong with grits for lunch?" she asked.

"I thought people usually ate grits for breakfast."

She smiled. "Down here we eat grits for breakfast, lunch, *and* dinner."

"Anything else?"

"A large sweet tea."

"How about dessert?"

Deborah shook her head. "I'll pass on dessert."

What she needed was comfort food. For some people it was mashed potatoes but for her it was grits. Reaching into his shirt pocket, Asa took out his BlackBerry, calling in the order to Jack's Fish House as he walked out the door. Walking behind him, she locked it, then took the HELP WANTED sign out of the window.

She couldn't believe her string of good luck. First she'd found an empty store in a prime location in move-in condition, and she'd just hired someone who was more than a clerk. He would become her assistant. And it was obvious he was either well-educated and/or an avid reader, and that gave him a distinct advantage when interacting with readers who preferred literature to popular fiction. The furnished apartment would become a perk for Asa—that is, if he decided to move out of the boardinghouse.

Peter programmed the television, resting on its stand on a drop-leaf table that she'd used in the other store for a collection of potted plants. The plants were now in the back porch and she would transport them to the shop for the grand opening. Deborah watched as he worked quickly to hook up the tuner, speakers, and the DVD player. Using the remote device, he turned on the television, smiling.

"Nice picture," he crooned.

Deborah nodded, smiling. "Thank you."

"Do you leave it on during the day?"

"I turn it on early in the mornings when there's not much activity, but once the regulars come to sit and read I'll turn it off and put in an MP3 with a collection of soft music. For those who just want to watch television I mute the sound and turn on the closed captions."

Peter adjusted his Atlanta Braves baseball cap. "It sounds as if you're going to have a nice place here."

"It is going to be nice," Deborah said with a modicum of pride. With the delivery of the concert piano, and once she positioned tables and chairs, hung framed prints of classic book jackets, and added the homey touches with plants, a refreshment table with Muffin Corner sweet breads, and an urn with hot water for tea, The Parlor would provide a place for·residents and tourists to come, browse, and sit a while.

"I'm done here. If there's anything else you need, just call me," Peter said, smiling.

Deborah reached into a pocket of her jeans and took out a check, handing it to him. "I want to put in track lighting and a couple of ceiling fans."

The electrician pocketed the check without looking at it. "Do you want me to pick up the fans and the lights?"

"Yes. I want fans similar to those upstairs."

"I'll pick them up today and install them before the end of the week. Thank you again, Mrs. Robinson."

Deborah nodded. "Thank you."

He left through the rear door, and a minute later she opened the front door for Asa, who cradled a shopping bag to his chest.

Chapter Seven

Deborah closed and locked The Parlor door behind Asa. "Something smells delicious."

Asa peered into the bag. "That's either your shrimp and grits or my crab patties and black-eyed pea soup."

"I'm so hungry that I could eat a whole pig in one sitting. Come on. We'll eat upstairs."

He followed Deborah to the back of the store, his gaze following the gentle sway of her slim hips in her fitted jeans. There was something very sexy about the young widow. Asa hadn't wanted to believe she had a seventeen-year-old child, wondering if perhaps she had been a teenage mother. A very young teenage mother.

There were things he wanted to know about this woman. What made her laugh, what she liked to do when she wasn't at work or caring for her children. During the walk between the bookstore and the restaurant Asa couldn't steer his thoughts away from Deborah Robinson. There was something about her that he found disturbing. Not disturbing like ominous or unsettling, but a welcome distraction from what had become his daily routine.

He hadn't come to Sanctuary Cove to get involved with a woman but to heal and wait. And he was still waiting—the last time he'd e-mailed the contact person at DWB as to a potential date for his application's approval the reply had been his application was still pending. Asa had thought about checking out of the Cove Inn and driving north to Myrtle Beach, but that had been before he'd seen Deborah. He'd changed his mind because there was something about the beautiful widow that rekindled feelings he believed had died when he'd buried his wife and son.

Deborah opened the door at the top of the staircase. When Asa had come in before, the heat on the second floor was unbearable. She'd since opened all the windows and turned on the ceiling fans, and now it was cooler, more comfortable. The fans were noisy, but functional.

"I'm going to have my son put an air-conditioner in the window later this afternoon," she told Asa.

"Where is the unit?"

"It's at my house."

"I can install it," Asa volunteered. He placed the shopping bag on the kitchen countertop.

Pressing her back against the refrigerator, Deborah gave Asa a long, penetrating look. "So, you'll stay?"

He nodded. "Only if you intend to hire me."

She stood up straighter. "I thought we already assumed that you were hired."

"I never deal with assumptions."

"Do you want it in writing, or will a verbal confirmation suffice?" she asked, smiling.

He angled his head. "I wouldn't mind a verbal confirmation."

Her smile grew wider. "You're hired."

"Thank you, boss."

Deborah narrowed her eyes. "That will be the first and last time you'll refer to me as your boss. It's Deborah."

He nodded. "Yes, Miss Deborah."

"You just won't quit, will you?"

"No, Miss Deborah."

She rolled her eyes upward, then turned before Asa could see her smile. Instinct told her he was going to be good for The Parlor and good for her. He was an interesting man with above average intelligence. She didn't know why he'd come to the Cove, and it didn't much matter. Outsiders who came to the Cove were welcomed and treated with respect, and when they prepared to leave it was always with an open Lowcountry invitation to *come back real soon*.

She turned on the water in the sink, letting it run until it was clear, then reached for a sponge and a bottle of dishwashing liquid. She wiped down the countertop, then the table in the dining area. "You can wash up in the bathroom while I set the table."

The day before she'd filled the cabinets with plates, cups and glasses from an old set she'd put aside for Whitney *if* he decided to live off campus. She had just finished setting out plates for two when Asa returned. Whitney still hadn't told her whether he wanted to attend Howard University in Washington, D.C., or Bennett College in Columbia. Although he'd been leaning toward Howard Deborah knew his ambivalence had come from losing his father. When Whitney mentioned that he'd promised Louis that he would take care of his girls if anything happened to him, she knew he was wrestling with his conscience, that he didn't want to leave the state because he felt he had to protect his mother and sister.

What her son hadn't realized was that she didn't need as much protection as he did. Even if he chose Bennett he would be leaving home for the first time in his life. Her children had never gone to summer camp like some of their friends and classmates, and whenever they did leave the state it was to go to Florida to visit their grandparents. Pearl McLeary-Williams's sister had moved to Florida to be close to her grandchildren, and whenever Crystal and Whitney went to visit they had children their own age with which to interact.

"I like the colors in the bathroom."

Deborah's head popped up when Asa joined her in the kitchen. "I decided on brown and green because I like chocolate-mint ice cream." The half-bath resembled a tropical oasis with dramatic browns contrasting with cool greens. There were chocolate towels, a jade-green chenille rug, a citrus-scented diffuser, votive candles, and a quartet of small framed prints of Chinese characters symbolizing health, love, luck, and long life, all selected with a discerning eye.

"Is that why you painted the walls in the bookstore green?"

Folding paper napkins, she placed them at the place settings. "I can't take credit for that. The walls were painted by the former owner. However, I did order two area rugs in a tartan plaid with browns and greens."

Reaching into the shopping bag, Asa removed takeout Styrofoam containers and two oversized foam cups filled with iced tea, watching as Deborah put serving pieces, flatware, white dinner plates with a cobalt-blue trim, and tall ice tea glasses on the table.

"I think I'm going to like hanging out here. There's a lot more space than in my suite at the boardinghouse." The apartment was one continuous space without walls. There were three doors: the one leading into the apartment from the bookstore, another leading out to a staircase to the parking lot, and the one to the bathroom. There were two ceiling fans with blades that resembled large brown banana leaves.

Deborah's hands stilled. "Too bad it holds heat. It's probably brutal up here in the summertime."

"It shouldn't be too bad with the fans and air conditioner," Asa said. "I meant what I said about going home with you to get the air-conditioner. After I put it in the window, I'm going back to the boardinghouse to change. If we work together we should be able to finish shelving the books by tomorrow."

"You don't have..." The ringing of her cell preempted whatever she was going to tell Asa. "Excuse me." Reaching into her back pocket, she retrieved the tiny instrument. It was the moving company. "Hello."

"Mrs. Robinson?"

"This is she."

"This is Bobby from shipping, and I'm calling to let you know we have a cancellation, so if it's all right with you we'd like to pick up the stuff from your house and deliver it to Sanctuary Cove tomorrow morning."

Deborah squeezed her eyes shut and rubbed her temple. "May I call you back, Bobby?"

"Of course, Mrs. Robinson. When do you think you'll get back to me?"

"I have to call someone to see if they can be at my house to let in your men."

Deborah ended the call, then scrolled through her cell directory for Sherilee's number. Closing her eyes again, she groaned when it went directly to voicemail.

"Sherilee, this is Debs. Please call me as soon as you get this message. The movers are coming tomorrow instead of Friday. Let me know if you'll be available to let them in." Hanging up, she began gnawing her lip between her teeth.

"Is there something wrong?" Asa asked when Deborah continued to bite on her lip.

Blinking as if coming out of a trance, she shook her head. "It's nothing that can't be resolved."

"Are you sure?"

"Very sure."

"You don't look very sure," Asa countered.

Deborah forced a smile. "How do I look?"

"Like a woman with a dilemma. It's obvious you can't be in two places at the same time."

She nodded. "I'll figure something out."

Asa pulled out one of the chairs at the table. "Please sit down and eat."

She sat, staring up at him over her shoulder. "Thank you."

Rounding the table, he sat opposite her, watching as she removed the top from an aluminum dish and ladled a portion of creamy grits topped with large pink shrimp, crumbled bacon, chopped scallions, and melted cheese onto her plate.

"Is that all you're going to eat?"

Deborah stared at the food, then at the man sitting

across from her. "Do you realize there's enough here for two people?"

"What if we share?" he suggested. "I'll give you half my soup and a crab cake and I'll take half your shrimp and grits."

Her expression brightened. "Okay." Pushing back her chair, she stood up, Asa rising with her. She took another bowl from the overhead cabinet and a spoon from the cutlery drawer. "Please sit down, Asa. You don't have to stand."

"Sorry, old habit." Deborah could tell Asa was old school, rising when women entered the room, or stood up. He opened doors for them and seated them. He had impeccable manners, something missing in a lot of men nowadays.

Asa ladled soup into the bowl, handing it to Deborah. "I've eaten in a lot of places, but the food from Jack's should definitely be Zagat rated."

"I don't think Otis and Luvina would welcome that kind of attention."

"Why not?"

"Folks here are humble and live very simple lives. The last census documented that about eight hundred people live in Sanctuary Cove. Eight hundred residents who don't want their Main Street changed, or an influx of outsiders impacting their quality of life. We tolerate tourists who come here in droves during the summer because the tourist dollars keep us afloat. Everyone knows everyone else; we have little or no crime and it's not unique for people to leave their doors or cars unlocked. A Zagat rating would bring people to Jack's year-round, shutting out the locals.

"The Cove Inn is our Four Seasons and the Waldorf-Astoria all rolled into one, and Jack's is our award-winning LeBernardin and Brasserie. The dishes at Jack's haven't changed despite the talk about black cuisine being viewed as being out of sync with what now defines healthy eating. All you have to do is look around the Cove and I doubt you'll find more than a dozen overweight people. We also have the distinction of living well into our late eighties and nineties. Do you want to know why?"

Asa nodded. The look on his face told Deborah he was quite pleased with the delicious shrimp and grits that made Jack's famous. "Tell me why," he said after swallowing.

"Because a lot of the food we prepare, especially the vegetables, is grown locally, without the harmful chemicals and pesticides that poison our bodies. The chickens come from a farm in Haven Creek and the pigs, too. Most residents have gardens and sell their surplus to restaurants and all the seafood comes from local fishermen." She flashed a winning smile. "Fresh air, fresh food, no industry polluting our air and the ocean as our playground. Life couldn't be better."

"You sound like a spokesperson for the Lowcountry tourist bureau."

Picking up her glass of tea, Deborah took a sip while staring at Asa over the rim. "If I sound a little passionate it is because I loved spending summers here."

"Where did you grow up?"

"Charleston. My father was born here, as were his parents, grandparents, and as far back as we can document."

"So, you're Gullah."

Her smile grew wider. "Down to the marrow in my bones."

"But, you don't sound like some of the people I've met."

"A lot of the older folks still speak the dialect."

"Do you?" Asa asked.

"No, but I understand it."

"How about your children? Do they understand it?"

"Yes." Deborah admitted. "They have friends in school who live on the island. They speak it when they don't want other kids who don't understand the dialect to know what they're talking about."

"I guess you can say it's like a foreign language."

Deborah nodded. "It is to those who don't understand it. The elementary schools on Cavanaugh Island are grades one through eight. All of the students are bussed into Charleston for high school, finally giving the island children a chance to mingle with each other and the city kids. Those who live in the Cove and who've never been to Haven Creek or Angels Landing meet those children for the first time in high school and usually form lifelong friendships."

"Do they marry one another?"

"I don't know."

Asa told Deborah about his attempt to tour the island, but how he'd had to turn back because he feared getting lost. "All I thought about was being forced to sleep in my truck with the windows rolled up, while praying some wild animal wouldn't get to me."

Throwing back her head, Deborah laughed until her sides hurt. "Don't you have GPS navigation in your car?"

"Yes. And what does that have to do with getting lost in the forest? Or should I say jungle? It doesn't work when there are no roads or streets. The next time I go sightseeing I'll take the causeway."

Deborah wanted to tell Asa that she'd never been to the Creek or Landing because of what her grandmother had told her about the people having tails and hooves. Once she was an adult she understood it was Sallie Ann's way of frightening her enough so she wouldn't go exploring and either get lost or bitten by some venomous reptile or insect. The causeway, which ran the length of the island, would take her past Haven Creek and Angels Landing before ending at the Cove. And she believed that was the reason why she'd continued to take the ferry instead of the causeway, which led directly to Angels Landing or Haven Creek.

Her phone rang and she answered it on the first ring. It was Sherilee returning her call. "Thanks for calling me back—on no, don't apologize, Sherilee. It's not the end of the world. Thanks, again." Punching a button, she ended the call.

"Is everything all right?" Asa asked.

Deborah met Asa's eyes, aware for the first time they'd changed color. Pinpoints of gold had been replaced with a deep chocolate brown. "There's been a change in plans. The movers are coming tomorrow instead of Friday, and that means I'm going to have to stay at the store to try and get as many books shelved to make room for the chairs, tables, and piano."

Asa leaned forward. "You're going to put a piano in the bookstore?"

"My maternal grandmother was a concert pianist. My mother inherited it, but when she and my father moved into a condo in Florida they gave it to me. It took up a lot of space in my living room, and there's no way it could fit in my house here, so I decided it would go nicely in the bookstore in keeping with the overall parlor design." She smiled. "And before you ask, I do play."

"What do you need me to do?"

Lines of confusion appeared between her eyes. "What are you talking about, Asa?"

"Judging from your conversation you can't be at two places at the same time. So tell me what you want me to do."

Deborah knew she couldn't afford to look a gift horse in the mouth. Asa had come along at a time when she truly needed someone to help her. "Can you begin working this afternoon? I'm going to have to try and put away as many books as I can before the movers arrive tomorrow. I can't see myself moving and stacking cartons in corners just to have to move them later."

Asa nodded. "What else do you need?"

The timbre of his mellifluent voice changed, seemingly caressing her like a feather on bare skin, and Deborah couldn't stop the shudder that eddied over her body. "I'll need you to be here when the movers arrive and show them where they should position everything."

"You're going to have to let me know where you want the piano. I'm certain the tables and chairs can be rearranged if you decide later on that you want to move them."

Relief swept through her as if she'd been denied air but could now breathe. "I'll pay you extra for—"

"I don't want or need your money, Deborah."

"But you can't work for nothing, Asa."

"Living rent-free in this apartment is payment enough. The Cove Inn isn't the Waldorf, but the prices can get steep for the suites, two meals a day, and room service. So, I'm willing to barter working in the bookstore with free rent."

Deborah knew he was right about the rates at the mansion-turned-boardinghouse, but she felt uncomfortable not paying him for the hours he would put in at the bookstore. "I'll agree, but only if you let me pay you for your meals."

"No." Asa's face was a mask of stone.

"You can't work for free," Deborah insisted.

"I won't be working for free. How much would you charge someone if you were to rent this apartment?"

The question caught her off-guard. "I don't know," she answered truthfully. "I've never been a landlord."

"Neither have I," Asa replied, "but I know people who rent summer homes on Southampton, Long Island, starting at two thousand dollars a week. And don't forget the summer season begins with the Memorial Day weekend and runs through the Labor Day weekend. That's nice money if you can get it. Now, think of what you can charge tourists who come to the Lowcountry for the summer."

"I'd never charge someone a thousand a week for this place."

"What you could charge is a lot more than you'd be paying me. Now, may I make a suggestion?"

Deborah paused, her gaze meeting and fusing with Asa's. There was just a hint of arrogance in his query. "Of course you may."

"We drop the subject. Let's finish our lunch, go pick up the air-conditioner, and I'll put it in the window. Then I'm going back to change my clothes and we'll see how many books we can shelve before it gets too late."

"I'll drop it, Asa, but only if we can agree to the terms of your employment." His eyes narrowed suspiciously. "Please don't look at me like that."

"Like what?" he shot back.

"Like I'm going to pronounce a death sentence. I'm willing to agree not to pay you a salary in lieu of free lodging, but..."

"But what, Deborah?" Asa questioned when she didn't complete her statement.

"I'd like to give you a hundred dollars a week for your meals."

"Damn, woman. You're like a dog with a bone. You just won't let it go."

She successfully hid a smile, picking up a napkin to wipe the corners of her mouth. Deborah knew she'd rattled Asa Monroe. Something told her the man was used to giving orders and having them followed without question.

"What is it going to be, Asa?"

"Make it fifty a week and you have a deal."

Deborah angled her head. "What's with you and money?"

"I don't need it as much as you're going to need it."

"What's that supposed to mean?"

"You're setting up a small business when there's no guarantee that it will remain viable. And that means you're going to need to save every dollar, not give it away. I don't need your money, Deborah. I love being around books so much that I'd be willing to work for free *and* pay rent for this apartment. I'll agree to accept fifty dollars a week just so we can end what has become very tiresome to me."

She extended her hand, excitement showing on her face. "Deal."

Asa took her hand, his thumb caressing her smooth knuckles. "Deal."

Believing she'd scaled a small hurdle, Deborah concentrated on finishing her lunch. She may not have been the traditional employer, but there was no way she was going to permit someone to work for free. And she knew instinctually Asa Monroe was worth more than fifty dollars a week, perhaps even ten times that amount. His intelligence, take charge approach, and the fact that he was a very attractive man was certain to bring customers into The Parlor—female customers in particular.

"Are you always this trusting?" Asa asked, breaking the comfortable silence. "Hiring someone without references?"

Propping her elbow on the table, Deborah rested her chin on the back of her fist. "I know you don't have any outstanding warrants because our sheriff runs the license plates of every outsider through a national criminal justice database. Don't forget there are only two ways off the island. And if you decided to break the law, I doubt you would get very far with Sheriff Hamilton waiting for you at the pier. If he doesn't catch you then you'd have to try and get past the roadblock on the causeway set up by the Charleston police."

"You can't tell me there's no crime on the island."

"There is. That's why we have a sheriff and several deputies. There are domestic disputes, problems with graffiti, an occasional drunk driver, and I'd heard there were a rash of burglaries over on Haven Creek before they discovered it was a cousin of one of the residents who had a serious drug problem. The man who caught the guy in his house beat him so severely that he had to be airlifted to the hospital. Unfortunately for the victim the man whose house he broke into was a former Vietnam vet suffering from PTSD. If he'd killed him it would've been the first murder on Cavanaugh Island in over thirty years."

"Why isn't the island listed on any 'best place to live and raise children' lists?"

"It isn't for the same reason why we don't have a Zagat-rated restaurant." Pushing back her chair, Deborah stood up and began clearing the table. She hadn't taken more than a step when she found her wrist trapped in Asa's strong grip. As he towered above her, the heat from his body added to her own. "What are you doing?"

"I'll clean up."

"You don't have to, Asa."

He gently tightened his hold on her arm. "Yes, I do. This is my place; therefore I'll clean up."

Tilting her chin, Deborah flashed a sensual smile. "Slow down, Asa. You won't be able to lay claim to this palatial estate until I give you a set of keys."

"Do you have an extra set?"

She nodded. "Yes. They're at my house. Let's clean up together, then we'll leave."

Working in tandem, Deborah washing and Asa drying, they were able to put the kitchen in order within five minutes. They took the back staircase to the parking lot where Asa had parked his vehicle under the shade of a palmetto tree. Opening the passenger-side door, he helped her up, waiting until she was seated and belted in before he sat beside her.

Chapter Eight

Asa started up the Range Rover, backing out of the space. "You're going to have to tell me how to get to your house."

"Once you pass the Cove Inn I'll tell you where to turn off." Deborah stared out the side window rather than look at him. "Slow down, Asa, before you're stopped for speeding."

"I'm going thirty miles an hour."

He could see her staring at him from his peripheral view. If he didn't have to keep his eyes on the road, he'd focus all his attention on her lovely face. "That's ten miles too fast."

Easing off the accelerator, Asa gave Deborah a quick glance. "If I go any slower I'll be standing still."

"There are no stop signs on the island, and you never know if a dog, cow, pig, or even a chicken will dart out across the road. If you hit and kill someone's pet or livestock you'll have to make restitution to the owner."

Asa slowed even more. "You're kidding. How can someone identify their chicken from someone else's?"

"I knew all of my grandmother's yard birds. Whenever I called them by name, they'd come running."

Asa's laughter reverberated inside the Range Rover. "Next you'll tell me you had to get up before dawn to milk the cow."

"I did."

"Seriously?" he asked.

Deborah laughed when she saw his shocked expression. "Why do you find that so hard to believe? There was a time when most people living in rural areas owned livestock. I didn't start milking the cow until I was around ten or eleven. My grandma would skim off the cream to make butter and buttermilk, then boil and strain the milk before letting it cool enough to store in the refrigerator. I don't know whether it was actually the milk, but everything on the Cove seemed to taste better, especially Grandmomma's buttermilk fried chicken."

"Ah, youthful innocence," Asa drawled.

"Why are you so cynical?"

"Am I being cynical or honest, Deborah?"

"Cynical, Asa. Make a right turn when you see the red barn. My house is at the end of the road on the left."

"To be continued," Asa said under his breath, as he maneuvered into the driveway of the large, white, two-story house with navy blue shutters. It was larger than the house he'd pictured and wholly Southern in design, from the distinctive front porch to the white wicker chairs, rocker, and swing covered with floral-print cushions. There was even a colorful patchwork quilt draped over the back of a wicker loveseat positioned near a matching low table so that it made for the perfect place to begin or end the day.

Shifting into park, Asa left the engine running and

came around to help Deborah down. His two hands spanned her waist and he held her longer than necessary. Feeling her fingertips on his shoulders, he tightened his hold, enjoying the softness of her body, the subtle fragrance clinging to her skin that he'd been unable to identify or forget.

"Please put me down, Asa."

He complied even though he had wanted to crush her to his body as a reminder of what he'd had and continued to miss: the warmth and smell of a woman's body. Asa wanted to tell Deborah he was sorry when he wasn't, so he decided not to say anything. He followed her to a side entrance. The air-conditioning unit outside the house indicated a central cooling system.

"How old is this house?" he asked as Deborah unlocked the door.

"The original deed documented it was built in 1909, but it was expanded many times over the years. I was told that my great-grandfather added the second floor a few years after he'd married my great-grandmother. It took him about four years to complete the project, because as a master carpenter and furniture-maker his skills were in demand here and on the mainland. I had to update the electrical system to accommodate several computers, and then decided to renovate the entire house. My husband and I had planned to use it for our permanent residence once we retired, but my children, who loved vacationing on the Cove, prefer living here to Charleston."

It was the first time Deborah had mentioned her late husband and Asa wondered if it had been as traumatic for her to lose her spouse as it was for him to lose his. If it had been, then she appeared to have adjusted well to being widowed. She'd relocated from Charleston to Sanctuary Cove, while he'd left all that was familiar, traveling from place to place as he waited for approval from DWB.

"How does your daughter feel about making the Cove her home?"

"She loves it here." Pushing open the door that led into the mud/laundry room, Deborah told Asa about Crystal wanting to put in a vegetable garden. "I'm certain she would've done quite well growing up on a farm."

"Do you plan to get a cow and chickens?"

Deborah gave him a sardonic smile. "Very funny," she drawled. "Here are the units. Do you think you're going to need both?"

Asa stared at two cartons labeled *air-conditioner* in a bold black marker, sitting on the floor in a brick-walled pantry. Mason jars filled with labeled fruits, vegetables, relishes, jams, and preserves lined the many shelves. The pantry was cool, much cooler that the outdoor temperature.

"I think one will do. Two air-conditioners going at the same time may blow the fuse. And, don't forget you have one in the shop."

"I'm going to put in some ceiling fans. I doubt I'll have to use the air until early May. Even though we don't officially have winter, sometimes it gets a little cool."

"What do you call cool, Deborah?"

Crossing her arms under her breasts, she smiled up at Asa. "Low sixties."

"That's short-sleeve and shorts weather."

Her smile grew wider. "Maybe for someone in New York or Boston, but any time the temperature drops below seventy folks start complaining."

Bending from his knees, Asa picked up the carton, shifting the weight until he could carry it without putting a strain on his back. "After I put this in, we should turn on both units to see if the electrical system can support them."

"Let's go before you throw your back out carrying that thing."

Asa and Deborah retraced their steps and the route, returning to the bookstore. He spent a quarter of an hour putting the unit in the window, making certain it was secured, then used the remote device to turn it on and program it to shut off in half an hour.

Both units were humming when he returned to the parking lot to drive back to the boardinghouse. Impulse and curiosity had gotten him a position in a Lowcountry bookstore and a different place to live while he bided his time on the island.

In just a short time his life had changed again—this time it promised a respite from the grief and guilt that had become so much a part of his day-to-day existence. Not only could he lose himself in the many titles that lined the shelves in The Parlor, but he could also interact with the customers who would come in to either browse or buy. Working the part-time, temporary position was certain to make his wait on the island a lot more gratifying.

And having Deborah Robinson as his employer was something he'd looked forward to. She was gorgeous, very smart, and a bit feisty, and claimed a strength that did not diminish her femininity. Yes, he mused, working at The Parlor was certain to become a pleasant and unexpected diversion.

• • •

Deborah sat on the floor in the bookstore, texting her son: Working late. Have Crystal reheat leftovers & make salad 4 dinner. Luv Mom.

Crystal had given her a crash course in texting, claiming she didn't have to type out every word and letter. As a former English teacher she still didn't use all the abbreviations and symbols that had become a language so inherent to the adolescent lexicon, but she had to admit texting was faster.

She'd lowered and closed the wooden blinds over the bookstore's plate glass window and had emptied three more cartons, flattening and stacking them in a pile where they would be picked up for recycling, when Asa tapped on the door. Pushing to her feet, she walked over and opened it. He'd changed into a black tee, jeans, and running shoes. The muscles and tendons in his arms and biceps bulged under the weight of a carton of bottled water.

"Can you take the shopping bag please, Deborah?"

She took the plastic bag from his fingers, peering inside to find another bag, this one also in plastic. "What did you buy?"

He smiled. "Dinner. I stopped at the supermarket and picked up a couple of salads from the deli section. I bought a Caesar with shrimp and a Thai salad with steak. I had them put the dressing on the side. I'm going to put a few bottles of water in the refrigerator."

"My, my, my. You've thought of everything."

"My motto is always plan ahead."

Deborah realized her instincts were right when she'd hired Asa. He was always just one step ahead of her, because she'd planned to call and have dinner delivered. "I'll bring up the salads."

"That's all right. I'll come back for them," Asa said.

"I'll leave them on the table." Picking up her MP3 player, she inserted the wire into a port in the tuner, then punched a button and the melodious voice of Anthony Hamilton singing "Ain't Nobody Worryin'" filled the space. She was swaying and singing along with the Commodores' "Three Times a Lady" when Asa returned for the salads.

"You like dancing?" he asked.

"I do, but I haven't danced much since my kids were born. As a working mom I never seemed to find the time to go out dancing."

"Although you're still a working mom, would you dance with me?" Asa asked, smiling and extending his hand.

Deborah hesitated, then placed her hand on his outstretched palm. "Yes, I would." Her voice was low, calm. Asa's arm went around her waist and he swung her around in an intricate dance step. He'd tightened his hold on her when she tried extricating herself from his firm grip.

"Asa!"

He smiled. "Yes, Deborah."

"Please let me go."

"Why? I love this song."

The heat in her face had nothing to do with the exertion, but from embarrassment. Suddenly Deborah realized anyone walking by the shop could see them. "Someone will see us."

Asa pulled Deborah closer. "Unless they have x-ray vision, they won't be able to see through the blinds." He chuckled softly. "If they're that nosey, then they'll get an eyeful. Relax. We're only dancing, and the song will be over soon."

She wanted to relax, but it wasn't easy. Not with his hard body pressed to hers. Not when the man holding her to his heart was a stranger. Not when he reminded her that the man she'd loved beyond description was gone and would never return. Yet, what bothered her most was she couldn't remember the last time she'd danced with Louis.

Resting her forehead on Asa's shoulder, she closed her eyes. The selection ended, segueing into the Marvin Gaye classic "What's Going On?"

"Thank you for the dance," Asa said in her ear.

Pulling back, Deborah stared up at him, meeting his amused gaze. "You're welcome."

He released her, breaking the spell. The next two hours were spent unpacking and shelving books as music flowed throughout the store.

Her cell phone rang and she scrambled off the floor to retrieve it. It was her daughter. "Hi, Crystal. What's up?"

"Whitney and I are just leaving school. He waited for me because I had cheerleading practice. He told me you texted him about heating up leftovers."

"Yes I did."

"Can we eat at Perry's before we come home?"

Deborah knew Perry's was a hangout hamburger spot for high school students. She took a glance at her watch. It was after four, and she knew it would be dark before her son and daughter returned to the Cove. It wouldn't be the first time they would stop off to eat before coming home, but they no longer lived in Charleston.

"Not tonight, baby."

"Why not, Mom?"

Crystal's whining grated on her nerves. "Please put Whitney on the phone."

"What's up, Mom?" Her son's deep voice came through the earpiece.

"I want you to come home now."

"Chrissie wants to eat with her friends."

"Chrissie can eat with her friends when she doesn't have to go to school the next day. I want you home before it gets too dark."

He sighed heavily. "Okay, but Crystal's about to catch an attitude."

"What she shouldn't want is for me to catch one. Call me from the house phone once you get there. Good-bye."

Deborah ended the call and placed the phone on a padded folding chair. She could always count on her daughter to try and push the envelope. She knew the rules: no socializing on school nights. If it had been a Friday night, Deborah might have considered letting her hang out with her friends. But not when she had to get up even earlier now that they lived on the island to make it to school on time. And Crystal always had a problem waking up— even with an alarm clock.

Brushing off the seat of her jeans, she walked into the bathroom and washed her hands. She stared at her reflection in the mirror over the vanity and the face that stared back at her was that of a stranger. It had been weeks since she'd gone to the salon to have her hair trimmed and styled; she needed a mani/pedi and a hydrating facial. In other words she needed a beauty makeover. The Beauty Box was several doors from the Muffin Corner and Deborah knew she had to make an appointment before her grand opening.

Drying her hands on a decorative guest towel, she left the bathroom. With Asa's assistance, they'd shelved most of the books. Only six cartons remained. "I'm going out for a few minutes to stretch my legs. Do you want me to bring you something from the Muffin Corner?"

Reaching into the pocket of his jeans, Asa took out a money clip. "I'll have large black coffee with a shot of espresso."

Deborah waved her hand. "Put your money away. I still owe you for lunch and dinner."

"I'm sorry, boss—I mean, Miss Deborah."

Deborah narrowed her eyes, then smiled. "Don't give away the store."

It had been after eight when Deborah turned off the lights, locked up The Parlor, gave Asa her set of keys, and selected a spot for the piano for when the movers arrived. Miraculously she and Asa had finished shelving all the books. She'd gone home to take a leisurely bubble bath. Deborah hadn't realized how tired she was until she lay in bed. She remembered Crystal coming into her room, but could not remember what they'd talked about.

Today was to become as hectic as the day before. She'd gotten up early to go into Charleston to supervise the movers as to what she wanted delivered to the bookstore. She was also expecting the delivery of the mattress and other furnishings for the second floor apartment. The receptionist at the Beauty Box had managed to squeeze her in, but she had to be there at four, or she would have to wait until Saturday for her favorite stylist to fit her in.

Her cell phone rang, and she answered it before it rang again. "Hello."

"Good morning, Deborah."

A smile tilted the corners of her mouth. "Good morning, Asa. How are you?"

"Good."

"Where are you?"

"I'm at the store."

"I'm leaving Charleston now, and I'm going to try and make the next sailing." Taking the ferry would get her there faster than taking the causeway, because it was a direct route.

"I'll see you when you get here."

Deborah ended the call; walking in and out of the rooms she checked to make certain the movers hadn't forgotten anything. The linen closet was empty, as were the closets in all the bedrooms. She and Whitney had loaded up the trunks of their cars with clothing they would take with them. Every year she would go through her children's closets and drawers to pack up what they'd outgrown or no longer wore, donating used and gently used clothes. Unnecessary clutter had become her pet peeve. Deborah had also packed up pots and pans, linens, and cleaning supplies for Asa's apartment.

She lingered when she should've been in her car driving for the pier, her fingertips caressing the backs of chairs, the surfaces of tables, lamps she'd waxed and dusted for as long as she could remember. The bed where she'd lain and made love with Louis would go to a single mother who'd lost everything. The furniture in her son's and daughter's rooms would go to other children whose need was much greater than any Crystal or Whitney had experienced in their young lives.

Let it go, Deborah. It's time to say good-bye, her silent voice taunted. Deborah took a final look around, and then walked out of the bedroom, down the hallway and the staircase to the first floor. Reaching for her handbag, she went to the door, opened it, then closed and locked it for the last time.

"Deborah!"

She turned around to find Barbara in a bathrobe standing on her porch and sipping from a large mug. "Hey you."

Barbara came down off the porch. Tears shimmered in her eyes. "I guess this is it."

"No, it's not," Deborah countered. "You know you and your family are welcome to come to the Cove anytime you want. And I hope you're coming to my grand opening tomorrow. I'm getting my hair done this afternoon," she added when Barbara stared at the hair she'd pulled into a ponytail.

"Of course, Deborah. I wouldn't miss it for the world. I changed my shift just so I could be off. What time should I get there?"

"I'm opening at noon, and the ribbon-cutting will be at one."

"Will you need help setting up?"

Deborah smiled and shook her head. "No. I hired someone to assist me in the store."

"Good for you." Barbara hugged Deborah, taking care not to slosh coffee on her white cotton pullover. "I'll see you tomorrow."

Deborah returned the hug, kissing her now ex-neighbor's cheek. "Tomorrow. Got to go, because I want to get to the Cove before the movers."

"Can I bring Nate and Janelle?"

"Of course. Maybe they can stay over to give you and Terrell a night to yourselves."

"I'd love that, but I promised my mother-in-law we would take her out to dinner."

"Perhaps another time then." Deborah glanced at her watch. She had thirty-five minutes before the next sailing. She looked up at the overcast sky. It was cool, but felt warmer because of the near one hundred percent humidity. If it was going to rain, then she hoped it would hold off until she reached the island.

An hour later, Deborah maneuvered into her parking space as the movers' van pulled up next to her. They'd arrived at the same time. Her stomach did a flip-flop when she saw Asa standing in the doorway dressed entirely in black: golf shirt, slacks, and slip-ons. There was something about his standing there, arms crossed over his chest, that was so male and virile. It took her breath away. He glanced her way and smiled. She returned it with one of her own. She didn't know what she would've done if he hadn't been there to help her. He was more than an employee. He was a godsend.

Stepping aside, Asa winked at Deborah when she walked in through the back door. "Mabel dropped off the muffins and coffee. Today's special is carrot-molasses."

She saw a tray of assorted muffins covered with cellophane and an urn of coffee on the table, along with hot/cold paper cups, small paper plates, and a dish filled with packets of sugar and sugar substitutes and a bowl filled with ice and prepackaged milk and half-and-half. Deborah had stopped at the Muffin Corner the night before and arranged to have the sweet breads delivered to the store to offer the workmen who would be coming and going throughout the morning. The smell of the brewing coffee was intoxicating.

"As soon as the coffee finishes brewing I'm going to get a cup."

"How do you take yours?" Asa asked Deborah.

"Very light with half-and-half."

"Sugar?"

"Yes please. Two."

"Mrs. Robinson."

Deborah turned to find the foreman of the work crew striding into the store. "Yes."

"We're going to either have to take off the door and the frame to get the piano inside or remove your plate glass window."

Deborah shuddered to think what would happen if they broke or cracked her window. "What is easier for you?"

"Take off the door and the frame," Asa said before the man could respond. "The window might be easier, but if there's any trouble replacing it, we could end up with leaks whenever it rains."

"Bring it through the back door," she said, confirming Asa's directive. "You and your men are welcome to coffee, muffins, and breakfast breads."

"Much appreciate the offer, ma'am."

One man in the three-man team quickly took the door off the hinges, then the frame, as the other two lowered the piano on a hydraulic lift and wheeled the dolly into the shop with relative ease. "Where do you want this, ma'am?"

"Position it in front of the window." Deborah had decided she wanted the piano near the front of the store, where passersby would be intrigued enough to want to come in and browse. Before leaving the night before, she'd had Asa tape newspaper over the front door to conceal the interior from onlookers.

The men replaced the legs on the magnificent concert piano, positioning it perfectly. Thankfully it came with casters, which made moving it around easy. Cordovan-brown club chairs with footstools and loveseats were set up to form a reading corner where customers could read or watch television. A generous supply of glass coasters were stacked on the coffee and side tables.

Deborah picked up an all-in-one computer and cash register off the floor, placing them on a mahogany writing table. She set a landline telephone on a matching desk, the file drawers filled with orders and receipts. Another mahogany piece—this one a buffet server that would provide a surface for the urn of hot water and packets of tea and condiments—faced the desk and writing table against the opposite wall. Once the rug was down, the ceiling fans installed, and the hand-painted pots with live green plants in place, The Parlor would resemble an actual parlor.

Asa stood with his back to the front door, surveying the bookstore as if it were his first time. The reading area was inviting, with twin floor and table lamps with Tiffany-style shades. He had visited countless bookstores—small and large—but none had the warmth and homey charm of The Parlor. Setting up the tea bar was an ingenious idea, because Deborah had mentioned she wanted to revive the ritual of afternoon tea with pretty tablecloths and china cups with matching saucers. The bar would be reserved for a small gathering of eight with tiny cakes, cookies, and tarts to accompany the various blends of tea.

"What do you think, Asa?"

"It's wonderful. Once people come in they're not going to want to leave. You have a nice selection of titles, so you should do okay."

"I have to do more than okay."

"What are you concerned about, Deborah? It's everything that you want and need."

"The Parlor has to be more than a bookstore, Asa. I have to come up with something to keep the customers coming back again and again. And it can't only be because of three o'clock afternoon tea."

Unconsciously, Asa's brow furrowed. "Why are you serving tea at three?"

"Haven't you noticed, with the exception of a few businesses, most places close between the hours of twelve and two?"

"Yes, I did. Why's that?"

"It's an island tradition that goes back about three hundred years. The summer sun is so brutal that it is dangerous to stay outdoors during that time of the day, so everyone and everything stops. The custom isn't adhered to as much during the winter months, but during the summer all businesses close down—even the restaurants, post office, and supermarket. Some people who've been to Europe refer to it as siesta, so when you hear folks talk about taking siesta you'll know what they mean."

"Are you going to observe the ritual now or during the summer months?" Asa asked.

"I'll keep the tradition year-round. It will give us a chance to put everything in order. It will also give us time to relax with a midday snack and set up for tea."

Lowering his arms, Asa rested a hand on Deborah's

back. She stiffened, then relaxed against his outstretched fingers. "I just thought of something."

Shifting slightly, she met his eyes. "What?"

"Did you have a book discussion group in your Charleston bookstore?"

Deborah shook her head. "No. I'd tried setting one up, but most of my customers were too busy to commit."

"I think it would work well here," Asa said, "because there are a lot retirees and snowbirds. You can hold it every two weeks, which means they would have to buy at least two books a month. That would definitely guarantee sales."

"Are you certain you never ran a bookstore before?" she joked.

He smiled, attractive lines fanning out around his eyes. "Very certain."

"What did you do before you retired?"

"I worked in a hospital."

"Were you a doctor?"

Asa's chest tightened. "Yes," he quickly changed the subject before she could probe further. "So, how are you going to run this book club of yours?"

"Well, if I'm going to moderate the discussions, then I'll have to read the books, too."

"You're a former English literature instructor. Select something you've already read."

Deborah froze. "Who told you I was a teacher?"

"Mabel did when she dropped off the muffins and coffee. She said she'd expected you to become a librarian because you were always obsessed with books."

Deborah paled for a moment, but shrugged it off quickly. "And I'd predicted that she would become a pastry chef. Whenever there was a cooking contest Mabel always came in first place. She's established a reputation for making the best piecrusts in the Lowcountry."

"Does she ever sell pies in her shop?"

"Pies and cakes are special orders. Her husband Lester is the cake man."

"Are you going to get them to provide the tea cakes? And will the ladies be required to wear fancy hats whenever they come for high tea?" Lifting his chin, he peered down his nose as if he'd detected something malodorous.

Deborah gave him a soft punch to his shoulder. "Stop it! It's not nice to begrudge our genteel Sanctuary Cove ladies."

Asa rested his hands on her shoulders. "I wouldn't dare. After all, you just happen to be one of those genteel ladies."

"You think?"

He nodded. "I know. You are incredible."

Asa fought against the tumult of emotions that left him feeling off-balance. It was as if he was metal and she was a powerful magnet, drawing him in, holding him captive. With each encounter he found it more and more difficult to relate to her not as an employer but as a woman.

She looked up at him, an unsure expression on her face. "Please, Asa..."

His hands fell away. "I'm not coming onto you, Deborah."

She took a step back, putting some distance between them. "Did I imply you were?"

He angled his head, giving her a long, penetrating stare. "No. But, if it makes you uncomfortable, then I won't touch you again."

"Did I say it made me uncomfortable?" she replied smoothly.

Asa crossed his arms over his chest in a gesture that had become very familiar to Deborah. "You don't have to say it. You freeze up even if I inadvertently brush against you. I'm not a sexual predator, so put your mind at ease that you're not going to be attacked when you least expect it. I'm forty-six years old and I've never had to force my attentions on any woman, and I'm not about to do it now."

Deborah watched him walk to the back of the bookstore. "Where are you going?"

He stopped but didn't turn around. "Out for a smoke."

Her eyelids fluttered. "But you don't smoke."

Asa turned, glaring at her. "Maybe it's time I start."

The seconds ticked as they continued to stare at each other. "My husband wasn't a touchy-feely person," she finally admitted.

Asa nodded. "Well, maybe what you need after a stressful few days is a friend who is."

He extended his arms, beckoning her closer.

She took a step, anchoring her arms under his shoulders, and found herself enveloped in his embrace, making Asa feel things he didn't want to feel. The runaway beating of her heart slowed until it resumed a normal rhythm.

"I'm sorry I snapped at you," Deborah said, burying her face in the crux of his shoulder.

Asa pressed his mouth to her hair, the curls piled atop her head tickling his nose. "I think we've done enough apologizing for one day, and definitely no pity parties."

Asa heard Deborah's audible sigh before she pulled out of his embrace. A tap sounded at the front door. "You're right. That's either the electrician or the furniture delivery." As she walked away, Asa realized how much he already missed having his arms around her.

Chapter Nine

Whoever it was, Asa cursed their timing. Holding Deborah, burying his face in her hair, felt so natural, as if he'd executed the motion countless times. She looked nothing like Claire, but holding Deborah had reminded him of what he missed.

Asa *was* a touchy-feely person, and touching Deborah made him feel more alive than he'd been in over a year. She had become a constant reminder that he was a man with physical urges he had managed to repress. Women had come on to him at the boardinghouse, but with them he'd felt nothing.

However, it was different with Deborah. Asa didn't know whether it was because they'd lost their spouses, or if it was glimpses of vulnerability he saw in Deborah that appealed to his protective instincts, but he knew that he wanted her for more than friendship.

Snapping out of his thoughts, Asa realized it hadn't been the furniture delivery, but the electrician, who'd arrived carrying an oversized sailcloth satchel containing his tools.

Peter Raney returned to his van and brought in cartons filled with the ceiling fans and track lighting Deborah had requested.

"Where do you want the fans, Mrs. Robinson?"

"I'd like you to replace the light fixture in the front and the one behind the loveseat with the fans. I have Tiffany-style globes to cover the other naked bulbs. But, there is one more thing I'd like you to do." The slightly built, pale man had a sparse graying pate and watery blue eyes that looked like they belonged on a heavy-lidded owl, and the bored expression on his face did not change.

"What's that?"

"I need a doorbell."

Peter squinted. "I just may have one in my bag. May I suggest something, Mrs. Robinson?" Deborah nodded. "I think you should replace your front door with a decorative one with beveled glass. It would let in light while still providing some privacy."

A blush made its way across her cheeks. There was no doubt the electrician was referring to the newspaper taped to the door to keep out prying eyes. "I'm planning on hosting my grand opening tomorrow."

"I can have it installed today," Peter said. "I'll measure the doorframe, then call my son and have him pick up one on the mainland. I'm not certain how much you want to spend, but a nice fiberglass door will probably run you, including installation, around seven-fifty. You'd want a storm-type door that will convert from glass to a screen to protect it from the saltwater. That's probably another three hundred. Both doors are a nice investment that will enhance the look of your store. What else do you need?"

"There are two ceiling fans in the upstairs apartment that work but make a lot of noise."

He gave her a rare smile. "I'll check them first. If they're bad, then I'll have my boy pick up a couple for you when he goes to get the doors. By the way, it looks real nice in here."

"Thank you. I know every dollar spent in the bookstore is a needed business expense." She paused before turning back to Peter. "You can put in the doors."

Asa came up behind Deborah when the electrician went to measure the door. "He's right about replacing the front door."

She glanced up at him over her shoulder. "What about the back door?"

"There's no need to replace it because it's made with reinforced steel. Are you going to install a security system?"

Deborah shook her head. "No. Only the bank and the pharmacy have security systems that are connected to the sheriff's office. The pharmacy has to have one because of the drugs and because it also houses the post office. In case you haven't noticed, all of Main Street, including the business district and waterfront, is monitored by cameras. Unfortunately some kids decided it was fun to leave their tags around the Cove. Though not a serious problem yet, the town council voted to install them. As soon as they went up the vandalism stopped."

"The sheriff looks like he's no-nonsense." When Asa had sat in at the town meeting he'd noticed that Jeffrey Hamilton hadn't smiled once.

"He gave the Marine Corps twenty years before becoming sheriff. Jeff would lock up his grandmother if she spat on the sidewalk. He grew up on the Cove, but has relatives in Angels Landing and Haven Creek. Folks called him Sheriff Buford Pusser from the *Walking Tall* movie after he caught some kids who'd come over from the mainland shooting up drugs in the schoolyard late one night. One came at him with a baseball bat, while another pulled a gun. He managed to get the bat and that was all she wrote. The boy with the gun ended up with two broken arms and the other was so lumped up that he couldn't see out both eyes for at least a week."

"Damn," Asa drawled.

"That's what I said when I heard the story. He's the sheriff for the entire island. He also supervises part-time deputies in the other towns."

"Why don't they have their own sheriffs?"

"They did at one time, but when they restructured their budget the mayors decided to pay Jeff to police their towns, too. The deputies are retired police, probation, and corrections officers who accepted the positions to supplement their pensions." Knocking interrupted their conversation, this time on the back door. Deborah smiled at Asa. "That must be the furniture delivery." She walked to the door, Asa following close behind.

He opened the door for her. "Yes?"

A burly man in a pair of overalls touched the brim of his oversized cap. "I have a furniture delivery for..." He squinted at his work order. "It looks like D. Robinson."

"You can bring it in." Waiting until the man went back to his truck, Asa turned to Deborah. "You can show them where you want them to put the furniture, while I'll hang out down here."

"You'll have to move the piano to put down one rug, and the other will go in the sitting area."

"Don't stress yourself, Debs. I'll take care of whatever it is you need."

"No, you didn't call me Debs."

Asa winked at her. "Yes I did. Don't you call yourself that?"

Her dark eyes sparkling in amusement, Deborah stared at Asa's smiling mouth. "Yes, but only my good friends call me Debs."

Asa leaned closer. "What about me, Debs? Am I not your good friend?"

He held his breath, hoping that she considered him a friend, wanting to become so much more. He was friend, protector, and guardian angel. "Yes. Right now you're my best friend."

He winked at her. "I like that. I've known a few girls who were called Debbie, but not Debs."

"Mabel shortened my name to Debs and it stuck. Very few folks on the Cove call me Deborah. My mother named me after her mother, who thought I was the best thing to come along since sliced bread because I was her first grandchild."

"Is she still alive?"

"No. She died two years ago. She'd moved to Florida because she couldn't take the cold weather, but when she was diagnosed with dementia my parents relocated to be close to her. When she began going outdoors alone and the police would bring her home dehydrated with second and occasionally third degree burns, Mom knew she had to put her in a skilled nursing facility. Once there she declined rapidly, losing control of her bodily functions. I flew down to see her and the doctor had to sedate me. I lost it when I saw her strapped to her bed. But I understood why they had to do it. She'd begun hallucinating and calling for my grandfather who'd died many years before. I was in the airport on my way back to South Carolina when my dad called to tell me that my grandmother had passed away. She was lucid for the first time in years and had told him that she wanted to see me. That was a dark period in my life because I'd lost three grandparents within the span of five years. I guess that's why I tell my children every day that I love them."

"I know you're a widow, but you're lucky to have your children."

Deborah pulled her lips between her teeth. "I'm more than lucky. I'm blessed. Do you have any, Asa?"

A beat passed. "No, I don't." He was saved from having to explain how he'd lost his only child when one of the delivery men, balancing a box spring on his shoulder, came through the door.

Deborah nodded to the man. "Please follow me. It goes upstairs."

She preceded him up the staircase, standing aside while he placed it on the springs of the massive antique iron bed. It had taken a lot of straining, but Asa soon appeared to help and together, they'd managed to pull the bed from the corner to the middle of the room. With the bed dressing, shades, wardrobe, and other accessories the apartment began to take on a homey atmosphere.

Peter, who'd taken the cover off the wall switch, flipped it several times and the blades to the fans turned slowly until they were whirling on the fastest speed. "The noise was because they were off-kilter."

Deborah smiled, causing Asa's heart to skip a beat. "Thank goodness for that."

"I'll replace the wires because they look a little frayed."

"Thank you, Peter."

Deborah stored the rest of the linens in the drawers at the bottom of the wardrobe after she made up the bed. When she'd ordered it she thought of what Crystal had said about moving into the apartment once she attended college. There had to be enough space for her to hang her clothes and drawers to store her lingerie, tees, and whatever else she needed to wear. There was still another three years before her daughter would graduate high school, and that was enough time for her to decide whether she would attend a local or out-of-town college. Or maybe Whitney would make use of the apartment should he decide to attend college in Charleston, rather than going away to Howard.

She overheard Peter, who'd replaced the cover to the wall switch, call his son and tell him what he needed, while she tore open the package to the slipcovers. Cursing under her breath, Deborah saw that she had to steam the wrinkles and creases.

"What's the matter?" Asa asked when she returned to the bookstore and opened the desk drawer, reaching for her key fob.

"I have to go home and get my steamer."

"For what?"

"I bought slipcovers for the chair and sofa, but they're wrinkled."

Asa took the key fob from her loose grip, pushing it into the pocket of his slacks. "No, Deborah. I'm not moving in tonight, so the wrinkles can wait. They'll probably fall out over time, so don't stress yourself out about it."

"When are you moving in?"

"Probably not until Monday or Tuesday. And I'm certain when I do move in the apartment will be lovely."

A smile like sunshine brightened her face. "The ceiling fans are quieter now."

Deborah didn't know why, but she wanted Asa to lower his head and kiss her. Not a passionate open-mouth kiss, but one that would allow her to see if he was as sweet as he looked. He stared at her under lowered lids. "Good."

"And I made up your bed."

"Thank you."

Deborah's eyebrows lifted slightly. "I hope Peter will be finished by four, but if he isn't can you hang out here until he is? I have a hair appointment and probably won't be finished until six."

Asa nodded. "No problem."

Pushing her hands in the back pockets of her jeans, Deborah pulled the denim taut over her hips as she stared at the rug under the piano. "Did you have a problem moving the piano?"

"Piece of cake," Asa crooned, walking over to the piano and sitting on the bench. Resting his hands on the keys he began to play, his fingers caressing the ivory.

Deborah felt her pulse quicken. She played piano, but even after years of lessons and recitals her skill wouldn't begin to match Asa's. Closing her eyes, she swayed gently. She opened them when Peter walked over to listen and they shared a knowing smile. No words were needed.

"That was real pretty," Peter said when the last note faded. Asa nodded. "Excuse me, but I'd better get to work."

Sitting on the bench beside Asa, Deborah leaned into him. "Where did you learn to play like that?"

He stared at his hands resting in his lap. "Practice, practice, and more practice."

"I practiced until my fingers bled, and I still couldn't play 'Bella's Lullaby' like you just did."

A hint of a smile tilted the corners of Asa's mouth. "So you recognized it?"

"There's no way I wouldn't. My daughter is obsessed with the Twilight Saga. She's read the four books at least twice and I've lost count how many times she's watched the DVDs."

"These young girls seem to be fascinated with vampires."

"Well, you have to admit that Edward is somewhat of a sexy vampire."

"Please don't tell me that you were one of those mothers who stood in line with their daughters to catch the midnight premiere."

Deborah folded her hands at her waist. "I was. There was no way I was going to let my child go to a movie theater that time of night without my supervision." She flashed a sheepish grin. "I think I would've enjoyed the film more if I hadn't had to deal with a theater filled with teenage girls screaming hysterically whenever Edward kissed Bella."

"I can't believe you bought into the hype."

"Why?"

"I don't know. I just wouldn't take you for someone who would go for a vampire flick."

"It was a paranormal romantic film."

"And that makes it different?"

"Of course it does," she argued softly.

Asa reached for her left hand. "Play something for me."

"What?"

"Anything, Deborah."

She searched her memory for a piece she could play without music, deciding on a Chopin nocturne. She hadn't played more than a dozen notes when Asa began playing with her. They shared a grin, he winking at her as their fingers flew over the keys as if they'd practiced together in the past. Deborah knew playing with Asa made her step up her game, and she lost herself in the music.

They segued from classical music to the show tunes from Andrew Lloyd Webber's stage productions: "All I Ask of You," "Don't Cry for Me Argentina," and "I Don't Know How to Love Him." Overcome with emotion, Deborah collapsed against Asa. Playing with him had been a way for her to open up herself to release the grief that had hung over her like a shroud. The songs he'd selected were sadly haunting and evocative. It was as if he, too, was in pain and needed to surface from a dark place filled with sadness and melancholy.

Covering her mouth with her hand, she cried silently. "I'm sorry," she sobbed, sliding off the bench. She hadn't taken more than three steps when he caught her wrist, spinning her around to face him.

Cradling her face between his hands, Asa stared at Deborah's tear-stained face. "I'm sorry." Reaching into a pocket of his slacks, he took out a handkerchief and gently blotted her face.

She managed a half-smile. "There's no need to apologize. I get a little sentimental when I hear certain songs."

Asa put the handkerchief back in his pocket. "You're not a very good liar, Deborah."

Deborah's temper flared, but she managed at the last possible second to clamp her teeth together to keep from spewing curses. She was upset because Asa had made her feel vulnerable, and after only two days he'd come to know whether she was lying or telling the truth. Was she that transparent, or was he just perceptive? She'd told him about her family, but little about herself. He knew she'd been a teacher, had owned a bookstore in Charleston, and was widowed with two teenaged children, but not much else. She hadn't told him her age, where she'd attended college or what she'd planned for her future. "Excuse me, but I'm going out for a smoke."

"But you don't smoke." He'd repeated what she'd said to him earlier that morning.

"Maybe I do. Maybe I don't. I'll right be back," she replied with a sad smile.

As Deborah opened the door and walked out into a light drizzle, she could hear the sounds of Andrew Lloyd Webber music being played on the piano. She stood still for a moment, allowing the melody to envelop her, before heading to the parking lot.

Deborah walked into the Muffin Corner, the wind chime affixed to the door jangling musically. She folded her body down on a chair at the only unoccupied table, waving to Mabel who'd come from the rear of the shop.

"What's up, Debs?"

She pulled her wet blouse away from her skin. "I'll have your largest cappuccino with plenty of sugar and whipped cream."

Mabel made Deborah's coffee, adding a generous amount of whipped cream, and then came over to sit down opposite her. "What in the world set you off? You look like a ruffled cat."

Taking a sip of the hot liquid, Deborah moaned softly as the perfectly made coffee warmed her throat and chest. "Thanks for the compliment," she said facetiously. She immediately apologized when Mabel's face fell. "I guess I'm a little stressed out trying to get the store ready for tomorrow."

"When I dropped off the muffins I noticed that you'd shelved all the books."

Deborah took another sip, licking the cream off her lips. "I couldn't have done it without Asa Monroe."

Mabel gave her a mischievous smirk.

"Don't look at me like that, Mabel."

"Like what, Debs?"

"Like the cat that just licked the cream off Sunday dinner's dessert."

Mabel affected an impassive expression. "Is this better?"

Deborah laughed when she felt like crying again. She could not have found better friends in Mabel and Barbara. They always knew what to do to make her laugh. She told her friend how she'd come to hire Asa.

"I still would have been unpacking books if it wasn't for him," Deborah concluded.

"The man is smooth as creamy peanut butter."

"What are you talking about?"

"Breeding and elegance, Debs. That's something you're born with, and the man definitely has a monopoly on both."

Cradling the mug in her hands, testing its warmth against her palms, Deborah had to agree. "He's very intelligent and extremely talented."

"Could it be that you like him?"

"No! No," Deborah repeated in a softer tone. "How can you say that when I just lost my husband?"

"Losing your husband has nothing to do with finding yourself attracted to a man. What if Louis were alive? Would you still think your Mr. Monroe intelligent and creative?"

"He is *not* my Mr. Monroe, Mabel. He happens to be someone who is vacationing on the Cove for the winter, and come spring he'll be gone like so many of the other snowbirds. He wants to work and I need someone to help me manage the bookstore. End of story."

Mabel applauded slowly. "Bravo, Debs. Nice speech."

Deborah's hands fell away from the mug as she began to massage her temples. "I came here to de-stress, Mabel. I don't want to talk about Asa. What I do want to discuss with you is afternoon tea."

"Afternoon tea?" Mabel repeated.

Deborah nodded. "Yes." Throwing back her head, Mabel laughed. The sound was so infectious that Deborah laughed with her. "What's so funny?"

"Are you talking about tea time when ladies put on their fancy hats and lace gloves and nibble on cucumber sandwiches?"

"Yes." Deborah revealed to the pastry chef what she'd planned for weekday afternoons at The Parlor. Deborah also told her about the book club, leaving out the fact that Asa had given her the idea. The less she mentioned his name the easier it would be for her to dismiss the strange sensations that he made her feel, which were far more frightening than the tales her grandmother had told her about the people on the north side of the island.

Mabel flashed her trademark gap-toothed grin. "I like

it, Debs. I remember hearing my great-grandmomma talk about the rich ladies who'd lived in the big houses. Their so-called grand mansions were falling down around them, yet they still managed to get together most afternoons for tea."

"Bless you, Mabel Davis-Kelly. You just gave me my first title for the book club discussion: Kathryn Stockett's *The Help*. And I'm going to place an ad in the *Chronicle* advertising the book club. I have to make certain to emphasize that we will be reading and discussing literary and popular fiction. Those who want to read literature will be in one group, and those who prefer popular fiction will be in another. Each group will be required to read two titles each month and every two weeks we'll have the discussion. The highbrow ladies will meet every other Tuesday, and the ordinary folk every other Wednesday."

"I know what you're up to, Debs."

"What's that?" she asked, grinning from ear to ear.

"I bet those snooty heifers will want to read the literary stuff, and us regular people will go for the popular stuff."

"You know you ain't right," Deborah drawled.

Mabel sucked her teeth loudly. "I'm as right as rain and you know it. What if they buy their books on those electronic readers, then join the group?"

"The criteria for joining will be that they have to buy the book from The Parlor."

The wind chime jangled again, and Mabel stood up. "I'll have Lester make a few cakes for your grand opening. It will be our homecoming gift."

"Thanks, friend. We'll talk later about what I'll need for my afternoon tea."

"It's not going to be that complicated, Debs. Whatever muffin is the special for that day I'll make into loaves and cut them into little squares. And for those who have a nut allergy I'll make shortbread cookies." She waved her hand. "Don't worry. I'll hook you up real nice."

Deborah squeezed Mabel's hand. "I don't know what I'd do without you."

"Yeah, you would. You'd look for another gap-tooth gal to make you laugh."

"You know you're crazy, Mabel."

"Yeah, I know. Crazy like a fox. Let me go and take care of this customer before she starts spreading gossip that I ignored her even though I can't stand her old ass," she said sotto voce.

Deborah watched in awe as Mabel interacted with Hannah Forsyth. Hannah had been the librarian when Deborah was a teenager, and nearly three decades later the woman was still in the position. She was also the Cove's historian and a notorious gossip. If she'd been a Hollywood gossip columnist, she would've become wealthy selling information about the residents of the island.

Deborah finished her coffee, pulled a bill out of the pocket of her jeans, left it on the counter, and walked out. The drizzle was now a heavy steady rain. Sprinting out the door, she ran through Moss Alley and around the back to The Parlor. By the time she made it into the store she was soaked through.

She stopped short when she saw Asa staring at her as if she were an apparition. "What's the matter?" When he didn't answer she looked down to see what he'd been staring at. Her white blouse was pasted to her chest and the outline of her breasts was clearly visible though her sheer white bra. Curbing the urge to cover her chest, she hunched her shoulders.

"Why don't you go upstairs and dry off?" Asa suggested.

Deborah nodded only because she couldn't speak. It was as if her voice had been locked in her throat, rendering her completely mute. Turning on her heels, she raced up the staircase. Peter was nowhere to be seen and for that she was thankful. Walking into the bathroom, she stripped off her blouse and bra, spreading both over the shower door. Reaching for a towel under the vanity, she blotted the moisture from her arms and chest.

Deborah stared at her reflection in the mirror over the vanity and then closed her eyes as the area between her thighs throbbed when she recalled the naked hungry lust in Asa's eyes. Moaning softly, she bit her lip when the throbbing increased until she felt as if she were coming out of her skin.

I need him. A rush of guilt assailed Deborah's traitorous thoughts. She'd buried her husband six weeks ago and now she found herself lusting after a man—a stranger who made her feel something she did not want to feel: desire. Pressing her fist to her mouth, she waited until the throbbing eased, then wrapped the towel around her body, tucking the ends together over her breasts. Her jeans were damp, but tolerable.

Deciding on a bit of ingenuity, Deborah draped her blouse and bra over the back of the dining area chair. Bringing it within a foot of the stove, she turned on the oven, waited for it to heat up, and then opened the oven door. She'd read stories about people using their oven to heat their homes, but she didn't think it would take that long for her clothes to dry and she'd installed carbon monoxide detectors on both levels. Her drying method may have been a little primitive, but the result would be the same if she'd used her programmable dryer at home.

Settling down to the chair, she picked up the remote and turned on the flat-screen TV resting on the table across from the bed and seating area. She was so engrossed in a Victorian-period drama that she almost didn't hear the soft rapping on the closed door.

Sitting up straight, she pressed a hand over the towel. "Yes?"

"It's Asa. May I come in?"

Though her head said no, her unsteady voice replied, "Yes."

Chapter Ten

Asa held the doorknob for a full minute before deciding to enter the room. Slowly, he closed the distance between them and sat on the sofa. He tried swallowing the lump that had risen in his throat when he found that he couldn't pull his gaze away from the erotic sight of the soft swell of Deborah's breasts rising and falling under the towel. Asa also couldn't get the image of her erect nipples showing through her wet blouse out of his head. It hadn't mattered that he was a doctor and seeing a naked human body held as much appeal as a dead bug on his windshield. But it was different with Deborah Robinson. She was a very special woman who reminded him that he was a man whose physical urges hadn't died when he'd buried his wife.

Sandwiching his hands between his knees, Asa stared at the pattern on the rug under his feet. The chocolate-brown comforter with its large green leaves, the pile of bed pillows, the white window blinds, off-white slipcovers, and the oak wardrobe in an alcove had turned what had been a cold, empty space into an inviting apartment where he hoped to spend many relaxing hours.

"I like your dryer." His head came up when Deborah laughed; the sound was like music to his ears. He liked her best when she was laughing.

"It's said that necessity is the mother of invention. Maybe I should put in a stackable washer/dryer."

"Don't bother, Debs. I send my clothes out to be cleaned and laundered."

"Doesn't the boardinghouse have laundry service?"

He nodded slowly. "The first time they did my laundry I got someone else's underwear. And that told me either they wash everyone's clothes together, or they got mixed up in the folding phase." He stood up. "I came up to check on you."

"I'm going to give my very unique dryer another half an hour, then I'll be down."

"Take your time, Debs. Peter put up the track lights. He's now working on installing the fans."

Asa wished there was more information he could give her, if only to be in her presence a second longer. When he could think of nothing else to add, he turned and walked away, her image emblazoned in his mind.

"Look at you!" Crystal squealed when she saw her mother walk in through the side door. She'd just finished taking clothes out of the dryer. "Oh, Mom, you look *faboolicious*."

"I decided it was time to get my hair done."

Crystal reached for her mother's hand. "You also got a mani."

Deborah wiggled her toes, painted a soft raspberry

color in a pair of flip flops. "And a pedi, and my eyebrows plucked," she added.

"Can I get my hair and nails done?" Crystal asked.

"Sure. But what's the occasion?" Her daughter only visited the salon when she wanted her hair cut. And she claimed she couldn't sit still long enough for a manicure and pedicure.

"I want to go to the school's Valentine's Day dance next month. Whitney's going, so I'll be with him. Please, Mom."

Wrapping an arm around Crystal's waist, Deborah led her into the kitchen. "Is there someone special that's going to be at this dance?" She dropped her handbag on a stool near the wall phone and sat at the table with her daughter.

Crystal affected a bored expression. "He's not special."

"What is he?"

"He's just a friend. He lives in Charleston. He asked me to go to the dance with him, but I told him I'm not allowed to date, so we're going to meet at the school."

Reaching across the space separating them, Deborah reached for Crystal, holding her hand gently. "It's not that you're not allowed to date. It's just that I think you're too young to get involved with a boy."

"You were twenty—only five years older than me when you married Dad."

"That's true, but I'd graduated high school and was close to finishing college. Remember, your father had finished and he was teaching. That meant he could support a family. If you get too involved with this boy and heaven forbid you get pregnant, where do you think you'll end up? By the way, how old is he?"

"Sixteen."

Deborah shook her head. "Fifteen and sixteen. Even if you got a job flipping burgers you can't work full-time, and that means how are you going to pay rent, buy food, and take care of a baby?"

Crystal rolled her eyes. "I'm not going to get pregnant."

"And why not, Crystal?"

"Because I'm not going to have sex."

"You say that now, but what if you get caught up in the moment and it happens? I've always been open with you when it comes to sex and birth control. After your Dad and I were married we decided we would wait five years before we would start a family. It didn't happen because one night we got caught up in the moment and I found myself pregnant with Whitney. Two years later you came along."

"Was I a 'caught up in the moment' baby?"

Deborah tunneled her fingers through her now bone-straight tresses. Whenever she wore her hair straight, she was reminded of photos of her mother, who had been the consummate hippie with long, curly auburn hair, bell-bottom pants, sandals, colorful dashiki, and love beads.

"No, baby. We planned to have you."

"That's nice to know. Back to the dance, Mom. I want a dress and heels."

This boy must really be something if my daughter wants to put on a pair of high heels, Deborah mused. "Do you know what type of dress and heels you want?"

"Not yet. I've been going through magazines looking for one. Shoes aren't as important."

"That's where you're wrong, Crystal. Accessories can make or break an outfit. You can look through my closet and try on a few of my shoes and see what style you like." She and her daughter had the same size foot, and Deborah's weakness had always been shoes and handbags.

"Can I wear the pair with the black silk bow?"

"Don't even try and go there, Crystal Robinson. I'm going to let you try my shoes on, but you're not going to wear them. Besides, those heels are four inches, and I doubt whether you'd be able to walk in heels that high."

"I have almost a month to practice."

"How tall is this boy?"

"He's taller than me."

"Will he be taller than you when you put on four-inch heels?" Deborah questioned.

Crystal scrunched up her face. "I don't know."

"Find out how tall he is before we buy your shoes. At sixteen boys don't like it too much when a girl is taller than them."

"I don't like being tall."

"I'm tall, Crystal, and so is your grandmother. Learn to accept it." Pearl Williams was five-ten, Deborah five-eight and Crystal was five-nine—and still growing. She glanced at the clock on the microwave. It was after seven. "Where's Whitney?"

"He's in his room typing a sample article for his meeting with Mr. Wilkes tomorrow. I should let you know that there's talk going around the school about Whitney."

Deborah closed her eyes. What she didn't want was a repeat of what had happened to Louis. "What kind of talk?" she asked, opening her eyes.

"Some kids are saying he's gay. That he doesn't like girls."

"What does Whitney say?"

"He doesn't say anything. I know he likes girls, because he's been talking and texting one who lives in Haven Creek."

"I take it the other kids don't know this?"

"He says it's none of their business."

Deborah smiled. "Good for him. I'm not going to say anything to him about what you just told me, but I hope she's at least a nice girl."

"I don't think she's a ho, but I don't know her like that."

"I hope you don't talk like this around that boy you like."

"I don't," Crystal confirmed.

"Then why me, Crystal?"

"Because you're cool like that, Mom."

Smiling, Deborah ruffled her daughter's hair. "Yeah. I guess I am cool like that. I'm glad you found a boy you like."

"He's nice, Mom."

"That's even better. Where does he live again?"

"Charleston."

"I'd like to meet him," Deborah said.

Crystal's eyebrows lifted. "Really?"

"Yes, really."

"Can he come tomorrow for the grand opening?"

Deborah nodded. It had been a while since Crystal seemed so upbeat about someone or something. "Of course. After dinner I want you to call his mother and I'll talk to her."

Crystal's expression changed, the excitement in her eyes fading quickly. "How is he going to get here, Mom? Darius doesn't drive. That's his name. Darius."

Deborah knew her daughter was flustered because her words came out choppy. "Don't worry about him getting here, baby. If his mother says he can come, then she can drop him off at the ferry and I'll have Whitney meet him at the pier."

Springing up from her chair like a jack-in-the-box, Crystal wrapped her arms around her mother's neck and kissed her cheek. "You're the best, Mom."

Deborah hugged her back. "I thought I was cool."

Crystal kissed her again. "That, too."

"What are we going to make for dinner?"

Crystal jumped and ran over to the refrigerator, holding the door open while she peered inside. "I defrosted some ground beef yesterday because I wanted burgers. But we can always use it for chili."

Deborah rose to her feet. "Chili sounds good. There should be some kidney beans in the pantry," she said as she walked to the half-bath to wash up. "See if the lettuce is still good. I'll put together a salad."

"How about garlic bread, Mom?"

"That sounds good," she called out from the bathroom.

She returned to the kitchen to find Whitney standing there in bare feet, holding several printed pages. He wore a white tee and jeans. She could never understand his aversion to wearing shoes.

"Hey, you look nice."

"Thank you, Whit." It had been weeks since her children had seen her made over, and having them compliment her buoyed her spirits.

"Mom, can you look these over when you get a chance?"

Deborah tossed the paper towel on which she had dried

her hands into the wastebasket under the countertop. "Are you sure you want me to see them before they're published in the *Chronicle*?"

"What makes you so sure that Mr. Wilkes is going to hire me?"

"The news he prints is old and tired, Whit. Hannah Forsyth's column about the history of the island is repetitious. People only buy the paper because they're hoping for something new. I've read the articles you've published in your school paper, and they are a lot better than what's in the *Chronicle*. If it wasn't for the ads, Eddie would've closed up shop a long time ago."

"Let's hope he doesn't close down until I get some articles in print. These are about Grandma Sallie Ann. I need you to tell me if I got the facts straight."

Deborah nodded. "Okay. I'll look at them after dinner. Leave them on the table in the back porch. And I promise not to take out my red pencil."

Whitney cut his eyes at his mother. "Real funny, Mom. I meant to ask you if you've read Grandma's letters."

"Yes, and burned them."

"Why?"

"What's in them was for my eyes only."

"Were they X-rated?"

"No, Whit. They were very personal. Things that happened before she married my grandfather. I plan to start reading her journals tonight. I'm willing to bet they'll be less personal. And if they are, then I'll let you read them for yourself. Maybe one of these days you'll write a book about her."

"Why haven't you written a book?" Whitney asked his mother.

"What would I write about? My life hasn't been that exciting that someone would want to read about it."

"It doesn't have to be nonfiction."

Deborah opened a cabinet and took out the pressure cooker. "I'd rather read books than try to write one."

"If I do write one, will you edit it for me?" Whitney asked.

"Yes, I will. Remember, I want you and Crystal to come to the grand opening tomorrow. In fact, you should write about it. I know it smacks of nepotism, but who cares."

"What are you wearing, Mom?" Crystal asked as she cradled two large cans of beans to her chest.

"Probably a blouse and dress slacks."

She set down the cans. "Can I pick out your shoes?"

"Don't pick out anything that will make her look like a hoochie, because you know there will be photos," Whitney warned his sister.

Deborah gasped. "I beg your pardon, young man. For your information none of my shoes come even close to hoochie status. So, mind your mouth."

"I guess I'd better take my foot out my mouth and get out of here while I can still walk," Whitney whispered under his breath.

"Good advice, brother love," Crystal drawled facetiously, laughing when her brother left the kitchen. "What if we have chili burgers instead of chili con carne?"

"You're the chef tonight and I'm the sous chef. It's whatever you decide. What do you want me to do?" Deborah asked.

"I need you to cut up several onions, garlic, bell pepper, and a few jalapeños."

"How much is a few, Crystal?"

"Three, four."

"No pepper mouth. I'm not going to eat food so spicy that I'm reliving it days later."

"Okay, Mom. Two jalapeños."

Deborah sat up in bed, her journal on her lap. Crystal had outdone herself when she added cubes of pepper jack cheese and finely chopped jalapeños to the ground beef patties, cooking them on the stovetop grill until they were tender and juicy with just enough heat to tantalize the palate. The garlic butter slathered on toasted hamburger buns and covered with a thick piquant chili along with an accompanying Greek salad had surpassed what they would've eaten at their favorite restaurant. She could see Crystal growing her own vegetables and serving them for dinner.

Reaching for a pen, she opened the cloth-covered book.

January 14th—I don't know what's happening to me. I find myself thinking about Asa when I least expect it. And I find myself wanting him when I don't want to. I say *want* because I don't want to need him. Needing Asa would make me dependent upon him, and that would prove disastrous when it comes time for him to leave the Cove. However, whenever I am around him I feel good—very good.

He's been a perfect gentleman, not giving me any indication that he wants more than friendship. But, I have to be honest when I say I don't know what I would do if he did. I'm still in love with Louis. I will always love Louis, and right now there is no room in my life for romance or another man.

Deborah closed the journal, placed it in the drawer, and turned off the bedside lamp. As she lay down to fall asleep her mind was flooded with images of Asa. His face, his smile, his tall, strong body, his hands. She loved his hands and the way they felt when he touched her. She thought about the way they skimmed the keys when he'd played the piano, envisioning his fingers caressing her naked body as they had the ivory. She imagined what it would feel like to have him stroke her most intimate places, bringing herself to climax before she realized what she'd been doing. Exhausted, she finally fell asleep, but not before trying to convince her heart that she was *not* falling in love with Asa Monroe.

Chapter Eleven

As Deborah maneuvered her car into the lot behind Moss Alley, she spotted Asa's truck. She shut off the engine and exited her car, but instead of entering the bookstore from the back door, she came around to the front. She wanted to see the new door in the bright daylight. The rain had stopped at dawn and the heat had returned with the rising sun. The weather was perfect for a grand opening. It was Saturday, the weekend, and a time when tourists came to the Sea Islands to shop.

Deborah had a sudden memory of years before. When she'd first told Louis her intent to stop teaching and open a store, he'd looked at her as if she had taken leave of her senses. Although in the end he'd given her his support Deborah knew he'd believed she would fail. However, she proved him and the other skeptics wrong because The Parlor offered the public what other bookstores hadn't—a nostalgic down-home, small-town charm that was wholly Americana. Those were past times when life was hard, but simple. Most people didn't have much, but they were content with their existence. Sunday dinners were family-oriented and national holidays meant fireworks, picnics, and county fairs. When her customers walked into The Parlor they felt that and more. Most were repeat customers, some who sat and talked long enough to form friendships. The homey atmosphere was what she'd tried to evoke, and had with much success.

This was what she'd duplicated with the Cove's bookstore. The piano was certain to garner a lot of interest, and the fact that she *and* Asa could play the magnificent instrument—he a lot better than she—was a double asset. There had been a time when she'd played for her children every night before putting them to bed. She'd gone from playing nursery rhymes to pop and show tunes to classical compositions once they'd begun taking lessons.

She still played duets with Crystal, who'd taken to the instrument like a duck to water, and Deborah attended her many recitals. Whitney, who'd hated to practice, stopped playing altogether when he turned ten. Crystal had continued taking lessons until she was thirteen. Deborah knew that Deborah McLeary would be proud to know that her precious piano hadn't been sold or left to gather dust in some warehouse, and that her namesake had kept it in concert-ready condition.

Standing outside the bookstore, she stared at the newly installed doors. The glass on the outer door was spotless. Moving closer she peered at the designer door, with its pattern reminiscent of those designed by Frank Lloyd Wright. Peter Raney was right. The beveled glass distorted objects inside the store, while the blinds covering the plate glass window concealed the piano and everything beyond it from view.

The day before, Deborah had set up her computer and printed a sign with the store's hours of operation, and set it in a silver frame that she placed in the window for all to see. Whitney had been given the task of designing a business card and the result was in keeping with the locale. Green lettering on buff-colored parchment with the image of a palmetto tree advertised the Cove's first and only bookstore.

Returning to her car, she opened the trunk and retrieved the hand-quilted runner for the table where she would place the live plants. She'd just put the key in the lock when the door opened and Asa stood, gaze fixated on her.

"Welcome to The Parlor." He bowed low as if she were royalty.

Deborah was too stunned to react, her breath catching in her throat. Asa had exchanged his casual attire for a white shirt, dark-gray silk tie, and a pair of charcoal gray suit trousers with a faint pinstripe. His footwear was a pair of Stacey Adams black leather slip-ons. He looked and smelled incredible.

She recovered quickly, giving him a modified curtsey. "Thank you, sir. You're here early," she said when he stepped aside to let her in.

"I decided not to wait and moved in earlier this morning."

Deborah smiled. "Good for you."

"You look beautiful."

Deborah froze, her eyes meeting Asa's. She'd wanted to tell him how handsome he looked, but he had complimented her first. A swath of heat swept over her, settling in her chest before moving lower. When she'd gotten up that morning she'd wondered about his reaction to seeing her with makeup, heels, and a different hairstyle. What she hadn't understood was why she was concerned about his reaction to her appearance, but seeing the way he was looking at her made it all the more clear. She wanted him to think her pretty, because she liked Asa Monroe.

Lowering her eyes and giving him a demure smile, Deborah said, "Thank you." As she turned to put the finishing touches on the store's appearance, she could feel the heat from Asa's gaze on her back.

Asa stared at the woman he'd grown to care for during his stay on the island. The electrician and his son had installed the doors before Deborah was to leave for her hair appointment, so he left after they did to return to the boardinghouse to pack. When he'd sat down to eat with the other guests he realized it would be the last time he would dine with them. Just knowing he would have a place to eat, sleep, and read in peace had made it difficult for him to contain his excitement. And for the first time, he'd joined the others in the parlor for cordials. That night when he went to bed, there was luggage sitting by the door. And when he finally fell asleep he'd dreamed of a beautiful woman with curly hair and a face like the angels in Renaissance paintings.

But the Deborah Robinson he knew had morphed into a sophisticate who belonged on the slick pages of *Town and Country*. The curls were missing and in their place was a sleek coif that swayed around her face and neck whenever she moved her head. Parted off-center, the smooth dark-brown strands with streaks of gold looked like threads of liquid silk. A light covering of makeup enhanced her dark eyes and full mouth.

How, he mused, could a woman look so utterly sexy in a tailored white blouse and black slacks? Some men liked their women in a state of undress, while he preferred his women clothed so he could imagine what they looked like without them. And right now his imagination had gone into overdrive. A single strand of large pearls, matching studs in her ears, and a pair of black cloth-covered pumps with decorative silk bows complemented her incredible look.

"What are you going to put on the table?" Asa asked.

"I have potted plants in the trunk of my car. I thought having live green plants would add a nice touch."

"I'll bring them in. What else do you need me to do?"

Deborah turned and patted his chest. "Nothing. Just look gorgeous for the ladies."

"So, I'm going to be your piece of meat."

Deborah ran her hands along his solid shoulders, smoothing the pristine shirt. "You're more than just meat. You're filet mignon."

Asa shook his head, smiling. "I prefer well-done rib eye with garlic butter or prime rib with horseradish."

Her smile matched his. "I'll keep that in mind when I treat you to dinner."

"Let me go and get those plants."

Deborah glanced at the time on the cable box. She had twenty minutes before The Parlor would open for business. She turned on the fans to circulate the warm air and lit scented candles, and the glow from track lighting and the sound of soft music set the stage for when she would finally open the door to welcome her first customer.

Asa came through the back door, kicking it closed behind him while carrying a plastic crate overflowing with greenery. "I'll leave you to arrange them however you want."

"Put the crate on the floor and I'll take care of them," Deborah called out. "Can you come over here for a minute?" She waited for Asa to come to where she sat at the desk, opening the top drawer and handing him a key on a black elastic band. "That's the key to the drawer in the writing table. Please open it."

Asa sat down at the table and opened the drawer, revealing the built-in compartment with stacks of bills in denominations from twenties to singles. There were also compartments for coins. "Nice."

"We need enough cash on hand to make change for customers." She punched several buttons on the cash register and the drawer opened. "You'll have to put in a pin number to open the register."

"A little security to keep someone from reaching over and dipping in the till," Asa said, nodding.

Deborah nodded. "I had to learn that the hard way. One time when I'd stepped away from the front someone walked in, opened the cash register, and scooped up whatever money was there before I realized what was happening. That's why I bought this one and I don't leave much cash in it. The credit card machine is connected to the landline telephone." She'd plugged in a cordless phone extension in the apartment and had an additional handset on the writing table. "All daily receipts will go here, orders in this one," she said opening and closing drawers in the desk. "I keep thinking I'm forgetting something."

"Stop worrying, Debs. Everything is perfect."

She smiled up at him. "I couldn't have done it without you."

"Yes, you would have. It may have taken a bit longer, but you would've done just fine."

Deborah stared at Asa's delectable mouth inches from her own, willing him to kiss her. Kiss her and remind her that she was a woman who'd realized she still had needs— sexual needs that had to be assuaged. Her gaze did not falter as she inhaled the citrus-blended fragrance that made up Asa's cologne and aftershave. She felt unable to move or speak as Asa came closer.

Her breasts felt heavy, nipples tightening in arousal as her chest touched his. Deborah's eyes closed; her heart stopped when his mouth brushed over hers. Asa's kiss was gentle, yet persuasive and she kissed him with a hunger that belied her noticeable calm.

"Deborah," Asa whispered, his heavy breathing echoing in her ear.

"Asa, I..."

His mouth moved over hers again, swallowing her words, while devouring her softness. "Don't talk, baby," Asa pleaded. "Please don't say anything." His lips left hers, trailing feathery kisses under her ear, along the column of her neck. "You smell delicious."

"Thank you," Deborah mumbled dreamily.

Asa kissed her again. "You taste delicious." Both were breathing heavily when the kiss ended. "That was for good luck, Debs."

"Thank you," Deborah said again in a husky whisper. The breathlessness of her own voice made her blush.

His smile was as tender as a caress. "As soon as you arrange the plants we can open the door."

Deborah didn't want to believe Asa could appear so calm when her insides were quivering like gelatin. Her mouth was tingling from his kisses. Asa had stoked a fire that grew hotter every time they were together.

Deborah set out hand-painted ceramic pots on the quilted table runner stitched with irregular shapes and various fabrics that her great-grandmother had pieced together. When her grandmother had shown Deborah her collection of quilts she had a story to tell about each of them. There were pieces that had come from a tattered apron, a worn tie, dress, work pants, shirt or jacket. The quilts were a textile history of her family and the time in which they'd lived.

Taking a step backward, she surveyed her handiwork before glancing over at Asa. She watched as he slipped his muscular frame into the suit jacket before adjusting his shirt cuffs and tie. He looked up at her then, their gazes locking before he walked over to meet her by the counter. Her shoes added at least three inches to her slender height, putting the top of her head at his nose. Deborah's chest fluttered at the thought of being this close to him, reminding her of the kiss they'd shared. She shook her head free of the thoughts and instinctively reached up to adjust his tie.

Raising his left arm, Asa stared at his watch. "It's ten." Reaching for her hand, he tucked it into the bend of his arm. "Are you ready?"

Deborah's eyes moved slowly over his face. "I was born ready."

Throwing back his head, Asa laughed loudly. Walking to the door, he propped it open to allow for The Parlor's first customers to come through. Deborah stood at the counter, staring out at the clear glass, while Asa opened and raised the blinds over the plate glass. The bookstore was situated on the west side of Main Street, and that meant the sun would not reach them until late morning.

Within fifteen minutes of opening a young man from the local florist walked in carrying a large potted plant wrapped in shiny green paper tied with a bright red bow. Deborah indicated where he could set the plant, signed the receipt, and gave him a tip. She plucked off the attached card. "It's from Lester and Mabel Kelly."

Asa ran a forefinger over the large green waxy leaves. "It probably will be the first of many you'll receive today."

The words were barely out of his mouth when Eddie Wilkes walked in with a large vase of long-stemmed roses in hues ranging from pure white to near purple. "Congratulations, Debs. The place looks fantastic. Where should I put this?"

Asa came over and took the vase. "I'll take it."

Eddie stared up at Asa. "Mr. Monroe, isn't it?"

"Just Asa is fine."

Eddie nodded. "Asa it is." Shifting his attention, he took a step closer to Deborah. "You did good, girl." He leaned in to kiss her, but she turned her head at the last possible moment, his mouth connecting with her jaw. "If I'd known twenty years ago that you were going to look like this I never would've let you go."

"Shame on you, Eddie," she chided. "You're lucky Asa doesn't know your wife, or he would be forced to repeat gossip. And you should know how fast gossip spreads in the Cove."

"Kitty knows all about you."

"She knows what, Eddie?" Deborah asked. They'd gone out twice. The first time was their senior prom and the second time it was to hang out on the beach with a group of kids in their graduating class.

"That we're old friends."

She smiled. "You're right. But I don't want your wife to get the wrong idea and come after me with something. I heard through the rumor mill that not only is she jealous, but has a hair-trigger temper."

A rush of color darkened Eddie's face. "She does go off every once in a while. I just came to drop off the flowers," he continued without taking a breath. "I have to get back because I have an interview with your son. The boy has a lot of talent, Debs. It's not often I meet someone whose writing is equal to their verbal ability. Kudos to you and Louis for producing a fine young man."

Deborah forced a smile she didn't feel. Every time someone mentioned Louis's name she felt as if she'd been stabbed. She didn't want to play the grieving widow, but she also didn't want to be reminded that she'd lost her husband whenever someone offered their condolence. What she wanted was to heal and move on. Her sole focus was to take care of her children and to make certain her business remained solvent.

"Thank you, Eddie."

"I'll see you later when I cover the grand opening ceremonies."

Seconds later, Asa, who'd overheard the conversation, placed a gentle hand on Deborah's shoulder. "You okay?"

"Of course. Why wouldn't I be?" She started to move away from his touch, but he squeezed her softly.

"How long were you married?"

A beat passed. "Eighteen years."

"I have to assume that you went to bed and woke up with your husband for most of those years."

"The only time we were separated was when he had to attend a conference or if I took my kids on vacation without him."

"The most difficult thing to adjust to now that he's gone is sleeping alone, right?" He didn't wait for her to answer. "You get into bed expecting him to be there, but he's not." Asa removed his hand and chuckled. "Lucky for you, your old friend Eddie seems more than willing to warm your bed. Not that I'd let a man like that near you . . ."

"So, what are you going to do, Asa? Become my protector?" Deborah rolled her eyes at Asa's macho talk, but she had to admit his protectiveness was flattering.

He grinned. "I will if I have to."

"There are quite a few single men on the island you may have to fight off," she teased.

"Don't worry, Debs. I'm up for the task."

Deborah sobered quickly. "I'm honored and appreciate your willingness to protect me, but at this time in my life I'm not interested in hooking up with a man. I don't care who or what he is. My first priority is my children."

Before Asa could respond, the door opened and two women walked in. One zeroed in on him like a heat-seeking missile. "Mr. Monroe. Fancy meeting you here," she crooned, "and how nice you look."

Deborah lowered her arms. She estimated both women were between forty and fifty, and it was obvious they were sisters. Both had the same platinum blond hair color, sea-green eyes, and coloring as translucent as fine bone china.

They wore white camp shirts, and black cropped pants and black-and-white striped espadrilles. They were tall and much too thin.

"Welcome, ladies. I'm Deborah and Asa is the bookstore's manager." She extended her hand, smiling as each one shook it.

"I'm Dora Levin and this is my twin sister Cora Varney."

Deborah angled her head. "Do I detect a New England accent?"

"We're from Massachusetts," Dora confirmed. "We plan to stay in Sanctuary Cove until mid-April. We've been at the boardinghouse," she finished, sliding her gaze back to Asa.

"You have a very good ear," Cora crooned.

"I spent four years at Bennington College." Deborah added.

Dora's eyes brightened like spotlights. "We went there, too. But, of course we're a little older than you. Did you like it?"

"I loved it," Deborah replied. "My first winter I felt as if I'd never get warm, but by the time I was a sophomore you wouldn't have known I was born in the South if I didn't open my mouth to speak. You're welcome to browse, and hopefully you find something you'd like to read. I also want to let you know that we're having a ribbon-cutting ceremony at one. This will be followed by an open house with refreshments."

Cora, the less dominant twin, spoke up. "We must get together and reminisce. I wonder if the same professors we had were still there when you attended."

"But, of course," Deborah agreed, smiling. "If you're

going to be here until April, then I think you might be interested in several activities we are hosting here at the store." She raised her brow, a playful smirk crossing her lips. "I'm certain Mr. Monroe will be more than happy to tell you about them."

Chapter Twelve

Asa cut his eyes at Deborah. He wanted to tell her that the sisters weren't as benign as they appeared. One was widowed and the other had never married and both were barracudas. No man, married or single, was exempt when they decided to target one. Dora had even attempted to compromise Jake Walker, who'd pretended he was hard of hearing.

You owe me, he mouthed to Deborah as he led the sisters to the seating area. She responded by blowing him a kiss.

It had to be word of mouth that brought a steady stream of people into the bookstore. Those who'd come to browse claimed seats when Asa sat down at the piano and began to play a medley of show tunes and movie soundtracks.

Mabel arrived, pushing a trolley with covered trays of cookies and tarts, as well as a sheet cake. Her husband carried in a large coffee urn, while Deborah set up another one filled with hot water for tea. The Kellys provided sugar, sweeteners, milk, cream, fresh lemon slices, plates, forks, and spoons.

There was another delivery, this one from Jack's Fish House. Otis set out platters of catfish fritters, shrimp with dipping sauces, and a seafood salad. He kissed Deborah, wishing her the best, stating he had to get back to the restaurant because he had to cater a party later that evening.

She was pleasantly surprised when a clerk from the local wine and liquor store walked in with a case of assorted wines and packages of colorful plastic cups. "I didn't order wine."

He smiled. "Mr. Monroe did." Reaching into the pocket of her slacks, she took out a bill, but he backed away. "I can't take that, Mrs. Robinson. Mr. Monroe took care of the tip. Good luck with the bookstore."

"Thank you." Walking over to the piano, Deborah rested a hand on Asa's back and put her mouth to his ear. "You're going to have to set up the bar."

Smiling, he continued to play. "Where?"

"Where I have the plants. You can put them on the floor under the table."

Glancing up at her over his shoulder, Asa met her eyes. They were dancing with excitement. "As soon as you turn on the music I'll stop playing."

Murmurs and groans went up when Asa slipped off the bench, while Deborah called the mayor's office, asking if he could stop by earlier than one for his photo-op. Ten minutes later Spencer White strolled in with his official photographer and members of the town council, amid a smattering of applause. Crystal and Whitney came in behind them. Deborah hugged and kissed her children, and the photographer captured the tender moment. Crystal's friend Darius couldn't attend because he'd had an appointment with his orthodontist.

"Oh, Mom, everything looks so beautiful," Crystal whispered.

"Thank you, baby." Deborah thought her daughter looked very pretty with a long-sleeved black tee, short, flaring pink-and-black striped skirt, pink leggings, and black ballet-type flats. "You look so cute."

"Thanks, Mom."

Deborah looped her arm through her son's. "How was the interview?"

The dimple in Whitney's right cheek winked attractively when he smiled. "I got the job. My first assignment is to cover your grand opening."

"But isn't that a conflict of interest?" Deborah whispered.

"No it's not, Mom. It's a test to see if I can be an impartial journalist."

Deborah was filled with an overwhelming surge of pride when she stared at her son. "Do you want to interview me now, or later?"

Whitney pulled a small hand-held tape recorder from the pocket of his jeans. "Let's see how much we can get in before Mayor White gets started."

Deborah answered all of Whitney's questions, outlining the details for the book club discussions and afternoon tea, while Spencer strutted around the store pressing the flesh like a candidate on the campaign trail. She noticed the number of women crowding around Asa, grinning and touching his arm to get his attention.

"Who is the man in the suit?" Whitney asked when he saw the direction of his mother's gaze.

"Asa Monroe. I hired him to manage the store. If it hadn't been for him I doubt whether I would've opened today."

"I'm glad you decided to reopen the bookstore. And, it's good that you found someone to help you run it."

"Yes it is."

Glancing around, Deborah attempted to count the number of people who'd come to The Parlor and lost count at twenty-seven. Most were eating and drinking, but there were a few who'd taken books off the shelves and were either sitting or standing around reading.

Dora and Cora had their arms full of paperback novels. Deborah excused herself and went over to help them. "Please, let me take your books to the front and I'll put them aside for you." She had to get Asa to bring down a carton with reinforced paper shopping bags stamped with The Parlor Bookstore logo and website.

Deborah had placed the twins' books in a large sweet-grass basket under the writing table when Rose Dukes-Walker, the woman who had woven the basket, entered with her husband Jake. Rose was the local artisan and Rachel's sister. Many of Rose's sweet-grass baskets and quilts were in private collections throughout the country. She'd begun giving private lessons to those who wanted to learn the craft, which had come to the American South with enslaved Africans.

Rose handed Deborah a large hat box. "There's a little something in here for your bookstore."

Leaning down, she kissed the petite woman's silken cheek. "Thank you so much, Miss Rose. Whatever it is I know I will treasure it."

Rose patted Deborah's arm. "I'm just glad you decided

to come home. You're going to have to excuse me, but I'm going to rescue my husband from these hungry women. I don't know what it is about these women who come to the Cove. They think every man, whether single or married, is fair game. Rachel told me they were all over Mr. Monroe like white on rice. It's a crying shame that the poor man had to move out to get away from them."

Deborah didn't tell Rose that Asa had moved in over the store. It was only a matter of time before everyone would know. There were very few secrets in Sanctuary Cove. There was a running joke that if you wanted to keep a secret, then never tell it.

She caught Spencer's attention, and he motioned for her to join him outside. It took an interminable amount of time for the photographer to position everyone so he could get them in the photo. Deborah stood next to Spencer. Three of the four members of the town council flanked his left, while Whitney, Crystal, and Asa stood on Deborah's right. Asa and the head of transportation held the length of wide red ribbon while the mayor gave Deborah an oversized pair of scissors. At the exact moment she cut the ribbon several flashbulbs went off, followed by applause. The Parlor Bookstore was officially open for business.

Deborah flopped down on the loveseat, kicked off her heels, and rested her head on the arm. She was exhausted. When she'd opened the Charleston store it had been without fanfare. However, on the Cove it was as if everyone had turned out to browse, buy, and eat and drink their fill. Unfortunately Barbara had called to say she couldn't make it because of a multiple-vehicle accident on the interstate;

many of the patients were taken to her hospital and as an on-call nurse she had to report for duty.

The last customer had filed out minutes before six, and she and Asa closed and locked doors and pulled the blinds. Large plastic bags filled with the remnants of uneaten food and trash were deposited in a Dumpster in a corner of the parking lot.

Now, a smile parted her lips when she felt the heat from Asa's body as he leaned over her. "Wake up, Sleeping Beauty."

She smiled up at him. "I was just resting my eyes." He'd dimmed the track lights but hadn't turned off the ceiling fans. She saw that he'd taken off his suit jacket and tie and had undone several buttons on his shirt.

Cupping her ankles, Asa lifted her legs, sat down, and rested her bare feet on his thigh.

He stared at the slender groomed feet with the red polish on toes that were much lighter-skinned than her face. "You need a little sun on your feet."

"My feet are always pale."

"Even in the summer?"

Deborah nodded. "They don't tan. I guess I get that from my mother. When she was growing up her friends used to call her Casper because of her pale skin. As a redhead she had to stay out of the sun or burn to a crisp."

"Your mother is white." The question was a statement.

Deborah nodded again. "Yes. She and my father met when they were Civil Rights attorneys."

"Are you an only child?"

"Yes. My mother had had three miscarriages before she had me. I always wanted a brother or sister, but when my parents didn't have any more children I told them to adopt a baby. By then Mom had gone back to work part-time and she didn't want to start over with diapers, colic, and teething. What about you, Asa? Do you have any brothers or sisters?"

"Siblings aren't always so great."

"What do you mean?" Deborah asked.

"I haven't seen my brother Jesse in years. He always had a weakness for women, gambling, and drugs. I don't know if he's dead or alive." Exhaling audibly, Asa shook his head as if to push all thoughts of his estranged brother to the furthest recesses of his mind. Grasping Deborah's feet, he pressed his thumb to her instep. "Your grand opening was a rip-roaring success."

Deborah recognized he wanted to change the subject and was happy to oblige. "It was better than I could have ever imagined. I sold a lot of romances."

"That's because women love reading about love, and are also in love with love."

"Why are you always so cynical?"

"I'm not cynical, Debs. It's called being realistic."

"I had a few male customers who bought romance novels for their wives." Deborah smothered a moan when Asa massaged her feet. It was as if he had magical fingers. "That feels wonderful."

Asa applied more pressure. "I also give body massages."

"How much do you charge?"

"I offer reduced rates for my good friends."

"Oh!" she gasped. "That feels good." Asa's hands had moved from her feet up to her legs and calves.

"Why do you torture yourself walking in those stilts?"

Pushing up on an elbow, Deborah rolled her eyes at Asa. "They are not stilts."

"Aren't they called stilettos?"

"Stilettos are skinny heels that are at least four inches or higher. Mine are thicker and only three."

Lifting her legs, Asa slid them off his lap and stood up. "Don't move. I'll be right back."

Deborah sat up. "Where are you going?"

"Upstairs to change into something more comfortable," he said over his shoulder.

She lay back down, sinking into the butter-soft leather. Asa was right. The grand opening was more than a success. It was spectacular, the day's total sales exceeding her expectations. Asa had gotten customers to sign up for both book discussions, and she had spoken to Eddie Wilkes about advertising store specials and promotions in the *Chronicle*.

Deborah hadn't known what to expect when she'd introduced Crystal and Whitney to Asa, but both were friendly and respectful, and Whitney thanked him profusely for helping out his mother. Some women didn't have protective men they could rely on, but it was different with her. Her son and her store manager were there for her. It felt good, even safe, knowing they were around.

She knew she should get up and go home, but her body refused to obey the dictates of her brain. *I'll take a power nap.* It was the last thought she remembered before Morpheus claimed her.

It was only minutes, though it could have been hours, when she felt someone gently shaking her. "Wake up, Deborah."

Eyelids fluttering wildly, Deborah sat up as if she'd been impaled with a sharp object. "What-what?"

Hunkering down in front of her, Asa rested his hand

on the side of her face. "It's all right, Debs. I'm sorry if I frightened you."

Swinging her legs over the side of the loveseat, she dug her bare toes into the pile on the area rug. "I must have fallen asleep again." He'd changed into a tee-shirt with a faded Virginia Beach logo, jeans, and thick black socks.

Asa leaned in and pressed a kiss to her forehead. "You did. I thought we'd celebrate before you go home."

"Celebrate...celebrate how?" It was hard for Deborah to sound coherent when Asa was so close. In fact he was much too close.

Wrapping an arm around her waist, Asa eased Deborah off the loveseat. "Come with me."

"Wait! I have to put my shoes on."

Bending slightly, he scooped her up in his arms. "You don't need shoes."

She looped her arms around his neck to keep her balance. "Where are you taking me?"

Asa smiled down at her. "Do you always have to ask so many questions?"

"Yes. Especially when you play caveman."

"Superhero, Debs."

"Which one?"

Asa carried Deborah up the staircase to his apartment. "Batman. I've been told women like men in black leather."

Laughing, she shook her head, her hair swaying sensuously around her face and neck. "Don't tell me you're a freak."

"I plead the Fifth."

"You *are* a freak, Asa Monroe."

Asa carried Deborah into his apartment, placing her on the sofa and dropping down beside her. "I thought we would have our own private celebration," he said when she stared at the bottle of chilled champagne, two flutes, and an antipasto salad.

"You are just full of surprises."

He stared at her delicate profile. "Do you like it?"

Shifting slightly, Deborah gave him a long, penetrating stare. "Very much." Leaning forward, she pressed her mouth to his. "Thank you."

"You're welcome. Shall I serve you?"

She nodded. "Please." Deborah watched intently as Asa filled a plate with salad before expertly uncorking the bottle of champagne, muscles flexing as he filled the flutes. He handed her one, his fingers brushing against hers.

Raising his flute, he extended it to Deborah. "To The Parlor and beyond," Asa barked out like an announcer.

"You are so silly."

Asa winked at her as he took a sip of the bubbling wine. "Not bad."

Deborah put the flute to her mouth and took a swallow, holding it for several seconds before letting it slide down the back of her throat. First there was cold, then a slow building heat. Pressing a hand to her chest, she blew out her breath. "I'd better eat before I take another sip." Reaching for a napkin, she spread it over her lap, and then picked up a fork and speared a portion of the salad.

"You don't drink?" Asa asked when she set down her flute.

"Not on an empty stomach, and especially not when drinking champagne."

"I didn't know you'd be a cheap date," he teased.

She ate slowly. The spicy salad had triggered an unnatural thirst and Deborah drank two glasses of champagne when she normally wouldn't drink more than one. Setting down the flute, she slumped back and closed her eyes. "I think I'm under the influence."

"How can you say that when you've only had two glasses?"

"Like you said. I'm a cheap date." Raising her arm, she peered at her watch. "I'm going to have to get home."

Lowering his head, Asa buried his face in her hair. He knew he had to move, but didn't want to. They shared the sofa, her soft curves molded to his body. It was pleasurable, satisfying. What he felt wasn't much different than the aftermath of lovemaking.

He shifted, wrapping an arm around Deborah's waist until she was sitting between his outstretched legs. They lay together, her back pressed against him, their chests rising and falling in unison. "You can't drive home now if you think you're impaired. Why don't you wait until your head clears?"

"I have to call my children to let them know I'm going to be late."

"I'll get the phone." Deborah leaned forward while he slid out from behind her and went to retrieve the cordless receiver from the handset on the kitchen countertop.

She took the phone, punching in the numbers to her home. It rang three times before there was a break in the connection. "Whit, this is Mom."

"Hi, Mom. What's up?"

"I'm still at the store. I'll be home later."

"Shall I leave the porch lights on?"

"Yes, please. Where's Crystal?"

"She's in her bedroom. Either she's on the phone or the computer."

"Tell her not to stay up too late, because we're going to the early service tomorrow."

"Okay, Mom. Is there anything else?"

"No. See you later."

"Later."

Deborah hung up, handing Asa the phone. Their eyes met. "I'm going to give myself an hour to sober up, and then I'm going home."

"Why don't you lie down on the bed, while I put everything away?"

She affected a lopsided smile. "I'm good here."

"The bed is a lot more comfortable than the sofa."

"That would pose a problem. If I get into that bed I won't get out until tomorrow morning."

"Go lie down, Deborah. I'll wake you in an hour."

"I'll lie down, but only if you promise you'll wake me in an hour. I've never left my children home alone here in the Cove. It was different in Charleston because I had my neighbor look in on them."

"I promise to wake you. And, when you leave I'll follow you to make certain you get home safely. I can't have my boss charged with DUI."

Asa didn't know whether to stay where he sat or go to her. He knew if he joined Deborah on the bed it would shatter their already fragile friendship. It hadn't been easy working with her, and he had had to call on all of his self-control not to take her into his arms and do more than kiss her. For now, he thought about how it would feel to really kiss her with a repressed passion that would communicate without words how much he'd come to like and want her.

But he knew one kiss would lead to a caress and still further. He didn't want so much to be inside her as much as he wanted to feel her naked skin against his.

Deborah moved off the sofa and over to the bed. Turning back the comforter, she lay on the crisp cool sheets and closed her eyes. She didn't fall asleep. Her mind was a tumult of images like frames of film. She recalled the first time she saw Louis, the sound of his voice when he'd introduced himself to her. The next frame was her waking up in bed—naked with a naked man beside her. At first she panicked, and then she'd remembered where she was and who the man was. She hadn't recognized him without his glasses.

Her mind fast-forwarded to her wedding day. Her hands had shaken uncontrollably throughout the ceremony, especially when it came time to exchange rings. She'd worn her wedding band for all of four hours. Once she got back to her dorm, she'd taken it off and put it on a chain around her neck.

There came another frame, the images moving so fast she could hardly recognize the couple writhing on twisted sheets. Stop moving! the silent voice in her head shouted. The man and woman did stop, and a gasp escaped Deborah when she saw herself and Asa locked in a passionate embrace.

Deborah must have drifted off before she was jolted awake. Asa had turned off all the lights except the one on the range hood. She sat up. "Asa?"

"It's all right, baby."

His disembodied voice came from somewhere in the room. "Where are you?" He sat up and she could make out the outline of his body. He had been reclining on the sofa. "What time is it?"

"It's seven-forty. Go back to sleep, Deborah."

She tucked her hair behind her ears. "I can't. I've been thinking too much."

"What are you thinking about?" Asa asked, the soft tone of his voice soothing.

"My life."

"All thirty-eight years?"

"Very funny, Asa."

"Well, you sound as if you're eighty and you're reminiscing about what happened back in the day."

Deborah lay down again, cradling her head on folded arms. "Do you ever reminisce?"

"I try not to."

"Why not?" she asked.

"I plan ahead and try to look ahead."

"You make it sound so easy. Forget the past and only concentrate on the future."

"It works for me, Deborah."

"Hopefully one day it will work for me." She sat up and swung her legs over the side of the bed. "My head feels better. I'm going home."

Asa popped up, walking to the bed on sock-covered feet. "Are you sure?"

Deborah stood up. "I'm good."

Reaching for her hand, Asa laced their fingers together. "I'll follow to make certain you get there okay."

Leaning into him, Deborah anchored one arm under his shoulder. "Do you know what?"

"What, Debs?"

"You're the first male friend I've ever had since my

husband. I met Louis at eighteen and married him at twenty. We…"

Asa waited for her to complete her statement, seemingly wanting to know something about the man she had married. When she appeared reluctant to talk, he eased her arm down, pausing long enough to put on a pair of running shoes. Then he got the key to his truck and a small leather case containing his driver's license, and then led her out of the bedroom and down to the bookstore. She slipped into her heels and retrieved her handbag.

Asa then locked the rear door to the store, before catching up with Deborah as she walked to the Audi. The parking lot was unlit. If it weren't for the lights over the rear doors of the various businesses and the glow from a half-moon it would have been pitch black.

"There is one thing you should know, Deborah."

She blinked slowly. "What's that?"

"I'm willing to lend an ear or a shoulder if you feel the need to talk about your husband."

She managed a smile, but it looked more like a grimace. "Thank you, Asa."

He dipped his head and kissed her cheek. "Get in. I'll be right behind you."

Deborah slipped in behind the wheel, pushing the Start Engine button. The soft purr of the engine sounded unusually loud in the stillness of the night as she maneuvered out of the parking lot. It was just a few minutes to eight o'clock yet most of Sanctuary Cove's businesses were closed. In Charleston, most restaurants and clubs would be crowded with college students, tourists, or local residents going out for a night on the town.

It was different in the Cove because there were only

a few eating places and the single-screen movie theater showed new movies several months after they'd premiered in other major cities. Occasionally an out-of-town theater group used a converted warehouse to put on their productions.

She turned onto the road leading to her house. Peering up in her rearview mirror, she saw Asa following at a safe distance. A tender smiled parted her lips. Not only was Asa her friend, but he had also become her guardian angel. A most winning combination. Deborah still hadn't figured out why she felt so relaxed around him, even more relaxed than she had when she'd met Louis for the first time. Perhaps it had something to do with them not sleeping together. It wasn't that she wasn't physically attracted to Asa, because she was, but there was so much more to him and she was determined to find out what it was. The erotic images of them had left Deborah more shaken than she wanted to acknowledge, and she found the notion of sleeping with Asa intimidating because she was newly widowed.

Her smile faded as if someone had pulled down a shade, shutting out the light behind her eyes. A flicker of apprehension coursed through her when she thought about him leaving the Cove. And it was going to happen. Come spring he would get into his car like so many of the other snowbirds and return to his northern climes.

Following the sweep of her headlights, Deborah decelerated and then pulled into the driveway alongside Whitney's Corolla. Getting out of the car, her eyebrows lifted a fraction when she saw that not only had her son left the lights lit on the porch, but in every room.

Deborah waved to Asa, turned her heel, and mounted

the porch steps. She unlocked the front door, walked in, closed it behind her, and slipped out of her shoes. Tossing her keys in a small sweet-grass basket, she went about the task of turning off lights, leaving on the lamp in the entryway and the high-hat between the kitchen and pantry.

She climbed the staircase to the second floor, holding tightly to the banister in order to keep her balance. Her head was still a little fuzzy from the champagne. The door to Whitney's bedroom was closed, as was Crystal's. Carefully placing one foot in front of the other, she made it to her bedroom, closed the door, and fell across the bed— fully clothed. *I'll get up in fifteen minutes, and then take a bath*, Deborah told herself. Fifteen minutes became an hour, then two.

Chapter Thirteen

Light had brightened the sky, heralding the dawn of a new day. Deborah woke to the sound of knocking and someone calling her name. It sounded as if they were in a tunnel.

"Mom, may I come in?"

Rolling over, Deborah sat up. Not only was she incredibly thirsty, but her mouth felt as if it was filled with cotton.

"Oh!" she moaned. She'd slept in her clothes—something she'd never done.

"Mom, open the door."

"Hold on. I'm coming." Sliding off the bed, Deborah shuffled over to the door and opened it. The look on her daughter's face was something she would take to her grave. It was etched with fear as tears trickled down Crystal's face. "What's the matter, baby?"

Crystal fell against her mother, nearly making her lose her footing. "I've been banging on the door and calling you for almost five minutes."

Deborah, rubbing Crystal's back in an attempt to console her, kissed her daughter's cheek. "I was asleep."

"Why ... why did you lock your door?"

Blinking, Deborah tried remembering when she'd locked the door. She couldn't. "I don't know," she answered truthfully. "Why are you crying?"

Crystal sniffled, wiping the back of her hand over her face. "I thought you'd hurt yourself."

Lowering her arms, Deborah made her way toward the en suite bath. "Come and talk to me while I wash my face and brush my teeth."

"I have to wash my face, too."

Deborah stood at the double-sink, staring at her reflection in the mirror. She looked a hot mess! If she'd been Sallie Ann Williams she would've said she looked a *"dog's mess."* When she'd asked her grandmother what she meant by a dog's mess, her response had been she didn't know, but had grown up hearing people on the island mutter it whenever they disapproved of what someone looked like or wore.

Smudged mascara, eyeliner, and what had been a smoky shadow now made her look like a raccoon. Her eyes were a little red and her bed hair looked as if she'd been made love to. A blush darkened her cheeks when she thought of waking up in bed beside Asa. No doubt if she had, she wouldn't be in her clothes. She didn't want to think about her clothes: Her blouse was a mass of wrinkles and creases and the wool gabardine slacks Deborah had just picked up from the drycleaner would have to go back again.

Reaching for her toothbrush, she squeezed a glob of toothpaste on the bristles. With the flick of a switch the vibrating bristles spread the foaming paste over her teeth and gums. Deborah winked at Crystal, who after splashing water on her face had blotted it with a towel from an ample supply stacked on a low table. She swished a cupful of minty mouthwash around in her mouth, depositing it in the sink before applying a thick layer of cold cream around her eyes and over her face, gently wiping away the makeup with a soft, moist cloth.

Meeting Crystal's puffy eyes in the mirror, she drew a wide-tooth comb through her hair. "Why are you up so early?"

Crystal dropped her gaze. "I bet Whitney ten dollars that I'd get up before him, so I set my clock for five instead of six."

"I give you an allowance, so why would you need more money?"

"I need enough money to buy a crate and dog food."

Deborah shook her head, unable to believe what she'd just heard. "Did you just say 'dog' as in a canine pet?"

"Yes! Please, Mom, can I have a puppy?"

"First you want to put down a vegetable garden, and now you want a dog." She'd asked Hannah Forsyth for the name of a local landscaper willing to clear enough land for her daughter to start a vegetable garden and the man was scheduled to come the following morning to survey the area and give her an estimate of the cost.

"I want both."

"Do you realize the enormity of taking care of a garden? It has to be weeded and watered, and you have to stay one step ahead of the critters who decide it's easier to eat your vegetables than go foraging for food. Then there is the responsibility of taking care of a dog."

"I can do both, Mom. Please, Mom."

Deborah stared at Crystal. This wasn't the first time her daughter had talked about a dog, but Deborah hadn't warmed to the idea because she felt Crystal wasn't responsible enough to take care of it. Extending her arms, she wasn't disappointed when Crystal hugged her.

"What if we talk about this later?"

Pulling back, Crystal gave her mother an expectant look. "How much later, Mom?"

Deborah smiled. "Tonight. Now, what was up with all the crying?"

"I thought that something had happened to you."

"Happened how?"

Crystal worried her lower lip, as if carefully composing her thoughts so the words would come out right. "Remember my friend Roxanna?"

Deborah met her daughter's eyes. "Yes I do. What about her?"

"Remember after her father died in Iraq and her mother was sent away?"

Suddenly Crystal's histrionics made sense to her. She tightened her hold on her child. Roxanna's mother had tried to take her life when she'd lost her husband. After swallowing more than two dozen sleeping pills washed down with a bottle of whiskey, she was now in a vegetative state. The girl's grandparents had had to sell their Ohio home to move to Charleston to take care of their grandchildren, or they would have become wards of the state.

"What makes you think I would ever take my life and leave you and Whitney without a father *and* mother? Baby, I love you and your brother, and all I want is for you to grow up and become the best you can be. Things happen in life, things over which we have no control, but unless I was certifiably insane I would never think of taking my life." She kissed Crystal's short hair. "I want to live long enough to become a grandmother and spoil my grandchildren like my mother does."

Easing back, Crystal smiled. "You think Grandma spoils us?"

"Please, Crystal. You should know better than to ask me that."

"Do you think she likes Whitney more than me?"

Deborah's eyes narrowed. "Where did you get that idea?"

"She gives him money, but buys me whatever I want."

She had never noticed any sibling rivalry between her children, and loathed thinking Crystal harbored resentment of her brother. "Whitney is seventeen and will soon be eighteen. Come August he'll be off to college, and that means he's going to need money to put gas in his car or do his laundry, while you'll be here having all of your needs met. I give you an allowance so you can buy what I call incidentals. Other than that, what would you need money for? You're not starting any habits I should know about, are you?" Deborah gave her daughter a playful, yet stern look.

"Mama!"

"Don't 'Mama' me, Crystal! Why would you need more than what I'm giving you?"

"Like for a dog."

"Like I said, we'll talk about this tonight."

"I want a Bichon or a Yorkshire Terrier."

Deborah rolled her eyes. "What you want is a lot of noise."

Crystal affected a smile just like her late father, with

her eyes but not her mouth. At times it appeared to be more of a smirk. "They are good watchdogs."

"Where are you going to get your dog?"

"Grandma says she has a friend who lives on Isle of Palms who breeds small purebred dogs. Whenever I'm ready she will call her for me."

"Let me talk to your grandmother before the two of you make any more plans about bringing an animal into this house. Now, scoot while I take a shower."

"I'm making pancakes for breakfast. How many do you want?"

"One."

"One big one?"

"No. One medium."

"You want it with strawberries and cream?"

Deborah began unbuttoning her blouse. "That sounds good."

She waited until Crystal left, then closed the door behind her. Her daughter's head was all over the place. When asked what she wanted to be when she grew up Crystal didn't have a clue. But she refused to acknowledge the obvious: she was an incredible cook. Deborah could envision her daughter owning and operating a restaurant, serving homegrown vegetables. She also had a green thumb and a magic when it came to bringing plants back from the dead. Deborah called her the Plant Whisperer.

Stripping off her clothes, she ran a wide-tooth comb through her tangled strands, covered her hair with a bouffant shower cap, and stepped into the shower stall. Within minutes she felt revived and energized enough to face the day.

• • •

Deborah sat in the pew between Whitney and Crystal, listening to Reverend Malcolm Crawford read announcements before the closing hymn. His sermon, taken from the book of Ecclesiastes, chapter one, verse four, spoke directly to her: A time to weep and a time to laugh; a time to mourn and a time to dance.

She'd wept, mourned, laughed, and danced. And she had to thank Asa for the laughing and dancing part. Before he'd walked into The Parlor asking to be hired she'd hadn't laughed—really laughed—in weeks. And before she'd danced with him she hadn't been able to remember the last time she had with Louis. Perhaps it was because Louis hadn't liked to dance, claiming he'd been born with two left feet.

The image of Louis in her mind made Deborah think of Crystal. Her daughter's crying jag earlier that morning reinforced the idea that her children still needed her and she needed them to help her to stay strong. Asa Monroe had been doing the same thing without trying. His continuous displays of affection seemed effortless.

"My brothers and sisters, we have several new faces with us this fine Sunday morning. Some of you may recognize his face from television news footage, but I would like newly elected U.S. Representative Jason Parker, his lovely wife Alice, and their two beautiful children to stand up. Representative Parker, whose election district includes Cavanaugh Island, has decided to make Sanctuary Cove his legal residence. The Parker name isn't new on the island. In fact they go back more than two hundred years, when Cyrus Parker established a rice plantation on Haven Creek. On behalf of all the members of Abundant Life Christian Church, we welcome you home."

Deborah applauded with the other hundred-plus people sitting in the small, homey church. She'd recognized Jason Parker because he'd campaigned on the corner only steps from the Charleston store, shaking hands while a worker handed out campaign literature extolling his accomplishments. He and Alice were both tall and very blond, and their adorable children had inherited their parents' flaxen hair.

"We also want to say a prayer for Sergeant Nelson Lambert who has been deployed to the Middle East. Let us bow our heads and pray for Sergeant Lambert's safe return and for his wife, Samara, and their children to stay strong during his absence."

Deborah grasped Whitney and Crystal's hands, giving their fingers a gentle squeeze as she whispered a silent prayer. She prayed for the young soldier and his family; she prayed for her children; she prayed for her parents; she prayed for everyone but herself.

"Everyone please stand for our closing song, number one twenty-two in the hymnal, 'We Are Marching to Zion'." There came a rustling and flipping of pages as the organist played the opening chords to the upbeat hymn. The choral group began the first verse, then the congregation joined in, voices blending in sweet, rich harmony. The last note faded and Reverend Crawford raised his hands in a farewell blessing as congregants turned and filed out, hugging and kissing as if they hadn't seen one another in months when it had only been the week before.

Malcolm Crawford stood on the church steps, shaking hands with each and every member of his congregation. Not even infants were exempt from his greetings. He shook Deborah's hand, flashing his straight, white teeth.

"I was thinking of you when I sat down to write my sermon for today."

She nodded, returning his warm smile with one of her own. "Thank you."

"It's good to see you and your children in church. Nowadays too many young folks stray from the Lord. It's only when something drastic happens that they seem to look for Him."

"Lambs will stray, Reverend Crawford," Deborah said.

"I'm certain you've heard of the parable about the shepherd who left ninety-nine sheep to look for one that had been lost."

"I remember it well."

Deborah thanked the minister again and then descended the stairs. She had understood the meaning of his sermon—loud and very clear. She had wept, and continued to weep because she missed Louis. And his loss was never more profound than when she woke in the morning expecting to feel the warmth of her husband's body next to hers.

She had mourned—mourned the loss of her life partner and the father of her children. But lately she had begun to enjoy living—with her children, with her friends, with the residents of the Cove and with Asa. Excitement filled her chest as she remembered dancing with him.

Deborah knew it would take time to heal, but with each passing day she was beginning to feel stronger, more in control. Asa had told her everything would get better with time. Time—a moment, instance, and interval measuring the number of breaths she took. Grinning, she walked to the church's parking area with an extra pep in her step. Whitney would drop her back at the house before driving into Charleston for basketball practice. Crystal had asked to go with him, and after she pouted for a full two minutes he'd agreed to take her. Whitney had suggested Deborah not cook for them because they would stop at Perry's to eat with the other kids. That left her all the time in the world to sit back and fantasize about the man who'd been occupying her thoughts since the day they'd met.

As soon as she arrived home, she dropped her things in the living room, grabbed her journal and headed out onto the front porch. Opening the book, she stared at her latest entry:

January 16th—Well I think I'm going out of my head. Yes I think I'm going out of my head over you, over you. The first three lines of the Luther Vandross classic "Goin' Out of My Head" keeps echoing in my mind, and I know it's because of my feelings for Asa. I still don't know whether I made a mistake to let him kiss me, and for me to kiss him back. I also know anything other than friendship between us would spell certain disaster—at least for me emotionally. I'm not ready to become involved with a man, at least I don't think I am, but try telling that to my traitorous body. However, I'm honest enough with myself to now admit that I need Asa—if only to assuage a sexual frustration that is triggering erotic dreams.

Deborah closed the cloth-covered book and her eyes, willing her mind blank. However, she was unsuccessful when images of the intimacy they'd shared at her grand opening came flooding back. Trying to draw her attention away from naughty fantasies of Asa, she reveled at his ability to sign up twelve women for two book discussion groups, leaving it to her to select the titles. The novels were what she'd considered modern day classics, with a cross section of time periods and cultures: *The Help*, *Like Water for Chocolate*, *The Alienist*, *This Side of Brightness*, *Memoirs of a Geisha*, and *Water for Elephants*. She was certain some of the women had read the titles on the reading list, but it was very different to get another perspective during an active and in-depth discussion.

Her decision to close Mondays allowed her time to do housework, shop for groceries, do her banking, and visit the Charleston book distributor to restock her shelves. She added another item to her to-do list: shop for tea. Two hand-painted porcelain teapots, eight china cups, saucers, and dessert plates, encased in bubble wrap, were packed in a crate she would take to the store for her afternoon teas.

The phone resting on the cushion rang and Deborah opened her eyes and picked it up without looking at the display. "Hello."

"Good afternoon, darling."

She smiled. "Hello, Mama. How are you?"

"Sweating. These hot flashes are driving me crazy."

"What happened to your central air?"

"I have it cranked up to the highest setting, but Herman keeps turning it down because he said he's freezing. Enough about me. How are you, darling?"

Deborah told Pearl Williams about the conversation she'd had with Crystal earlier that morning. "Mama, you can't promise her something without talking to me first."

"I told her not to say anything until I spoke to you."

Deborah smiled. "Well, apparently your granddaughter didn't listen to you. I told her we would talk about it tonight."

"Are you going to let her get one?" Pearl asked. "Every child should have a pet. You had your cat."

"Muffin wouldn't let me hold her, but would invariably jump on the bed and sit on my face every morning at six o'clock. She wasn't a pet. She was possessed with an evil spirit."

"Deborah, you know I don't like it when you talk about those ignorant Gullah superstitions."

"I don't understand you, Mama."

"What don't you understand?"

"You've been married to a Gullah for more than forty years, and you've spent time on Cavanaugh Island, yet you still view *us* as ignorant."

"Not you, darling. And I resent your implication that I believe people are ignorant. It's the superstitions that are ignorant."

Deborah knew arguing with her mother would end in a stalemate. "What do you have planned for Whitney and Crystal when they come down at the end of February?" she asked, deliberately changing the topic of conversation.

"We're going to meet up with my sister and her grandchildren in Key West. Patricia is renting a bungalow and we're all going out on a charter boat to do some fishing. And of course Crystal and I will do a little shopping."

A little shopping, Deborah mused. Her mother was totally unfamiliar with the phrase. Pearl McLeary-Williams, who had grown up with a silver spoon in her mouth, had never had to struggle for anything. She had come into her trust at twenty-three, due to the death of her parents, and she and her sister had inherited equal shares to a multimillion dollar estate.

"You didn't answer my question about Crystal getting a dog."

"Yes, I'm going to let Crystal get a dog. It hasn't been easy for her, Mama, so right now I'm willing to give her whatever she wants—within reason, of course. But she can't get one until after she comes back from her *little* shopping spree with you."

Pearl's soft laughter came through the earpiece. "Whenever you're ready, I'll call my friend on Isle of Palms to let her know you're coming to look at her puppies. I'd have one right now if we were allowed to have pets. A house is not a home without pets and children underfoot."

Deborah chatted with her mother for another ten minutes, before ending the call. She didn't ask to speak to her father because her father was usually off fishing or golfing with a trio of retired businessmen.

Reaching for her laptop, she tapped a key and turned it on. Waiting for it to boot up, she went into teacher mode. Teachers in the lower grades usually put up colorful decorations celebrating the seasons or important holidays. As the owner and operator of an independent bookstore Deborah had to come up with a theme or promotion for each month. Luckily, she didn't have to concern herself with January because of the grand opening.

February was designated as Black History Month and of course there was Valentine's Day. Resting her fingers on the keys, she began typing. The Parlor would offer a fifteen percent discount for all books in the Black Studies and African-American Literature section. Romance, her bestselling genre, would be given ten percent off, but she also had to come up with something with a romance theme.

Her phone rang again, and Deborah picked it up, staring at the strange number with the 302 area code. "Hello."

"Deborah, Asa."

Her pulse quickened when his distinctive baritone voice caressed her ear. But her joy at hearing his voice quickly faded, replaced by concern. Why was he calling her when the store was closed? "What's wrong?"

He chuckled softly. "Nothing's wrong. It's just that I came downstairs to look for something to read when I found the envelope with your receipts on the desk. I didn't know if you'd thought you had taken it with you."

Deborah smothered a groan. She knew she would've freaked out when she arrived at the bank the next day with the anticipation of making a deposit. "I thought I had taken it with me."

"Do you want me to drop it off to you?"

"No, please don't bother, Asa. I'll come and pick it up. Besides, I have to drop off a box of things I'll need for tea."

"I'll be here."

She smiled. "I'll see you later."

Deborah went back to filling in her promotional event calendar. March was the month for spring and also St. Patrick's Day. She could feature the works of celebrated Irish writers, poets, and playwrights, many of whom were on her list of favorites: Oscar Wilde, W.B. Yeats, George Bernard Shaw, James Joyce, and Samuel Beckett. She didn't have much for April. That meant she would have to search the Internet for writers born in that month. May was Mother's Day and graduations. The list continued until she reached December. Saving what she'd typed on a flash drive, she dropped it into her handbag, pushed her bare feet into leather mules, and picked up the crate with the tea set. After locking up the house, she drove to the bookstore.

After a short drive, she turned down a narrow street and into the parking lot behind a row of stores. Twenty minutes later she emerged from De Fountain with a half-pint of chocolate mint ice cream and a pint of peach and strawberry gelato. Minutes later, when she maneuvered into her space at the rear of the bookstore, Asa was standing in the doorway.

A bright smile flitted across her features when she saw his legs for the first time under a pair of khaki walking shorts. A matching short-sleeve shirt and leather woven sandals completed his casual look. His five o'clock shadow told her he hadn't shaved.

Deborah handed him a small shopping bag with the ice cream. "Can you please put this in the freezer before it melts?"

Asa lifted his eyebrows when he peered into the bag. "What's the occasion?"

"There is no occasion. You've been feeding me, so I thought I'd return the favor and bring dessert."

He smiled. "Thanks. Where are you going?" Asa asked when Deborah headed back to her car.

"I have to get something out of the trunk."

"Is it heavy?"

"Not too heavy."

Reaching for her hand, Asa transferred the shopping bag from his to hers. "You take this upstairs and I'll get the stuff from your car."

"The trunk is open. You can bring in the orange crate, a box labeled 'paper,' and a canvas bag with the plant light." She made her way to the staircase while Asa went to unload her car.

The door at the top of the staircase was ajar, and when she walked in she was shocked to find it immaculate. The bed was made, there were no dishes in the sink, and not one article of clothing was on display. It was as neat as it had been before Asa had moved in. He was either an obsessive-compulsive or a neat freak.

When she returned to the bookstore she found Asa reclining on one of the club chairs, his feet resting on the matching footstool, reading *A Heartbeat Away*, a mystery thriller by Michael Palmer. He'd tuned the radio to a station featuring soft music and the overhead track lighting cast a golden glow on his salt-and-pepper head. The bag with the plant light was near the table with the plants, the crate with the tea set sat on the floor by the buffet server, and the box with the printer on the writing desk. Her handbag was on the desk chair. She placed the envelope with the cash and credit card receipts in her handbag.

Deborah busied herself with unwrapping the cups, saucers, plates, and tea pots, then storing them in the buffet before connecting the printer to the computer. Retrieving her flash drive, she pulled up what she'd stored. She was so engrossed in editing and tweaking what she'd typed that she hadn't realized Asa had put aside his book and stood over her until his intoxicating scent filtered into her nostrils. She could always tell when he was near by the cologne he wore.

She patted the desk chair. "Please sit down. I want to show you what I've been working on." With a click of the mouse, Deborah printed out the reading list and templates for the calendar, handing it over to him.

Asa studied the book titles. "I've read them all except *The Alienist.*"

Deborah smiled. "It's one of my personal favorites, and I'm certain you would enjoy it, too. It's a mystery/ thriller set in New York City in 1896. During that time people who studied abnormal psychology were called alienists. In the story, Teddy Roosevelt, a reform police commissioner, recruits an alienist to track down a serial killer who is slaughtering boy prostitutes."

"Don't tell me any more. I want to read it," he said. He noted Deborah had chosen an interesting and eclectic mix.

"I may have a few copies on the shelf. I've e-mailed my distributor in Charleston, asking him to set aside copies of these titles. I'll know by tomorrow if he has them in stock, and if not how soon he'll be able to get them."

Asa perused the calendars, noting the various holidays and other observances. "Where did you find these observances?" he asked, staring at the calendar for the month of July. "July sixth is fried chicken day and the thirteenth is beans and franks day."

Leaning to her left, she stared at the page. "I like ugly truck day on the twentieth. I thought we could tie some of these holidays and observances into store promotions. What do you think?"

"I think you're bright *and* beautiful."

Asa had finally said what he'd thought when he first saw Deborah walk into the town hall meeting. He had thought her stunning with her golden brown skin and curly hair with glints of red and gold. At first he'd wanted to categorize her as exotic, but that was a word used too loosely whenever the media described an exceptional looking woman of color. To him "exotic" meant foreign or alien and there was nothing about Deborah Robinson that was strange or odd.

Initially he'd believed she was too thin, but after working closely with her he realized she wasn't. She was slender with enough curves to make a man crazy. Her fitted jeans displayed long legs and blatantly curvy womanly hips. And she'd become a chameleon when she'd transformed from the girl-next-door into a genteel lady with her coiffed hair and chic blouse, slacks, makeup, and jewelry.

It had taken a night of soul-searching, tossing and turning in the antique iron bed in the apartment above the bookstore, for Asa to admit to himself that he was entranced with Deborah. It had begun at the meeting, continued when she'd offered to give him and Jake Walker a ride back to the Cove Inn, and did not abate when he'd peered through the plate glass window of The Parlor and spied the HELP WANTED sign. And God help him when he'd caught sight of her rain-soaked top...the things he had envisioned. He'd believed that he hadn't had an impulsive bone in his body, yet Asa had proven himself wrong when he'd walked in and asked to be hired. What he couldn't understand was his reaction to the newspaper editor flirting with her and his wanting to punch out the insipid little man.

Had he become bored living at the boardinghouse? Yes.

Had the other guests begun to annoy him? The answer was yes.

Did he want to remain in Sanctuary Cove until he received notification that his application to DWB was approved? Again, the answer was yes, but only because he'd grown tired of driving aimlessly from state to state, city to city, and town to town. Sleeping in a strange bed that he didn't have to change or make up had lost its appeal. Cavanaugh Island had become somewhat of a refuge, a place he could stay until he began the next phase of his life. Even the names of the towns on the island denoted shelter and protection: Haven, Sanctuary, Angels. Fate had brought him to Sanctuary Cove and some strange and unknown force had brought Deborah into his life. He knew their time together would be short, but he'd promised himself he would make it into something he would remember for much longer.

Asa wanted to take more than the memory of his deceased wife and son with him when he retired to his future lodgings, after treating people who lacked even the most basic medical care.

"Now I know why the ladies like you, Asa." Deborah's voice broke into his thoughts.

"What did you say?"

"I said I know why the ladies are drawn to you."

A frown of confusion appeared between his eyes. "I don't understand what you're talking about."

"You're quite the silver-tongued devil. You know exactly what to say to make a woman feel good about herself."

Realization dawned when Asa stared at Deborah as if he'd never seen her before. "You don't believe you're beautiful?"

"No, Asa."

"What are you then? Ugly?"

"No! At least I don't believe I am."

"How do you see yourself, Deborah?" Asa whispered.

Time seemed to stand still as Asa waited for Deborah's response. The look on her face told him she was searching for an answer that didn't come easily. Asa wanted to say so many things. He wanted to tell her that in order to move past her husband's death, she needed to deal with it; confront it head on so that she could move past the emotions, but he was afraid of her reaction. He didn't want to push her away but he knew this was what she needed to heal. That's how he'd managed to get over his own grief.

Just as he started to say something, she cut him off.

"I guess you could say that I'm attractive."

Asa's smile and the gold in his eyes sparkled like polished amber. "You're a lot more than attractive, Deborah. You're stunning."

Lowering his gaze, Asa stared at Deborah's mouth as a warning voice whispered in his head that they were treading out onto dangerous waters. If they weren't careful they would be pulled under by strong and dangerous currents, unable to make it back to where it was safe, comfortable. That was what he felt whenever he and Deborah shared the same space. He'd become her friend, someone he hoped she could rely on, someone she believed she could go to with a problem or dilemma.

As much as he wanted Deborah to trust in him he also ran the risk of loving and losing for the second time. He'd lost his wife and son, and if he fell in love with Deborah he would lose her also, when he eventually left the Cove at the end of the winter season. Asa's heart sank with that notion and he found himself wanting to pull her close. He leaned toward her, his breath feathering over her mouth.

"I feel beautiful when I'm with you," she whispered.

Asa stared at the length of lashes touching the top of Deborah's high cheekbones. "You should feel beautiful even when you're not with me, because you are. Inside and out."

Awkwardly, she cleared her throat and looked away from him.

"Thank you, Asa."

"Is that all I get? A thank you."

Shifting slightly, Deborah gave him a long stare. "What else do you want?"

The query was a hushed whisper as Asa's expression changed.

"At this very moment I don't know what I want," he said after an interminable silence. "I suppose 'thank you' will have to suffice. Let's get back to your monthly store promotions," Asa said, as if what had just occurred between him and Deborah had never happened. "What do you plan to do with the calendars?"

"I think I'll print out a stack and leave them around the bookstore for customers to pick up. The observances and holidays tied to store promotions will be highlighted in color. We can't highlight all of February because it's National Black History Month, but we can highlight Valentine's Day. I've been trying to come up with something other than featuring popular romance authors or collections of poems dedicated to romance."

"Turn off your computer, and let's go for a walk."

Deborah gave him a puzzled look. "A walk?"

Asa smiled. "I think a lot better when I'm walking."

She shut down the computer and within minutes she and Asa were strolling along Main Street.

Chapter Fourteen

Deborah went completely still, then managed to relax when Asa reached for her hand. She couldn't help but wonder what people were thinking when they saw them walking hand-in-hand. The day was warm and sunny and the streets were teeming with locals and sightseers.

The bank, as well as Jack's Fish House and the hardware store, were closed, as were a number of small mom-and-pop shops. The drycleaner was also closed but the adjoining Laundromat was open. De Fountain, nestled between the variety store and Rose Dukes-Walker's A Tisket A Basket—a take on Ella Fitzgerald's "A Tisket A Tasket"—was crowded. It had become a favorite with the locals because all of the ice cream, sorbet, and gelato were made on the premises. They'd begun serving exotic flavored pop with bizarre names that appealed to the island's teenagers before trying their hand at making ice cream. The first time Deborah bought a pint of peach gelato and chocolate mint ice cream she was hooked. Now, if the ice cream did not come from De Fountain, she wouldn't eat it.

"Have you thought about a raffle?" Asa asked after a comfortable silence.

The mention of a raffle piqued Deborah's curiosity. "What type of raffle?"

"It will be up to you to determine the criteria, but I'm willing to donate a basket with champagne, a chocolate assortment, gourmet cookies, and other goodies."

"Oh my goodness! You're a genius, Asa. We can have several baskets, each with a free book and a gift certificate that will have to be redeemed within thirty days." Deborah smiled at him, brainstorming. "If I give the winners any longer I might lose the opportunity to make them repeat customers. The rule is anyone who makes a purchase between now and February fourteenth is eligible to win."

"Do you want them to purchase a minimum number of books?"

"No," she said quickly. "That would be unfair to those who don't have the money to buy more than one book at a time. Even a single purchase should have as much chance of winning as a multiple purchase. I'll pick up a roll of raffle tickets and a fishbowl tomorrow. Then I'll stop by Rose's A Tisket A Basket and pick up a few sweet-grass baskets."

"Aren't they expensive?"

"Yes. But Rose will give me a discount. Please don't repeat this, but she inflates her prices for the tourists who come here in droves during the summer months. They are worth every penny, because it takes hours for her to weave a basket and basket weaving has become a dying art."

"How much would the round tray Rose gave you as a grand opening gift go for?" Asa asked.

"Rose could easily have sold that for up to fifteen

hundred dollars." Deborah still hadn't decided what she wanted to use it for.

"It's an incredible piece."

"I agree. Did you know that slaves wove baskets so tightly that they held water?"

"I didn't know," Asa admitted. "Do you know how to weave them?"

Smiling, Deborah shook her head. "No. Learning to hand quilt was enough for me."

"One of these days I'm going into Charleston to take the Gullah tour."

"It's fascinating. Put Middleton Place on your places to see. The tour of the gardens and grounds include an African American focus tour that explores the lives of slaves and freedmen at Middleton Place and other Lowcountry plantations. I took my son and daughter on the carriage tour when they were much younger and that was all they could talk about for days."

"How long has it been since you've taken the tour?" Asa asked.

Deborah counted back in her head. "At least seven or eight years ago."

"If I sign up to go will you come with me?"

"Sure," she replied offhandedly. "But it will have to be on a Sunday."

"Don't you go to church on Sundays?"

She smiled. "Yes. But I usually attend the early service, so I'm free from ten on. Why don't you come to church with me, then we can leave directly from there?"

"No."

Deborah was caught off guard by the sudden hostility in his voice. "Are you an atheist?

"No, I'm not an atheist."

"Are you agnostic?"

"My not going to church has nothing to do with being a nonbeliever. At this time in my life I'm struggling with my faith."

Asa didn't want to tell Deborah that he'd become embittered, blaming God for giving him a son, then taking him. He was no Abraham, with faith in God so strong and unwavering that he was willing to offer up his Isaac as a sacrifice.

If God had been testing Asa Monroe's faith, then his so-called faithful servant had failed, because he was still struggling with *"Why me, Lord?"* As a doctor he was more than familiar with the cycle of life and death but nothing could have prepared him for losing his wife and six-year-old son.

Deborah met his stony stare. "I'm sorry for being presumptuous."

Asa smiled, but the warmth did not reach his eyes. "There's no need to apologize."

"What would you think if I made room for a reading corner for teens and little children?" she asked, smoothly bringing them back to discussing the bookstore.

"What would you use? Little tables and chairs?"

"They would take up too much room. What if we use beanbag cushions? I bought one as a birthday gift for one of Crystal's friends. What made it special was that I had Pottery Barn Teen embroider her name on it. We can get probably about three in different sizes and colors. When we get back to the store I'll show you them online."

"You have books for teens, but not many children's books."

"You're right," Deborah said, agreeing with Asa. "A new family just moved to the Cove and they have two kids that are probably in the first and second grade. They're going to need picture and eventually chapter books. I'm also thinking about teenagers who will need another place to hang out during the summer. Why not at The Parlor for a couple of hours?"

Before he could respond, they arrived at the town square and found a bench under the sweeping branches of an antique oak tree draped in Spanish moss. Stretching out her legs and crossing her sandaled feet at the ankles, Deborah rested her head on Asa's shoulder and closed her eyes. The warmth of the sun filtering through the branches of the towering tree, the incessant buzzing of insects and the murmurs of voices lulled her into a state of total relaxation.

"Debs Robinson. Is that you?"

Deborah opened her eyes to find Hannah Forsyth standing a short distance away, hands resting at her waist. The librarian was stuck in another era, with her oversized glasses, teased champagne-pink hair, and blood-red lipstick.

A smirk parted Deborah's lips. "It sure is. How are you this fine day, Miss Hannah?"

"Fine to middling," Hannah answered. "I hadn't expected to find you out here and with Mr. Monroe at that. Shouldn't you be home taking care of your babies?"

Deborah struggled to control her rising temper. She didn't mind if folks talked about her, but she didn't want her children brought into something that had nothing to do with them. "I would if I had babies, Miss Hannah. But in case you've forgotten my children are old enough to drive. I hope you enjoyed the grand opening," she continued, not bothering to take a breath.

Hannah smiled, her mouth a slash of red in her pale face. "It was simply charming." Her gaze shifted to Asa. "How are you?" she asked Asa, who'd stood up.

"I'm well; thank you, Miss Hannah. Would you like to sit down?"

"No thank you. I was just trying to get some walking in, because my doctor claims I need more exercise. Have a good afternoon."

"You, too," Deborah and Asa said in unison.

Deborah took a deep breath, trying to calm herself as Hannah continued walking. "She's nosey as hell," she mumbled.

Asa sat, staring at Deborah's strained expression. "What's the matter?"

Deborah focused on the vibrant color on her bare toes. "It's going to be all over the Cove that the town crier saw us together."

"It shouldn't matter, Deborah. After all we do work together." A beat passed, then Asa's expression changed. "Don't tell me you're talking about us having an affair?"

"That's exactly what I'm saying."

"Since when did sitting in public together translate into having an affair?"

"Have you ever heard of 'small towns, small minds'?" she asked.

There came another pause. "It's nobody's business what goes on between us."

Deborah laughed. "You're preaching to the choir, Asa." She stood up. "Let's head back."

They walked back to the store in no time, spending the

next few hours researching websites for the items that would go into their Valentine's Day gift baskets. In the end Deborah decided she would order an assortment of Godiva chocolates, boxes of mini Baci by Perugina, and Charleston Cookie Company double fudge cookie whoopee pies and mini chocolate chip cookies.

"I'll order chocolate-covered strawberries with sprinkles from the Muffin Corner and imported cheese from the supermarket deli. I think one basket should contain sparkling cider, fruit and cheese for those who don't want a sugar rush. The largest basket will have the champagne and the other a bottle of red and white wine. Let me know if I'm missing something."

Asa angled his head. "I think you've covered everything."

Deborah stared deeply into his eyes. "Thank you."

"For what?"

"For bringing me back to center whenever I get excited about a new project."

Running a finger down the length of her nose, Asa gave her a tender smile. "You're like a different person when you get into something. It's as if I can feel your excitement."

"This is all very new for me. The Charleston bookstore was just a store, but this place feels like a real parlor. It's like coming home."

"It could be because this is where you really belong."

Her smile faded and her eyes grew serious. "Where do you belong, Asa?"

"Go home, Deborah." Suddenly Asa's face had become a mask of stone.

She blinked. "All you had to say is that you don't want to answer the question."

"I don't want to answer the question."

"Good enough." Deborah exhaled an audible breath. She noted the time at the bottom of her computer monitor. "It's a lot later than I thought. Do you want me to leave the computer on for you?"

Asa shook his head. "No. I have a Netbook and my BlackBerry if I need to access the Internet."

Deborah gathered her papers and the receipt envelope, pushing them into her handbag that occasionally doubled as a tote. She walked to the back door, Asa following. "Thank you again for your help."

Pushing her hair behind her ear, Asa leaned over, pressing his mouth to hers. This time it wasn't a soft brushing of lips. His kiss was a slow, warm caress that left her mouth burning with fire. "I'm sorry. And you're welcome," he said, finally releasing her. "Get home safe."

She blinked as if coming out of a trance. "Thank you." Deborah was breathing heavily, like a runner who'd just finished a long grueling race. Her knees were shaking when she walked to her car and got in.

The rear door to the bookstore closed as she put the car in reverse and backed out of the space. She wanted to lick her lips and taste Asa again, but curbed the urge because her mouth was still tingling from his kiss. If he could do that to just her lips she shuddered to think of what she would do if he kissed her body.

The smile that tilted the corners of her mouth was still there when she maneuvered into the driveway to her house, coming to a stop next to Whitney's car. She found Whitney and Crystal on the back porch watching a playoff football game. In the South, it was high school football on

Friday nights, college ball on Saturdays, and professional teams on Sundays.

"Who's playing?" she asked.

"The Panthers and Tampa Bay," Whitney said without taking his eyes off the screen.

"Who's winning?"

"Tampa Bay," they chorused in unison.

Deborah knew they were rooting for the Carolina Panthers, so she left, leaving them to their game. Not having to prepare dinner had freed up her time; she could put up several loads of wash and possibly dust and vacuum.

Her cell rang as she mounted the staircase. Pulling it out of her blouse pocket, she glanced at the display then answered. "How's it going, Barbara?"

"That's what I want you ask you. How was the grand opening?"

"Quite grand," Deborah confirmed. "What are you doing tomorrow?"

"Relaxing. Why?"

"Come to the Cove and hang out with me."

"What about the bookstore?"

"I close on Monday."

"What time do you want me to come?" Barbara asked.

"Any time is good for me. I'm up early to see the kids off to school. I'll make brunch."

"If that's the case, then I'll see you around ten."

Deborah stood on the porch, watching Barbara as she mounted the steps. She had covered the wicker table with a floral tablecloth, silver, china, and crystal for two. A serving cart with covered dishes was positioned next to the table.

They exchanged hugs and air kisses. "Thanks for coming."

Barbara flashed a wide grin. "Thank you for inviting me." She dropped her tote on a cushioned rocker. "Every time I leave here and go back to Charleston I ask myself why I am still living in the city. Don't get me wrong, Deborah. I love my hometown, but there is something about this place that's like another world." She sniffed the air. "It even smells different here."

"Sit down and sniff away." Deborah uncovered dishes with sliced melon, scrambled eggs, an assortment of breakfast meats, and lemony brioche. She also set out tiny jars of apple butter, and peach and strawberry preserves.

Reaching for a carafe of chilled fresh-squeezed orange juice, Barbara filled her goblet, then Deborah's. "You look different."

Deborah's hand stopped in midair as she spooned melon into a fruit cup. "Different how?"

"You look like you did before losing Louis."

"How is that?"

"Relaxed. Content."

Deborah smiled. "I am."

"Who is he, Deborah?"

"What makes you think it's a man?"

Barbara set down the carafe. "How long have we known each other? A long time," she said, answering her own question. "You didn't ask me to come here to keep you company. You asked me because you need someone to talk to. Someone you trust."

Deborah nodded. She ladled a spoonful of eggs onto her plate. "You're right. I need your opinion on something."

"I'm all ears," Barbara said.

In between bites of food, and sips of juice and coffee, Deborah told Barbara everything about Asa: how he'd helped her get the bookstore up and running, how she had come to depend on him. "I like him, Barbara. I like him more than I should."

"What's wrong with liking him, Deborah? He's gorgeous, and from what you've told me he's intelligent *and* a gentleman. In case you haven't noticed you have wonderful hair, good skin, and an incredible body for an almost middle-aged woman with two teenage kids. And you didn't have to dip into your kids' college fund to pay a plastic surgeon to look the way you do."

"Thanks for the compliment, but that's not helping me with my dilemma."

Resting an elbow on the table, Barbara gave her former neighbor a long, penetrating stare. "You are creating a dilemma where there is none. You are a single woman, Debs, and from what you've told me your Asa Monroe is a single man." She put up a hand. "Louis is gone, Deborah, and he's not coming back. And if the situation were reversed I'm certain you wouldn't want him to spend the rest of his life alone."

"Of course not."

"Then why are we having this discussion, Debs?"

Deborah ran a hand through her hair. "Louis is the first and only man I've ever slept with." The admission was a whisper.

Barbara slumped back in her chair and gave Deborah an incredulous stare. "You're kidding?"

"No. I was in my first year at Bennington when I met Louis. He'd come up to Vermont for a holiday weekend to ski with a few of his MIT classmates. They invited a group of us to their ski lodge for a party. I was seventeen and away from home for the first time, and I was always the nice girl because my parents were well-known attorneys and heaven forbid if I did something to embarrass them. There was something about Louis's nerdy appearance that appealed to me. I'd had too much to drink and wound up in bed with him. I think he felt worse than I did because he hadn't known I was a virgin."

With wide eyes, Barbara stared. "Did he use a condom?"

"I wasn't so drunk that I would've had unprotected sex. He kept apologizing and I kept telling him it was all right. We exchanged phone numbers and I thought I'd never hear from him again."

"But you did."

Deborah nodded. "He called me every other day and whenever he had a break he'd drive up to see me. By the end of my junior year I knew I was in love with him. Instead of returning to Boston for the summer Louis took summer courses, accelerating to graduate in three years instead of four so we could marry. We got married, but decided not to tell anyone.

"He got a teaching position in Boston and I'd either take the train down or he would drive up to Bennington on weekends. I finally tired of the subterfuge and told my parents. They weren't too happy, and there was nothing they could do because I was of legal age to marry. The day before my graduation Louis's aunt and my parents sat us down and told us what they'd planned. My dad, through his connections, asked a Charleston principal to hire his son-in-law, while Louis's aunt gave us enough money for a down payment on a house as a wedding gift."

"You talk about Louis's aunt. What happened to his parents?"

"He never knew his father, and when he was nine his mother dropped him off with her sister and never returned to pick him up. His aunt, who was a schoolteacher, petitioned the court to make her his legal guardian. And because he'd been abandoned by both parents his aunt overindulged him. She was gentle, kind, and extremely generous and Louis had adopted her best qualities. He would never have hurt anyone, so for him to have been accused, later, of getting a teenage girl pregnant...it nearly destroyed him. I kept telling him we were going to beat the charge, but I don't know whether or not he believed me."

"Did you ever doubt his innocence?" Barbara asked.

"Never. Louis didn't do well with guilt. If he'd slept with another woman it would've haunted him until he had to tell me. We'd had a good sex life, so there wasn't a need for him to go looking for another woman."

Barbara exhaled an audible sigh. "I know you may not believe this, but there are men who sleep with other women even though they're sleeping with their wives."

Deborah shook her head. "As much as I enjoyed making love to my husband, that wasn't happening at the time of the accusation. About a year ago Louis was diagnosed with hypertension. One of the side effects of his medication was impotence. That's also why he couldn't have gotten Melissa Perry pregnant."

Barbara emitted an unladylike snort. "All he had to do was say he had ED and none of that crap would've happened. Why didn't you say something, Deborah?"

"I couldn't. Louis made me promise not to tell anyone.

He was one of the good guys, and I'm not just saying that because he was my husband, but in the end he got a raw deal. People are so willing to believe the worst, and that's what made me so angry. If the principal and the school board hadn't been so quick to judge him I believe Louis would still be alive today." A wry smile twisted her mouth. "Now you know everything."

"I wish I would've known before," Barbara countered, "because promise be damned I would've told that school board where they could stick their bogus accusation. I don't know if I'll ever feel the same way about some of the folks Terrell works with. If things were different, then we wouldn't be talking about your Asa."

"He's not *my* Asa."

Barbara flashed a Cheshire cat grin. "You really like the man, don't you?"

Deborah nodded. "Yes. I told you I like him."

"Have your kids met him?"

She nodded again. "Yes. At the grand opening."

"Do they like him?"

"Crystal and Whitney said they did."

Barbara leaned over the table. "Invite him to Sunday dinner."

Deborah snapped her fingers. "Just like that. I invite him over to my house."

"You really are naïve when it comes to men, aren't you?"

"I'm inexperienced when it comes to dating. Remember, I had one serious boyfriend, and I married him. I never learned to flirt, because I didn't have to."

"And there's no need for you to learn. All you have to do is be Deborah. The man has danced with you, kissed you, and massaged your feet. The only thing left is his making love to you. Close your mouth, Debs," Barbara said when Deborah's jaw dropped. "I just hope you'll be able to deal with it when it happens."

Deborah thought about Barbara's prediction. She'd told her everything except that she wanted to sleep with Asa, probably because she had trouble admitting it to herself. "I don't have a problem sleeping with a man."

"What *is* the problem?"

She stared at the salt-and-pepper twists framing her friend's face. "I don't want to get emotionally involved."

Barbara placed her hand over Deborah's. "You're no different than most women. We live for love, and once we decide to sleep with a man we not only offer them our bodies but also our hearts. But you're ahead of the game, because you know Asa isn't going to stay. If you keep reminding yourself of that, then when he does leave you will have prepared yourself for it. I've slept with guys that I never should have even said hello to, and one or two that I'd believed I couldn't live without. Then I met Terrell and I wasn't very nice to him, because I felt he had to pay for what I had to put up with all the other scrubs. When he told me he wasn't going anywhere I knew he was a keeper."

"Terrell is wonderful."

"So was Louis," Barbara countered.

"But, I still love Louis."

"And because you do it should make it easier for you not to fall in love with another man. If Asa is offering, then take it. And if he's not then I want you to take it anyway."

Throwing back her head, Deborah laughed until tears

rolled down her face. Picking up a napkin, she blotted her cheeks. "You're unbelievable."

"No I'm not. I just believe in keeping it real. You've been celibate long enough, and if you don't use it you'll lose it."

"There are always—"

"Don't you dare say the 'v' word, Debs Robinson. There's nothing like the real thing."

Deborah sobered, asking, "How would you know?"

Barbara waved a hand. "Girl, please. There was a time before I married Terrell that I had so many sex toys that I had a name for each of them."

"What were their names?"

"Chocolate Thunder. White Lightning. The Stallion. And my favorite was Timex. It took a licking but kept on kicking."

"I thought it was ticking."

"That too," Barbara confirmed. "It came with a special battery that worked on solar power, and never had to be replaced."

"What did you do with them after you married Terrell?"

"I keep them in a box in the top of my closet. I never know when I might need them." She burst into laughter.

"You are crazy!"

Deborah and Barbara sat on the porch, talking and laughing as the sun reached its zenith, then they stood up together, cleared the table, put everything away, and retreated to the back porch to watch *All My Children*. When the show ended, Deborah offered Barbara the chance to see the new bookstore setup, but she refused, stating she wanted to get back to Charleston before she got caught in school bus traffic. Deborah herself left as soon as the taillights of Barbara's car disappeared, driving to the bank to deposit Saturday's receipts.

Stepping up to the teller's cage, she slid her deposit ticket, cash, and checks under the slot at the window. "Good afternoon, Jennifer."

The teller's head popped up, her blue-gray eyes sparkling in amusement. "Oh. Good afternoon, Debs. Miss Hannah was here just before you came in and she said it's a shame you were keeping company so soon after burying your husband. I don't think she liked me telling her that I didn't appreciate her gossiping about my friend, and that I was going to tell you."

Deborah's lips parted in a smile. "Thanks for letting me know." She and Jennifer Stewart were of the same high school graduating class. When Deborah went off to college Jennifer had stayed in the Cove to marry her high school sweetheart.

Jennifer flipped a wave of highlighted hair over her shoulder, frowning. "What I can't understand is why she feels the need to get into everyone's business."

"I don't think anyone has an answer to that question. Maybe I should give her something to really talk about."

Rolling her eyes and shaking her head, Jennifer said, "It would serve her right if it came back to bite her in the butt." She processed the deposit, pushing the receipt through the opening. "Try not to let her get to you, Debs."

"I have better things to worry about than Miss Hannah's gossip."

"Good for you."

Deborah walked out of the bank, trying not to lose her

composure. She had warned Asa about Hannah when she saw them together. After a while, it wouldn't matter who saw them because Deborah knew Asa wasn't going to stay in the Cove, that he was going to leave with the other snowbirds. She had at least another three months to prepare herself for the inevitable.

Chapter Fifteen

January 22nd—Yesterday Asa overheard someone in the store whispering about us having an affair and to say he was upset is putting it mildly. I told him to ignore it, let it go, and it took a while before he was calm again. When I mentioned the ditty about sticks and stones, he shocked me when he said he wanted to go to the library and openly confront Hannah Forsyth.

Talk about putting fuel on the fire. He went to the pharmacy and bought a supply of condoms, making certain Grady Forsyth saw him so he could pass the information along to his "nosey-ass wife." I actually think he got a kick out of doing that.

Hannah came into the store today to pick up a book I'd ordered for her, and Asa put on a show, calling me darling and sweetheart. I thought the poor woman was going to have a stroke when we shared a tight hug. Once she left I playfully chastised him for misbehaving, but he claimed he'd been on his best behavior. What I couldn't tell him was that I enjoyed being in his arms and having him call me *his* darling. And if I were a bolder woman I would admit to him that I want to be his sweetheart and so much more.

February 1st—When I walked into The Parlor earlier this morning Asa was at the piano playing ragtime. He winked at me, smiled, and continued to play. It wasn't his day to work, but he hung out in the store, taking personal requests from the customers. I've finally realized the days he is scheduled to work we have a lot more customers than when he isn't there. I know the women come to see him and although I've told him this, Asa says I'm imagining things. It's as if he's totally oblivious to his charm. But I'm not and sometimes I wonder if the attentions shown to him spark a bit of jealousy in me.

It was the second Tuesday in February and Mayor White had asked Deborah if she would host the monthly town hall meeting at The Parlor; meeting rooms at the library and town hall were undergoing much-needed repairs that included installing new windows and roofing. She told him he and the members of the council could use the space if he sent someone over to move the furniture, then at the conclusion of the meeting move everything back. Spencer told her his men would be over at three to set up and she was forced to cancel afternoon tea and close the store at noon.

Deborah still couldn't believe how successful her Valentine's Day promotion was until she saw the fishbowl filled with colorful red tickets. Two weeks ago the ad had appeared in the biweekly paper, outlining the rules for winning three gift baskets filled with fine wines, gourmet chocolate, cheese, and other delectable goodies. The following day a steady stream of men and women came into The Parlor to purchase books or cloth-covered journals. And to enter their raffle tickets.

Book club members had picked up their books and were scheduled to return at the end of the month for their discussion meeting, and afternoon tea had become a favorite for a group of retired women who arrived on the stroke of three every day. Deborah served hot and cold tea with butter cookies, miniature tarts, and brioche from the Muffin Corner; on several occasions she made dainty sandwiches. The women seemed to favor her spicy chicken salad made with mango chutney, mayonnaise, and curry powder. Then Asa had surprised her when he produced a platter of round avocado and bacon sandwiches on cracked wheat bread, salmon pinwheels, and date and walnut sandwiches for those without nut allergies.

Before the meeting, Deborah stood at the front door, staring at the rain sluicing down the glass. It had been raining steadily for two days now, leaving the streets empty. She had placed the CLOSED sign in the window.

"I doubt if the ladies would have come to tea today even if we hadn't closed early," Deborah said when she felt the heat from Asa's body as he came up behind her.

"Do you think the mayor will call off tonight's meeting?"

Turning, she looked up at Asa. "I doubt it. The only time he's ever canceled a meeting is when council members don't show up, and that doesn't happen too often. Spencer ran on a platform of transparency, so he wants to keep townsfolk abreast of everything that's going on in the Cove."

Pushing his hands into the pockets of his slacks, Asa angled his head. One hundred percent humidity left Deborah's hair in tiny ringlets. "Why don't you come upstairs? I'll make lunch for you." Between twelve and two he usually retreated to his apartment to eat or watch the midday news while Deborah either went home to eat or ordered takeout.

She smiled. "What's on the menu?"

"Shrimp ravioli with lobster and a garlic butter sauce."

Her eyes lit up. "You're kidding?"

"Nope. I made it last night for tonight's dinner."

"You're a man of many talents. You said you're not married, so why hasn't some woman scooped you up?" Deborah asked.

Shock crossed over Asa's handsome features as he stood momentarily speechless He continued to stare at her. "I was married once," he said, recovering his voice and changing the subject. "Are you going to join me for lunch, or would you prefer we go out?"

"If I go out, then I'm not coming back. I'm like a cat. I don't like getting wet in the rain."

"Let's go up to the penthouse," he said jokingly.

Reaching for her hand, Asa led her over to the wall switch where he turned out all the lights, plunging the bookstore in total darkness. He flipped the switch on the wall at the bottom of the staircase. Resting his hands on her waist, he guided her gently up the stairs. When he opened the door to the apartment, Deborah noticed the difference in temperature immediately. It was at least ten degrees cooler here than it was downstairs.

"The penthouse is cold," Deborah remarked, rubbing her bare arms.

Asa walked to the wardrobe and came back with a cotton pullover sweater. "I'll turn off the air, but put this on until it warms up."

She pulled the sweater over her head, adjusting the sleeves and hem. "It's a little big, but it will have to do."

Asa winked. "It's cute."

Deborah glanced around. She hadn't been in his apartment since the Sunday following the grand opening. It was clean and neat—everything in its place. "Your apartment is immaculate."

"What did you say?" Asa called out from the bathroom where he was washing his hands.

"I said your place is very neat."

He stuck out his head as he dried his hands. "I don't do well with clutter."

"I wish my son felt that way."

Asa came out of the bathroom and opened the refrigerator. "He'll grow out of it."

Deborah moved over to the table, watching as Asa removed a large plastic container from a shelf. "When?"

Smiling, Asa gave her a sidelong glance she found so endearing. "When he goes to college and lives on campus. I had a roommate that was a complete slob. I sat him down and told him either he cleaned up after himself or I was going to request a new roommate. We worked out a deal: I would clean and he would cook."

Folding her arms under her breasts, Deborah watched as he filled a large pot with water and placed it on a burner. "I didn't know there were kitchens in dorm rooms."

"Well, we found ways around that," he replied, a look of mischief crossing his face.

"Could he cook?"

" 'Cook' couldn't begin to describe what Joey Farina could do. His parents owned a restaurant and he'd begun working there when he was ten. By the time he was sixteen he was in the kitchen. In the four years we roomed together he taught me how to make pasta and tomato sauce from scratch. I didn't have a pasta machine, but a rolling pin did the trick."

"Tell me what you need and I'll bring it over for you."

"You gave me enough pots and pans, dishes, glassware, and serving utensils, so I'm good for now," he said. Deborah had even given him a small electric food processor.

"Is there something I can do besides stand around and watch you?" Deborah asked. It wasn't that she didn't like just looking at Asa because she did. He was handsome, fastidious, and claimed an incredibly conditioned physique for a man his age. There wasn't an ounce of fat on his toned body.

"Do you want me to make a salad?" Deborah asked.

"Yes."

"What kind of greens do you have?"

Asa opened the refrigerator to browse. "Red leaf, radicchio, endive, escarole, and romaine."

Deborah stood up. "I'll be right back after I wash my hands."

She returned to the sound of music filling the space. Asa had turned the television on to a station featuring cool jazz. When Deborah opened the refrigerator she found it fully stocked. This was the same with the overhead cabinets. A countertop wine rack held two bottles each of white, red, and rosé. None were opened.

"Do you make your own salad dressing?" she asked.

"Yes. What about you?"

"There hasn't been a bottle of store-bought dressing in my house in over ten years," Deborah admitted, sharing a smile with him.

"There's a tin of anchovy filets in the cabinet on your right and a fresh wedge of parmesan in the fridge if you want to make a Caesar dressing."

"How about a basic vinaigrette with minced garlic and red wine vinegar?" She planned to make a mixed green salad with a Mediterranean flavor.

"Make whatever you like. I'm certain it will be delicious."

Standing side by side Deborah and Asa worked together as if it was something they'd done many times before. She washed, dried, and tore lettuce leaves while Asa dropped half a dozen lobster tails in a pot of boiling water. Within minutes they were bright red. He drained and cooled them, then split the shells with a sharp knife, removing the meat and dividing it into equal portions. He sliced the tender chunks into pieces and minced the rest.

"I'm going to set the table," Deborah said as she placed the bowl of greens on a shelf in the refrigerator.

"Please take down soup and salad bowls. There's a container of lobster bisque in the refrigerator. I would've attempted to make it myself, but the woman where I bought the lobster said they made the best fish soups on the island."

She took out the container. Asa had bought the soup from Sanctuary Harbor's Fishery, where Elias Fletcher owned and operated a seafood clearinghouse. Elias purchased the catch of the local fisherman and then sold it to mainland restaurants. "She's right, Asa. You have to try their conch soup."

"I ate conch soup once, and I didn't like it. They were too chewy."

"They probably weren't cooked long enough. Try the Fishery's and you'll change your mind," Deborah suggested.

She watched mutely as Asa opened a drawer in the refrigerator and removed a bottle of chilled rosé, recalling the last time she'd shared a glass of wine with him. Today would be different because she would eat first, then drink. And she wasn't going home until after the meeting; she'd gotten up early to roast a chicken with herb stuffing and new potatoes for the children. There was a note on the refrigerator telling Crystal to make a salad to accompany their dinner.

A delicious mouth-watering aroma permeated the kitchen as Asa filled bowls with the bisque topped with minced lobster; vinaigrette-tossed salad and shrimp-stuffed ravioli with lobster was the second and third course. He'd put the entire meal together within thirty-five minutes.

The homemade ravioli literally melted on her tongue, and there was just enough heat in the shrimp to offset the creamy pasta covering. "May I invite myself up for lunch every day?"

"The door is always open. Come up whenever you want."

"You may come to regret those words, Asa Monroe."

Asa smiled at Deborah over the rim of his wineglass. "I doubt that, Debs."

Asa didn't know why but opening night seemed so very long ago, when it'd only been a little more than three weeks. He felt as if he'd known Deborah even longer. She'd hired him to work no more than twenty hours a week, yet he spent more time in the bookstore than he did in his apartment.

In the mornings Deborah came in at nine to dust, vacuum, and straighten books before opening at nine-thirty. He usually came down around ten, filled the urn with hot water, and then went to the Muffin Corner to pick up an assortment of sweet breads. Throughout the day he checked the bathroom, making certain it was well-stocked and clean. Whenever there was a shipment of books he entered the quantity and ISBNs into the computer for accurate recordkeeping.

Most nights Deborah left at six in order to share dinner with her children, and this was when he missed her most.

He managed to fill up his days talking to customers, playing the piano and fielding phone calls, but at night when the lights were out and the store was silent, he was unable to hold back the sadness. Sometimes it crept up on him, as if on the silent paws of a stalking cat, catching him unaware, where he wanted to cry. Other times, after he'd locked the rear door and watched Deborah get into her car and drive away, he wanted to scream at the top of his lungs. He wanted to release the grief that reminded him that when he climbed the staircase and lay in bed he would be all alone.

It wasn't that he needed a woman for sex as much as he needed her for companionship, and of all the women he'd seen and met since becoming a widower it was Deborah Robinson he wanted. Asa knew their time together wouldn't be long, but that no longer mattered. He would take whatever morsels of affection she was willing to offer.

He'd ignored Deborah's warning about Hannah Forsyth, but when the woman's gossiping became a reality Asa knew he had reacted badly. He knew it wasn't his reputation that concerned him, but Deborah's, and Asa didn't want to think of how her children might react hearing that their mother was sleeping with a man so soon after losing their father. He knew it had been wrong to call her endearments in front of the nosy old woman, or to purchase condoms to fan the rumors, but he hadn't been able to help himself. And the truth was that even though he told himself over and over that he didn't want to make love to Deborah, as soon as the thought entered his head he knew it was a lie. There were times when he did withdraw from her, shut down, but only because he wanted Deborah with him 24/7. He resented her having to go home to her children, but then became racked with guilt for harboring selfish thoughts. He picked up his wineglass, staring at Deborah over the rim.

Leaning back in her chair, Deborah studied the man sitting across from her. Although they spent most of their days together he still was an enigma. She touched the edge of her napkin to her mouth. Asa *was* her friend but a part of her wanted him to become more.

Tenting his fingers, Asa stared at them. "It seems you have something on your mind. Why don't you tell me what it is?"

With an exasperated breath, Deborah told Asa about her mother's promise to her daughter about the dog. Once the words left her lips she felt silly for being bothered by such a small thing. But Asa didn't judge her and instead offered soothing words to help calm her sudden agitation.

"Sorry to hit you with my problems."

"It's not as if you divulged top secret information. You were upset and you needed to vent. I just happened to be here. There's nothing wrong with that."

"I shouldn't have dumped on you."

Pushing back his chair, Asa stood and came around the table, pulling her gently to her feet. "Stop it, Deborah. Stop beating up on yourself. You had a small disagreement with your mother. It probably wasn't the first time, and it certainly won't be the last."

Curving her arms under his shoulders, Deborah rested her head on his chest. "My mother hardly ever disagrees with me."

"Was that the first time?"

"No."

"So, what's the problem? The next time you talk to her you'll kiss and make up."

Deborah tightened her hold on Asa as if he were her lifeline. "Did I make a mistake?" she mumbled against his chest.

"What are you talking about?"

"Maybe I shouldn't have reopened the bookstore."

"Why? Where is this coming from?"

"My children need me. Especially my daughter."

"You shouldn't blame yourself for wanting to continue your business," he said tenderly. "Or is this about Miss Hannah Forsyth?" He led her over to the window, twirling her around as he swayed in time to the music. They glided toward the bed, Asa pulling her down to lie beside him. "Your children are not babies, Deborah. They are young adults, and don't need you to watch them 24/7. They go to school, have their friends and extracurricular activities. If you were home they would resent you monitoring their every move. The bookstore also provides you with an income so you can take care of them."

Deborah wanted to tell Asa that she really didn't need to work to support her children but she didn't. The monies she'd received from Louis's insurance policies and the money from the sale of the house in Charleston had given her financial stability. There was no mortgage on the house in the Cove, and she'd repaid the home equity loan she'd taken out to update the property. Even when she and Louis had needed to watch every penny Deborah never accepted money outright from her parents. They'd accepted the down payment as a wedding gift, and whenever her mother or father sent a monetary gift for her birthday or Christmas she would always use the money to pay off the mortgage. They had paid off a thirty-year mortgage in fifteen years. But the real issue now was Hannah's words, making Deborah second-guess her parenting skills.

"The bookstore keeps me sane," she admitted.

Placing an arm over her waist, Asa pulled her closer. "What would you do if you didn't have the store?"

A dreamy expression crossed her face. "I'd probably teach."

"Did you like teaching?" he asked.

"Yes. Especially on the college level. Nowadays I don't think I could cut it teaching high school students. There's too much crap going on with them."

"Define 'crap'."

"Bullying, gangs, drugs, etcetera."

Asa smiled. "That was going on when I was in high school, and definitely when you were, too. It appears to be more prevalent because we're living in an electronic age when everything happens in nanoseconds."

"Were you ever bullied, Asa?"

"No. Only because nobody messed with my brother Jesse. He is four years older than me, and he put the word out that if anyone stepped to me then they had to deal with him." Asa smiled, remembering. "If you looked at him sideways he'd just walk over and knock the hell outta you. He could pull A's without opening a textbook. He breezed through college and medical school, graduating at the top of his class." The smile faded. "Then he met a woman who turned him onto drugs. He started writing prescriptions to support their habit, and when he was afraid of getting caught he started stealing drugs from the hospital. The hospital administration couldn't prove he was stealing, but they always had someone watching him.

"When crack became popular he was in hog heaven. It was cheap and readily available, so he literally lost his mind. He would disappear for weeks, and when he'd finally surface he looked more dead than alive. Jesse would go cold turkey, clean up for a while, and then when he met another woman he'd relapse. Whenever he was low on money he'd go to the casino to gamble. Even in his drug haze he still had the ability to count cards. He'd win enough money to pick up a prostitute and score his drugs. Then it would start all over again, until he was banned from several casinos.

"He put my mother in an early grave and I saw my father age before my eyes the first time Jesse came home after spending several weeks in a crack house. My mother would wash him as if he were a baby and nurse him back to health, but whenever one of his women came around he would disappear. When Mom died after suffering a massive coronary, we held the body as long as we could while we waited for Jesse to show up. But he didn't reappear until two days after we'd buried her. When Dad told him what had happened he turned and walked out without saying a word. The last time I saw him he'd come to me asking me for money so he could leave Delaware. I don't know who or what was after him but I gave him all the cash I had in the house. I didn't ask who the people were because I didn't want to know. If it wasn't drug dealers, then it had to be loan sharks."

"Do you ever think about him?"

A wry smile parted Asa's lips. "Yes. I wonder where he is. What he's been doing and whether he's clean."

"I'll say a prayer for him."

Tightening his hold on Deborah's waist, Asa buried his face in her hair. "I'm sure he would appreciate it wherever he is."

"I'd like to invite you to my home for Sunday dinner."

She glanced up at him at the same time he lowered his head and brushed his mouth over hers. "Are you certain you want me to come?"

"Of course. You've met Whitney and Crystal, so it's not as if they don't know who you are."

"What time is dinner?"

"We usually sit down to eat around four, but you can get there about three-thirty."

"Do you want me to bring anything?" he asked.

"Yes. Yourself."

"Now you know I can't show up empty-handed."

Smiling and shaking her head, Deborah said, "Why is it so important to show up with something?"

Asa lifted his shoulder. "I don't know. I guess it's a black thing."

"It is a black thing," she confirmed. "I remember when a woman who my dad had grown up with invited us to Christmas dinner. We arrived empty-handed and even before we darkened the door the word had spread that Herman Williams had forgotten his home-training. He, his highfalutin' clean skin wife, and child came, ate and drank and left with only a thank you. Two days later she had to eat her words when a twenty-five pound Smithfield ham was delivered to her house with a thank-you note from my mother. It was apparent she had forgotten that highfalutin' folks don't tote food because it just might spill and ruin their fancy clothes. Back in the day they had their help bring over the hospitality offering."

"What the heck is clean skin?"

"It refers to a light complexion. Most folks around here believed my mother was mixed race because she has a short button nose and very curly hair."

"But, you said she is white."

"You know skin color means nothing; there are a lot of fair-skinned black folk. Around here people tend to look at the hair, features, and skin undertones. If it's yellow then you're suspect. But here on Cavanaugh there has been a lot of race mixing. So because of my mother's features, everyone assumed one of her parents must have been black."

"Gullah talk and superstitions. It's as if the Lowcountry isn't a part of the United States," Asa said.

Deborah laughed softly. "There's a lot of history here

most folks don't know about. Over on Angels Landing there are people who practice putting spells on and off folks. All that talk about working roots and ghosts would scare the bejedus outta me when I was younger."

"What the heck is bejedus?"

"Jedus is 'Jesus' in Gullah talk."

"Say something else and let me try and translate it."

Deborah searched her head for something she was certain would stump Asa. "E onrabble e mout."

Unconsciously his brow furrowed. "I understand mouth. Onrabble sounds like rattling on. You talk too much."

"Yeah, you're good. What's bonkey?" He gave her a blank expression. "That's behind," she explained. "We'll try another easy one: 'Waffuh do?'"

"What you do?"

"Close. It's what *to* do. If you listen closely you'll understand most of the words only because they've become a part of the black dialect and lexicon. Gullah is a blend of African and European languages. I'm certain you've heard people drop the ending to 'with' and it becomes wid. 'Tater' is potato. Now we even have tater tots. 'Jook'um' is to poke or stick. 'Sat-day' is Saturday. 'Ting' is thing. 'Nuff' is enough and the phrase I like is: 'E yent crack e teet.' That means he didn't open his mouth to speak. Some of the words are of African origin, from various tribes in West Africa, and the lilting accent makes it sound Caribbean."

"The culture sounds intriguing."

"It is. It's rich, colorful, and fraught with a lot of superstition."

Asa reached over and brushed a wayward curl off Deborah's cheek. "Are you superstitious?"

A mysterious smile softened her mouth. "The only thing I'm going to admit to is that I respect the superstitions, because I've seen many of them come to fruition. Are they unexplainable? Yes. But I still respect them."

"Give me an example."

"If an older person decides to 'put de mout on you' then you'd better watch out, because depending upon who he or she is your life isn't worth spit."

Throwing back his head, Asa laughed. "That's crazy."

Deborah's eyes narrowed as she glared at him. "So were the folks who had the *mout* on them."

Without warning, he sobered. "Are you telling me they went crazy?"

She nodded. "My grandmother left me her journals and the other night I read how a woman she knew was messing around with another's husband. The wife dressed her husband, and after he slept with the loose heifer her stomach *swole up* so big folks thought she was going to have triplets."

"Was she pregnant?" Asa asked.

Deborah landed a soft punch to his shoulder. "You're missing the point, Asa. No, she wasn't pregnant. But you thought she was when you could see things moving around her belly under her clothes. Grandmomma wrote: *de doctuh couldn't do nothin' to help de po chile.* Even though my grandmother was college-educated she would sometimes lapse into speaking and writing Gullah."

"What happened to the loose heifer?"

"Grandmomma wrote she got skinnier and skinnier while her belly continued to grow. When she finally passed away the doctors opened her up and found a tumor the size of a watermelon, weighing about thirty pounds.

Word went around that the growth looked like a hairy baby pig."

Asa rubbed the back of his neck, clearly agitated. "As a medical student I have witnessed medical procedures where tumors were removed from human bodies that were so hideous that some students bolted from the room or lost the contents of their stomachs. It only took one incident for me to learn not to eat before observing an autopsy or a surgical procedure. This definitely sounds like one of those cases." Asa shook his head as if trying to clear the images from his mind. "What happened to the cheating husband?"

"Grandmomma said his penis shriveled up like a newborn's and that put an end to his tomcattin'."

"Ouch!"

"My grandmother's journals are fascinating. After I finish reading them I'm going to give them to Whitney to read, because one day he may want to write a book about her."

"I read his article about the bookstore opening in the *Chronicle*. It was intelligent and impartial, considering he was writing about his mother."

"He plans to major in Communications."

"What college is he going to?"

"Howard has accepted him, and so has Bennett in Columbia. He doesn't have much more time before he makes his decision."

"Why is he waffling?"

"He'd decided on Howard before Louis died. Now, he feels as if he has to be close to home."

"Close to home or close to his Mama?"

"Probably both. I've told him that I don't have a problèm with him going to an out-of-state school, but it's apparent I haven't been too convincing."

"Columbia isn't Charleston," Asa reminded Deborah.

"I know. But it's only two hours away by car."

"Where do you want him to go?"

"I'm leaning toward Howard, because there are more employment opportunities in D.C. Wherever he decides to go, I'll support him one hundred percent."

"Where are you going?" Asa asked when she pulled out of his embrace and slipped off the bed.

"I need to clean up the kitchen." Deborah walked over to the table and picked up the soup bowls, cursing under her breath when a spoon slipped, falling against the sweater before it landed on the floor.

"Yuck! Now I'll smell like fish." Luckily the spoon missed her slacks.

Asa walked over and picked up the spoon. "Why don't you bring a change of clothes with you and leave it here since you've been spending so much time in the store? That way you won't have to go home to shower and change."

"That's a good idea," she said, frowning at the damp spot under her right breast.

"Take it off. I'll give you a shirt."

"Let me see the shirt."

"Don't worry, Debs; it will come at least to your knees." Asa walked to the wardrobe. He returned with a laundered long-sleeved shirt on a hanger. "Will this do?"

Smiling, Deborah nodded. "It will."

Taking the shirt, she went into the bathroom to change; she added a dollop of liquid soap on the spot, rubbed it gently before rinsing it with cold water, then hung the sweater over the shower rod. Slipping out of her pants, she folded them neatly over her arm. Asa was in the kitchen clearing away the remains of their lunch while she hung her blouse and slacks on a hanger and then on a rod in the wardrobe next to rows of slacks, shirts, two suits, and a navy blazer. His outerwear also included a trench coat, barn jacket, and a leather bomber. Shoes, ranging from sandals to two pairs of wingtips, lined a shoe rack. Slipping her feet into her ballet-type flats, she rejoined him in the kitchen.

Asa angled his head and stared at the woman wearing his shirt. Never would he have imagined having her there with him. With her tussled hair she looked as if she'd just been made love to and he instantly hardened at the thought. His gaze traveled downward to her bare legs, realizing it was the first time he'd seen them. They were long and smooth with curvy calves and slender ankles. His mouth watered.

"You look sexy," he croaked, when really he'd wanted to say how much he needed her in his bed, and not just for a few minutes. He wanted her to spend the night.

Chapter Sixteen

The Parlor was brightly lit. Rows of folding chairs took up more than half the space. The men had come as promised and had moved tables, chairs, and rugs toward the back of the store, leaving space for people to maneuver to the restroom and the rear exit. Deborah's treasured piano was pushed close to the plate glass window. Despite the inclement weather there was the usual number of attendees.

Mabel walked in with her husband and headed straight for Deborah. "Have you heard?" she whispered softly.

Deborah leaned closer. "Heard what?"

"Some strange dudes with fat pockets were asking around about abandoned properties here on the Cove."

"I thought I overheard someone mention developers the other day, but I try not to get into the business of my customers because I don't want them in mine."

"Well, Debs, I can't help but hear when they sit in my shop for hours drinking coffee and beatin' their gums. Even Lester, who hates these meetings, decided to come.

He owns some land north of your place that he inherited from his uncle. Someone called him the other day and asked if he was willing to sell it and Lester said *'hell no'* and hung up before the man could leave his name and number. To say he cussed a blue streak is putting it mildly."

"I suppose this is going to be a very interesting meeting."

"Sho 'nuff," Mabel drawled.

Deborah sat down in the back row while Asa elected to stand, leaning against the door leading to his apartment. Spencer White walked in wearing a sweatshirt, jeans, and boots, his expression solemn. The members of the town council were similarly dressed for the rainy weather. Jeff arrived a moment later, removing his cap and taking his seat on the end of the row of seats facing the assembled.

Spencer cleared his voice. "As soon as Eddie arrives we'll start the meeting."

The words were barely off his tongue when the newspaper editor walked in, struggling to close the outer door until Jeff got up to assist him. Before it had just been rain; now it was wind and rain. Eddie, sitting in the front row, removed a handheld tape recorder from his jacket pocket and turned it on.

"I'm ready, Mayor White."

Spencer cleared his voice again. "I'd like to thank everyone for turning out with the weather such as it is. If what I have to tell you wasn't so important for the Cove's future I would have canceled tonight's meeting."

"Quit jawin' and spit it out, son. You're not in the courtroom," said an elderly woman. "I'm certain these good folks want to get back home jest I like do."

A rush of color suffused Spencer's face. "Okay,

Grandma," he said, apologizing to his great-grandmother. "I've been approached by several men who represent a developer who want to buy up vacant homes and land to put in a casino, a golf resort with a number of hotels, and a conference center." There came murmurs and whispers until Spencer raised his hand for silence. "They not only approached me, but also the mayors of Angels Landing and Haven Creek."

"What did they say?" Lester asked. "Because I hope those bastards didn't ask you what they asked me."

"I spoke with Allen over in Haven Creek and they want no part of it. He claims it will inflate property values, forcing his people to move."

Luvina Jackson raised her hand. "What about the folks in Angels Landing?"

"The mayor said he took a survey and the vote is split fifty-fifty."

Rachel Dukes stood up. "If they decide to let them fat cats in, it will be a disaster. Everyone knows most of the land in Angels Landing is cursed." Nods and murmurs followed her pronouncement. It was a known fact that Rachel had been born with a caul over her face, which meant she had the gift of sight. Whatever Rachel predicted usually came to fruition. "Let them build and it will become nothing more than a fancy cemetery."

"I don't want them to build anywhere on Cavanaugh Island!" shouted Hannah Forsyth. "It shouldn't matter if the land is cursed or blessed. I've seen what developers have done to Hilton Head, Jekyll Island, and parts of St. Simons. They carve out sections where they put up fancy homes with gates. Then they have folks with guns patrolling the land we'd worked and claimed as our own for generations."

Spencer waited for Rachel to sit, then said, "We've heard the downside of permitting developers to build here. What if we limit their building? Give them an area of, say, eight hundred acres and let them deal with that?"

Elias Fletcher stood up. His formerly long red hair was now snow-white and hung midway down his back. He wore every year of the thirty he'd spent as a fisherman on his leathery face. Blue eyes flashing, he shook his fist at Spencer. "What's in it for you, Mayor Spencer? Did those sons of bitches offer to grease your palm if you convinced us to go along with their crooked scheme?"

"Watch your mouth, Elias," Spencer warned.

"No, Mayor, you watch yours. I've spent all of my life here in Sanctuary Cove and I have seen people come and go because they felt there was something better for them away from here. You were one of those who cut and run for a while when you were chasing that actress's skirt. So don't start with me, Sonny, because I'll give you more than you can take. We on the Cove have survived when so many other Lowcountry politicians have sold out their folks. Just make certain you don't become one of those, *Mayor White*." He'd spat out the title as applause followed his outburst.

Alice Parker stood up, waiting to be acknowledged and heard. Spencer, obviously shaken and embarrassed, pointed to her. "Yes, Mrs. Parker."

"It's Alice. I'm not one of those people Mr. Fletcher spoke about, but my husband is. His roots on this island go back more than three hundred years, and though he lived in other places, when it was time to start a family he had to come back. He wanted our children to benefit from the values this town believes in, and grow up in a place with a strong sense of history. If we sell to developers, then it's the same as selling our birthright. In a couple of generations you won't be able to find anyone with roots that go back years on Cavanaugh Island, because everyone will be a newcomer or outsider. If Cavanaugh Island has survived without golf courses, overpriced hotels, and companies that pollute our waters so fisherman will be forced out of business, then I say to hell with the developers. Sheriff Hamilton, you need to give them a personal police escort off the island with a warning if they come back they'll be shot on sight." The entire assembly rose as one, applauding, shouting, and whistling their approval.

Spencer waited until everyone was seated again. He smiled at Alice. "Are you certain you're not campaigning for something?"

She returned his smile, her complexion flushed. "Yes, Mayor White. I intend to run against you when you're up for re-election."

"Well damn," Mabel whispered under her breath. "The sister ain't no joke."

"I like her," Deborah whispered back. "We've never had a female mayor. It's time we get one."

"You ain't lyin'."

Spencer, who seemed to have recovered his composure, forced a too-sweet smile. "I'm going to poll the council, something we usually do behind closed doors, to get their take on what we've discussed tonight." One by one he called names. No one was in favor of permitting the developers to purchase land in Sanctuary Cove. "It's unanimous. I'll have my secretary send a letter to the gentlemen to let them know that we're unable to entertain their proposal at this time."

Grady, Hannah's husband, raised his hand. The pharmacist also doubled as the Cove's postmaster. "What is it you don't understand, Mayor White? The people have spoken. They don't want outsiders coming in and chopping up their land and offering others outrageous sums to sell out their legacy. Not now and not ever. So, when you word that letter make certain you don't say *at this time*. It's *never ever*!"

Hannah patted his back. "That's *my* man!"

Eddie spoke up for the first time. "Would you mind, Mayor White, if I print a copy of your letter in the *Chronicle*?"

Spencer, knowing he'd been overruled, nodded. "I'll make certain you get a signed copy. There's not much else to report except that repairs have begun on the library and the town hall. However, I'd like Sheriff Hamilton to bring us up to date on what he's uncovered about some suspicious activity in and around the business district."

All eyes were focused on the ex-Marine. A few sighs from women were heard when Jeffrey leaned forward. "Our surveillance cameras picked up two individuals lurking behind several stores after closing time. Business folk—make certain you check to see that all of your back doors are locked before you leave. And, because many of the parking lots are not lit, I suggest you install lights over the rear doors. Not only would it deter someone from breaking in, but their images would be more identifiable when we go through camera footage. I'm not certain what they're looking for, but let's not make it too easy for them."

"Are they kids, Sheriff?" asked the pharmacist.

"It's hard to tell, Grady. I'll let you know if I happen to

catch them. I've begun nighttime foot patrols, so tell your kids not to hang around behind the stores once the business district closes down for the night."

Deborah noted the thickness in Jeff's neck for the first time. He was massive. Unless someone was heavily armed, she felt sorry for anyone willing to go up against him. Jeff was handsome, although not nearly as handsome as Asa.

But Deborah didn't want to think about her growing attraction to the man living above her store. She related to him in a way she never had with Louis. Their relationship was smooth and easy.

The loud hum of voices and movement of furniture snapped Deborah out of her thoughts. The meeting had ended, and one by one everyone filed out except the men assigned the task of putting all of the furniture back. Working in tandem, they repositioned the piano, buffet server, desk, writing table, and seating arrangement, leaving Asa and Deborah to rearrange the plants and bean-bag chairs.

Asa, having closed and locked the door behind them, turned to Deborah. "That was quite a heated meeting."

"That's because it's about the island's survival," Deborah said.

"How can the island survive if it's stuck in time? Bringing in a hotel or a casino would inject new life in the island's economy."

"New life and all the social ills we don't need," she argued softly. "Developers have been good and bad for the Lowcountry Sea Islands, but in my opinion the negative outweighs the positives. It's like letting Wal-Mart, Sam's Club, Target, or Home Depot set up shop on Cavanaugh.

Every independent and mom-and-pop shop in the three towns would go out of business. The only exceptions would probably be Jack's Fish House, the movie theater, and the Cove Inn. Everyone else, including myself, would have to close down. The big companies claim they can lower unemployment rates, but at what cost, Asa?"

"What I found surprising is that no one wanted to entertain limiting how much land the developers could purchase and what they build."

"This isn't the first time developers have expressed an interest in Cavanaugh. Every few years they come back, hoping they'll get the residents to change their minds. What frightens everyone is the pollution that comes with growth. In the 1950s a growing industry along the nearby Savannah River polluted many of the marshes and creeks around Daufuskie. Health officials cited and closed up most of the valuable oyster beds. The fishermen lost their livelihood and moved away. One by one the stores closed and then there were none."

"Personally, I don't think they should have written off the entire proposal."

Deborah exhaled an audible breath. "You can't understand where we're coming from because you don't live here."

"Why should not living here make a difference when you're talking about progress?"

"Are you saying we're backward?"

"No, Debs. I'm just saying things could be better."

"For whom?" she argued. "It can't be for me and my children."

"That's because you have options," Asa retorted. "Your grandmother was educated; so was your father and so are you. Your children will be the fourth generation to attend college. How many others in the Cove can claim that distinction?"

"I don't know, Asa. However, that's not as important as making certain our predictable way of life doesn't change so much that we can't recognize it. Jason Parker moved back because he wanted to give his children a better quality of life than they would have in Charleston. Everyone looks out for one another. You saw how supportive they were at my grand opening."

Her eyelids fluttered wildly and then her expression softened. "When I wake up in the morning, I stand on the front porch and take a deep breath. Then I close my eyes and try to identify the different smells: the ocean, palmetto leaves, and sweet-grass. Even the earth smells are different. When I go to bed I'm not jolted awake by the sounds of police and fire sirens, or kids drag-racing down the street. I go to bed listening to crickets and wake up to them. I don't have to concern myself with traffic lights or stop signs. I love my little house, and there are times when I can almost imagine my grandmother calling me to come in and wash up before we sit down to dinner." She saw the strange look on Asa's face. "You probably think I'm a little crazy, but I don't want anything to change. At least not in my lifetime."

He shook his head. "No, Deborah. I don't think you're crazy. You're just passionate about what you believe in, and there's nothing wrong with that."

"It's been a long day and I'm a little tired." Going on tiptoe, Deborah kissed his cheek. "Good night and thanks for everything."

Asa rubbed her back. "I'll walk you out."

She retrieved her handbag from the desk drawer as Asa grabbed a large umbrella. "Don't forget to lock the door."

"Aye, aye, captain!"

Deborah rolled her eyes at him. Outside, he leaned over and opened the driver's side door for her. She got in and started the engine at the same time Asa closed the door. He stood back, arms crossed over his chest, while she put the car in reverse and maneuvered out of the lot with her wiper blades turned to the highest speed, then he bolted back inside out of the heavy rain.

Deborah pulled into her driveway, got out of her car, and sprinted to the porch and out of the rain. Crystal, singing at the top of her lungs, greeted Deborah when she opened the door. Unlike her mother, who was tone deaf, Crystal had a strong singing voice. She was sprawled on the living room sofa watching *Glee*.

Leaning down, Deborah kissed her cheek. "Hi, baby."

Crystal picked up the remote, muting the television. "Hey, Mom."

"Why are you watching TV down here?"

Crystal sat up straight. "I was waiting to talk to you."

Deborah sat down and stretched out her legs, crossing her feet at the ankles. She rested her head on the back of the sofa and closed her eyes. "What do you want to talk about?"

"Can you meet me after school on Monday so we can go shopping? I know what kind of dress I want."

"Of course. Where is it?"

Crystal chewed her lip. "It's in a boutique on King Street called Finicky Filly. And I also found my shoes.

They're Kate Spade." She scrunched up her nose. "They cost three hundred dollars."

Deborah's expression did not change. "Are they also at Finicky Filly?"

"No, Mom. I saw them at the Copper Penny."

"What else do you need?"

"I'm going to have to get my hair and nails done."

"What else, Crystal?"

The teenager rolled her eyes upward, then squinted. "I don't know."

"You're going to need a jacket or shrug in case it gets chilly. And probably a little purse with a strap you can wear across your body. A woman never goes out without a purse. It shouldn't be too big but large enough for your keys, lip-gloss, cash, and other personal items."

"This is my first dance and I want to really look good."

Deborah dropped an arm around Crystal's shoulders, pulling her close. "I'll make certain you'll look beautiful. You should think about letting your hair grow out. Not that it doesn't look nice, but I can tell you from experience that guys like girls with hair they can touch."

"Mom!"

"Don't Mom me. It's true. You'll find out once you're allowed to get a boyfriend. When I met your dad I had hair down my back, and whenever I set it or blew it out he couldn't stop touching it."

"How many boyfriends did you have before you married Daddy?"

Deborah hesitated, then decided to be truthful with her daughter. "Your father was my first serious boyfriend."

"Had you gone out with other boys before him?"

"Yes. They were more like group dates, when six or

eight of us would get together and either go to the movies or the mall. It was different when I spent summers here. There was only one movie theater and no mall."

"Where did you go? What did you do?"

"Me and my friends hung out at the beach. Most times we'd go swimming. By the time I was in my teens my parents would let me go to the beach on Friday nights. Every teenager in the Cove would show up with food and pop. We'd light a fire and have a clambake, then sing and dance to a boom box. Somebody's mother or father would come by and check to see if we had any alcohol, and then leave."

"Did you?"

"No. We knew if they caught us it was all she wrote. It wasn't so much about drinking, getting high, or having sex as it was about not having our parents clocking us."

"How late were you allowed to stay out?"

"We had a midnight curfew. That was long enough because we'd start gathering around seven, and with the heat and salt water we were plenty tired by midnight. I fell asleep many a night on the sand, and when I got back I still had to shampoo my hair and wash sand from every crevice on my body."

"Mom?"

"What is it, sweetheart?"

"Do you think you will ever date or marry again?"

"Would you want me to start dating?" Deborah asked, answering Crystal's question with a question.

Crystal lifted her shoulders. "I don't know. Daddy's gone and once I leave for college you'll be alone."

Deborah kissed her daughter's forehead, smiling and thinking about Asa. "I don't want you to worry about me. I'll be okay."

"Which friends did you like best? The ones in Charleston or here?"

"It's not about which ones I liked best, but who they were. The folks on the Cove are more laid-back. It's not about what you're wearing, what make and model car you drive, or the size of the diamonds in your ears. Don't get me wrong, Crystal. There are people who live on Cavanaugh that have a lot of money, but they don't flaunt or talk about it. And there are people who don't have enough, but you won't see them living in homeless shelters or waiting on line at a food pantry, because their neighbors take care of them. You're going to grow more veggies than we can eat or store, right?"

"What do I do with the extra?"

"Call Reverend Crawford and let him know. He'll arrange for you to bring them to the church, where they will be distributed to needy families. Even though Samara Lambert is a teacher, she is having a hard time making ends meet without her husband's salary. She is someone who would benefit from a food donation."

"Tell me about your prom."

Deborah thought about Eddie Wilkes. He'd asked her and she'd said yes. "I had a date for the prom. Why so many questions, baby girl?"

"A lot of girls in my grade have boyfriends, but I told them I couldn't have one because number one I'm too young, and secondly it would interfere with my schoolwork."

Deborah kissed her hair. "When did my daughter get so smart?"

"I was always smart." There was a hint of smugness in her voice.

"I'm not saying you're not smart, Crystal. What I mean is that you're able to stand up for yourself and not give in to peer pressure."

Crystal sucked her teeth. "I don't have a choice. You said I can't have a boyfriend and I can't even sneak around with Whitney shadowing me like I'm about to do something."

"Your brother is just trying to protect you."

"That was okay when the other kids were talking about Daddy. But there's no need for him to watch me now."

"I would've given anything to have had a brother. Even one who would've read my diary or snapped the heads off my dolls."

Crystal laughed. "Whitney never did those things."

"Well then, I guess he's a pretty good brother."

Crystal rolled her eyes, but smiled as she did. "Thanks, Mom."

"For what?"

"For agreeing to take me shopping."

"I told you I'd take you."

Crystal lowered her head and her eyes. "I thought you were still mad about Grandma and the puppy."

"You're giving it too much energy. I said what I wanted and needed to say to my mother, and as far as I'm concerned it's over." Deborah rose to her feet and picked up her handbag. "Don't stay up too late. And don't forget to turn off the lights before you go upstairs."

"I won't." Crystal unmuted the sound, folded her arms under her head, and went back to watching her favorite show.

After settling into her room, Deborah opened the drawer to the bedside table and took out her journal. It had been more than a week since she'd written anything in it. Uncapping her gel pen, she wrote the date:

> February 6th—Asa prepared dinner for me. We danced together again—and I find myself growing closer and closer to him. It is as if I need to connect to someone other than Whitney, Crystal, and the customers that come into the bookstore. The more time we spend together the more I like him. He is a wonderful friend and I know I'm going to miss him when he leaves to return to Delaware.

If she were truly honest then she would admit that Asa was becoming more than a friend. A knowing glance, a gentle caress, and a chaste kiss. These were hardly things shared by friends—especially between a man and a woman. When, she mused, had she become a coward?

Recapping the pen, she returned it and the journal to the drawer. She couldn't write anymore. Not tonight.

Chapter Seventeen

~~~

Don't forget to come straight home after practice."

"I know, Mom."

Deborah stared at Whitney's impassive expression, her hand resting on the door handle. "Is something wrong, Whitney?"

"No, Mom. I was just thinking about something." He exhaled audibly. "I'm going to have to leave now if I'm going to get to practice on time."

"I'll see you later," Deborah said as she pushed open the car door and got out. She stood on the macadam staring at the Corolla's taillights as Whitney drove off. They'd gone to early service without Crystal. Her daughter had overslept and Deborah had kept her promise not to become the girl's alarm clock.

She'd reminded Whitney not to hang out with his teammates following basketball practice because she wanted him home when Asa arrived for dinner. Having her children there made it look less like a date than an invitation—which it was.

Deborah mounted the porch steps, pausing before unlocking and opening the door. It was only after she'd announced to her son and daughter that she'd invited Asa to eat with them that she'd noticed a change in Whitney's demeanor. He'd looked at her, then mumbled "that's nice." Crystal had lifted her shoulders, but didn't say anything.

Then Deborah began to question herself. Had she acted impulsively when she'd asked Asa to come to her house? Or was the invitation one she would've extended to anyone of whom she'd become fond? It wasn't as if they hadn't had company for Sunday dinner before.

When Louis was alive they'd had Barbara and Terrell Nash and their children, Mabel and Lester Kelly, and of course her parents, Herman and Pearl Williams, as house guests and for holiday celebrations. She wasn't going to let her children's reaction to her inviting her friend spoil her excitement.

Tossing her keys into the small sweet-grass basket on the table in the entryway, she made her way to the half-bath off the kitchen to wash her hands. It was nine-thirty and Crystal still wasn't up. How, she thought, was her daughter going to get up and make it to class on time once she was in college? Or worse—to work when she got a job? Deborah knew she couldn't continue to agonize over Crystal's inability to wake up on time, because they'd talked about it over and over until she was at a loss for words.

She left the bathroom and flicked on the coffeemaker. There had been a time when Deborah would brew a four-cup carafe and drink four cups of coffee a day. That changed when Louis gave her a single-cup brewing system for Mother's Day, and she'd gone from four cups to one, or sometimes two, cups a day. She had always switched from caffeinated to decaf because she'd had a problem falling asleep.

Deborah had finished her coffee and a slice of cracked wheat toast topped with strawberry preserves when Crystal walked barefoot into the kitchen in a pair of pajama pants and a tank top. Her hair stood out like tiny spikes on her head.

"Good morning, Mom. Why didn't you wake me so I could go to church?"

"You know I stopped waking you up months ago. If you'd wanted to go, then you should have set your clock."

Crystal sat on a high stool at the cooking island. "I did. But I guess I didn't hear it."

"You didn't hear it, or you hit the snooze button?"

"I remember hitting snooze, but then I guess I went back to sleep." She ignored her mother's pointed stare. "I had cheerleading practice today."

Deborah did not respond. In the past Louis would've driven her to practice. He would pick up the slack, or pitch in whenever Deborah was unable to make a meeting or arrive home in time to start dinner. But Louis wasn't here.

Deborah rinsed her coffee mug, placing it in the dishwasher before opening the refrigerator to take out the fresh turkey she'd marinated the night before.

"Are you taking me to practice?"

Deborah set the large glass-covered dish with the turkey on the countertop. "No, Crystal, I am not taking you to practice."

Crystal pushed out her lip, slid off the stool, and stomped out of the kitchen. "It's not fair! I'm going to get kicked off the squad."

Deborah wanted to tell her that life wasn't fair. It had taken her husband and the father of her children from her in the prime of his life. And if Crystal was going to get booted off the cheerleading squad, she had no one to blame but herself.

"You can't live your life expecting people to wake you up, Chrissie. If you got up when you were supposed to, then you could've caught a ride with Whitney. Why don't you move your clock to a place where you can't reach over and hit the snooze button? Put it on your dresser, then you'll be forced to get out of bed to turn it off."

"It's still not fair."

Mentally dismissing Crystal and her antics, Deborah busied herself setting the dining room table with a hand-made crocheted tablecloth, china, silver, and crystal. A bouquet of flowers in a Waterford vase doubled as the centerpiece.

She'd ordered the fresh turkey from the supermarket. The produce section was stocked with a cornucopia of locally grown vegetables, and she'd selected fresh mustard and turnip greens and enough sweet potatoes for two pies.

Deborah had planned her menu to include roast turkey with herb/sausage stuffing, white long-grain Carolina rice, giblet gravy, greens with smoked turkey, and cornbread. She would cook enough so there would be leftovers. She'd just placed the turkey on the rack in a roasting pan when the telephone rang. Wiping her hands on a towel, she picked up the cordless receiver.

"Hello."

"Hi, Deborah. Babs."

"Hey! How are you?"

"Good, girl. I'm calling to ask you whether Whitney and Crystal can spend the night at my place after the school dance. You know Janelle's birthday is the fourteenth, and instead of a party I told her she could have a sleepover. I know Whitney's not going to want to be around a bunch of giggling girls, so he'll probably hang out with Nate."

"Crystal didn't tell me about the sleepover."

"I just thought of it this morning. I'd planned to have something at a restaurant at the end of the month, but then remembered Crystal and Whitney were going to Florida for the break."

"I don't have a problem with them staying over," Deborah said.

"Good," Barbara said. "Nate will tell Whitney and he'll give Crystal an invitation. I know I should have my head examined for entertaining a houseful of teenagers, but I'd rather have them here where I can keep an eye on them rather than drop them off at a restaurant. Janelle wants a D.J., but I told her I don't want the neighbors calling the police if it gets too loud."

"How many kids do you plan to invite?"

"No more than a dozen. That's why I'm handing out invitations. If anyone shows up without one, then they're not coming in. And you know how these kids do when they hear about a party. It becomes a mob scene and when you try putting them out or not letting any more in, they get stupid and come back with guns. I swear before goodness that I will not have a bunch of thugs crash my child's party."

"Have Terrell act as bouncer. I'm certain he could toss a few of them like he used to throw a football when he was a college quarterback."

"Please, Deborah. All the kids know my husband is all bark and no bite."

"I'm willing to bet he won't just bark when it comes to his daughter."

Barbara's high-pitched laugh came through the earpiece. "Anyone messing with Janelle will turn my teddy bear of a husband into a beast. And that's one side of him I witnessed once and don't want to see again. I just want you to know that your kids will be safe while they're here."

It wouldn't be the first time Crystal and Whitney would stay with their former neighbors, but it would be the first time they would attend a house party there while Deborah remained so far away on the Cove. She knew Barbara was apprehensive about hosting the party because there had been a rash of shootings when uninvited partygoers were denied access, but Deborah trusted Terrell and Barbara and was certain they would take the necessary steps to avoid a similar situation.

"I know they will."

Anchoring the receiver between her chin and shoulder, Deborah continued to talk while she put up a pot of boiling water for the sweet potatoes, then went into the pantry for a canister of flour to make pie crusts. She brought Barbara up-to-date about the bookstore. Deborah didn't mention Asa because she wasn't certain when Crystal would walk into the kitchen.

"I've been working double shifts," Barbara said. "We had eleven nurses retire at the end of last year and so far administration has only hired two to replace them. I am working harder than a pack mule going down the Grand Canyon. I keep telling Terrell that I'm going to quit and find a position as a school nurse. At least I'll have holidays and summers off."

"That was why I loved teaching, Babs."

"I know you have the bookstore, but would you ever consider teaching again?"

"That's something I thought about after Louis died and I closed the store," Deborah admitted. "I knew I was going to move to Sanctuary Cove, so I went online to look into vacancies for the schools on the island."

"Did you find any?"

"There is one opening for a language arts teacher in Haven Creek, for the upcoming school year. While I was thinking about whether to fill out the online application I found the vacant store, and you know the rest."

"It's nice that you have options, Debs. You have three elementary/junior high schools on the island from which to choose if you decide to go back to teaching. You'll probably have no more than an eight-to-one student-teacher ratio and field trips will be picking up seashells along the beach."

"Stop it, Babs. You know I'm a visual person. All you have to do is mention the beach and I'm there."

"Have you been to the beach since moving back?"

"Not yet. But soon."

"I envy you, Deborah. Every time I go to Cavanaugh Island I get mad as hell when I come back. Please, don't get me wrong. Charleston is beautiful, but the older I get the more I want a slower pace. I've been telling Terrell that as soon as the kids are up and out of the house we are moving. I wouldn't mind buying a little place in Sanctuary Cove and commuting."

"I know there are a few houses on the market. Some

are fixer uppers and one or two are close to move-in condition. Remember Congressman Jason Parker?"

"The Ken doll?"

Deborah laughed. "He's the one."

"What about him?"

"He moved to the Cove."

"No!"

"Yes. I saw his wife and kids in church last Sunday."

"But they live in a mansion on South Battery."

"They don't live there anymore," Deborah stated. "They bought a dilapidated house that had belonged to an eighteenth-century shipping merchant and renovated it. I've heard talk that it is one of the grandest homes on the Cove. It's apparent they wanted a slower, simpler way of life for themselves and their children. I happen to know of a foreclosed abandoned property that's going for around thirty thousand. It's small, but it would be the perfect vacation home. There's even enough land where you can build out and up. And with developers sniffing around like hounds after a rabbit, it's not going to stay on the market long."

She gave Barbara an overview of the last town council meeting. "I don't want to believe they're the type to cut and run. They'll probably resort to underhanded tactics, like having their people buy up vacant lots and homes and hold on to them while waiting for sentiment to change in their favor."

"I'm definitely going to talk to Terrell about looking into buying property on Cavanaugh. Maybe before the year is out we'll be neighbors again." Barbara told her, then said, "What's up with you and Asa?"

"He's coming for dinner," she whispered into the mouthpiece.

"Are you home alone?"

"No."

"Then you have to call me once he leaves and fill me in."

"I will," Deborah said in a normal tone.

By the time Deborah ended the call, she'd rolled out two pie crusts and boiled the potatoes. Crystal, having showered and combed her hair, returned to the kitchen to prepare breakfast for herself. She seemed to have recovered from missing practice when she talked excitedly about attending her first high school dance. Deborah told her about Janelle's birthday party and sleepover.

Mother and daughter worked together cutting, chopping, and sautéing as the kitchen was filled with delicious smells that tantalized their olfactory nerves. The basted turkey had taken on a light golden color, and the aromas from the roasting bird permeated the space.

Deborah finished preparing her dinner at one-forty, then retreated to her en suite bath to shower and change her clothes. Whitney, who had returned at two claiming he was starved, knew he wouldn't sit down to eat until their customary four o'clock. He showered quickly, also changing his clothes. When the doorbell rang at three-thirty, he went to answer it.

Asa smiled at the tall, lanky young man. "Good afternoon, Whitney."

Whitney opened the door wider. "Good afternoon, Mr. Monroe. Please come in."

Asa handed the boy a shopping bag. "This is a little something for dessert."

Whitney peered into the bag. "What is it?" he whispered conspiratorially.

"Mississippi pecan pie. I hope no one is allergic to nuts."

Whitney's eyes danced with excitement. "No one in this house. Come in," he urged when Asa held back. Going to the staircase, he called out, "Mom! Mr. Monroe is here."

Deborah skipped down the staircase and slowed when she saw Asa staring up at her. A slight smile parted her lips as she took in the sight of him. He wore a pair of black, sharply creased slacks, slip-ons, a white silk shirt opened at the throat, and a pale-gray lightweight jacket.

She stepped off the stair, extending her hand. "Thank you for coming."

Asa inclined his head. "Thank you for inviting me. Something smells good."

Crystal, who had come from the kitchen, stopped when she saw Asa standing in the entryway. She tilted her head to the side as if trying to remember where she knew him from, then her gaze shifted between Asa and her mother. She closed the distance between them, holding out her hand.

"Hello again, Mr. Monroe," she said, finally recognizing him from the bookstore.

Asa smiled at Deborah's daughter and shook the proffered hand. "Hello to you, too, Crystal."

Crystal released his hand. "Come and I'll show you where you can wash your hands. My Mom has a cow every time we come to the table without washing our hands. Well, you do, Mom," she added when Deborah gave her a *no you didn't say that* look.

Whitney handed his mother the shopping bag. "Mr. Monroe bought a pecan pie."

"I told him not to bring anything."

"No biggie, Mom. I'll eat it," Whitney volunteered.

"You do that, you'll be bouncing off the walls from a sugar rush." Looping her arm over her son's, they walked toward the kitchen. "Put the pie on the countertop with the others." When Asa emerged from the half-bath, she took his hand and led him to the dining room where Crystal had taken her seat. Deborah had removed the leaf in the dining room table and took away two of the six chairs for a more intimate seating. "You can sit here," she said, directing Asa to sit at one end of the walnut pedestal table.

Crystal stilled, glaring at Asa. Deborah noticed the change in her daughter's demeanor, wondering what had caused her to bristle.

"Asa, would you mind saying grace?" Deborah asked.

With wide eyes filling with tears, Crystal glared at her mother. The tears overflowed as she bit her lip to stifle the sobs. It wasn't until a sob echoed in the room that Deborah turned to look at her daughter.

A frown of concern lined her forehead. "What's the matter?"

"How could you, Mama?"

Whitney, who had entered the dining room, stared at his sister. "What's going on?"

Crystal pointed to Deborah. "Ask the *traitor*."

Deborah wanted to disappear on the spot. "Traitor? Crystal, honey, why would you say something like that?" she said, clasping her daughter's hands. "I'm not a traitor. I'm your mother," she responded softly. "What's wrong?"

Crystal's chin trembled as the tears continued to flow. "How...how can you have him sit in Daddy's chair when…" Her words trailed off in another round of heart-wrenching sobs.

Pushing back the chair, Asa stood up. "I'm sorry, but I think I need to leave."

Resting her hands on her hips, Deborah's eyes went from Asa to Crystal and back again. "No, Asa. You don't have to leave."

He held up his hands. "But…"

"Please, sit down, Asa. You too, Whitney," she said in a voice made her children stare at her as if they'd never seen her before. Although spoken softly, it held a hard edge.

Deborah sat opposite Asa, her eyes moving slowly around the table before coming to rest on Crystal. "If you have a problem, then speak on it. After that I intend to have a civil Sunday dinner without your disrespect."

Picking up the damask napkin at her place setting, Crystal dabbed her eyes. "I…I just remember Daddy sit…sitting there and I don't think it's fair that someone else should sit there when…"

"When what?" Deborah asked.

"I understand where Crystal is coming from," Asa said when the girl didn't answer her mother's query. "She feels betrayed because she believes I'm taking her father's place." He lowered his gaze, staring down at the tablecloth. He was so still he could have been carved from stone. A shuddering sigh escaped him. "I know how she feels to lose someone, because I lost my wife…and son…last year." He registered a gasp, and knew it had come from Deborah. "I waited a long time to become a father, but I would only have Isaac for six years."

Resting his elbows on the table, Whitney asked, "What happened to them?"

Pushing back his chair, Asa stood up and walked out of the dining room, then stopped. He didn't move for several minutes, then returned and sat down again. "My wife had taken our son with her when she went Christmas shopping. She was on her way back home when it started sleeting. The road had become very icy and when she came around a sharp turn she lost control of her car, crashing through the guardrail and slamming into a tree. The car exploded into a fireball and they were unable to get out. The medical examiner used their dental records to confirm their identities.

"I'd stopped eating and sleeping, and there were times when I thought about taking my own life because I had nothing to live for. It would've been so easy to die by injecting myself with a double dose of morphine."

"You're a doctor?" Crystal whispered.

Asa nodded. "Yes, I am a doctor, and my brother was a doctor, as were my father and his father. I'd planned for my son to become the fourth generation Dr. Monroe, but it was not to be."

"Why are you working in a bookstore instead of practicing medicine?" Whitney asked.

"I sold my home and my practice, because there was nothing for me in Delaware. It's been more than a year and I still hurt. I don't know whether I will ever stop hurting when I see a little boy my son's age."

"We miss our dad, too," Whitney confessed. "We were lucky because our father was cool. Maybe it was because he taught at a high school, but he understood where kids were coming from. In fact, he was voted the most popular teacher for three consecutive years. Kids went to him instead of their guidance counselors when they had a problem."

Deborah did not want to believe her children had opened up to Asa—a near stranger. And now she knew that whenever she'd glimpsed sadness in him it hadn't come from his estrangement with his brother, but because he'd lost his wife and child. Now she understood what he'd meant when he said that although she'd lost her spouse she had her children. He, on the other hand, had lost his spouse *and* child.

"I came here today because your mother invited me. And I have no intention of replacing your father. I'll be leaving Sanctuary Cove in a couple of months."

Crystal sniffled. "I'm sorry, Mr. Monroe. I didn't…"

"It's okay, Crystal," Asa said softly. "There's no need to apologize."

Whitney met his mother's eyes. "I also apologize. Not for my sister but for having similar thoughts. We weren't raised to be disrespectful, and I know we're going to hear it once you leave. Although this is my Mom's house I'd like you to come back and give us a second chance to show you that we do have home training."

Asa smiled. "If your mother invites me back, then I will definitely come, if only to enjoy a home-cooked meal."

A new and unexpected warmth eddied through Deborah when she met Asa's gaze. Her son's offer to invite him back was as shocking as Asa's revelation that he was a widower. She'd assumed a soured relationship, even divorce. They'd worked closely together, talked about any and everything, yet he had given no indication that he'd recently lost his wife and child. In fact, he had revealed only that he was a doctor, had worked in a hospital, had been married, and didn't have any children. She'd asked, and even though he hadn't been forthcoming, he had been truthful.

Now she said, "We'll talk about that later. Let's say grace, then eat before everything gets cold."

Asa bowed his head, as Deborah blessed the table. He picked up the platter of sliced turkey, holding it for Crystal while she speared several slices. He took some for himself, then handed the platter off to Whitney who held it for his mother, then served himself. The ritual continued until plates were filled, the food eaten then washed down with goblets of homemade brewed sweet tea and lemonade.

Asa took second helpings of everything, stating numerous times that Deborah had missed her calling and that she should have gone into the culinary arts. "Who taught you to cook?" he asked her.

Deborah set down her tea. "My grandmother."

"Mom said our grandmother couldn't cook until she took cooking courses," Crystal blurted out. Crystal swallowed a forkful of stuffing. "I would never have somebody cook for me."

"What if you had a career that took you away from home for days at a time? Or if you had to host a dinner party for twelve? Would you do your own cooking?"

She lifted her shoulders. "Probably."

"I doubt it," he said. "After standing on your feet for hours cutting, slicing, dicing, and checking meat for doneness, do you think you'd have enough energy to entertain your guests?"

"I don't think so," Whitney chimed in.

"Whitney's right," Asa concurred. "You wouldn't. That's why people have their parties catered. Perhaps you could be the one to cater the events, leaving the hosting to someone else. Have you ever considered going to culinary school?"

Crystal nodded with excitement.

"Where did you go to school, Mr. Monroe?" Whitney asked.

"Howard. Undergraduate and medical school."

"I've been accepted at Howard," Whitney said proudly.

"It's an excellent school, Whitney."

"That's what my mom says."

"Your mom is right."

Deborah felt a rush of emotion she couldn't explain. Whitney and Crystal were so comfortable with Asa and had told him things they never would have divulged to a stranger. She wanted Whitney to go to Howard and hoped that his conversation with Asa convinced him the school was the best college for his career choice.

Dinner became a leisurely affair, the quartet sitting at the table long after they'd eaten their fill. The discussion segued from college to the recent Super Bowl and high school sports. Whitney admitted to joining the basketball team because he needed another extracurricular activity.

When Deborah stood up to clear the table, Asa also stood. "Whitney and I will clean up."

Whitney popped up like a jack-in-the-box. "Of course."

Crystal placed a hand over her mouth to hide her grin. "That's a first," she whispered when they disappeared into the kitchen.

Deborah met her daughter's eyes. "You can help me serve dessert as soon as the men are finished."

Crystal leaned to her left. "I like him, Mom."

"Who?"

"Mr. Monroe. He's real nice."

"That he is," Deborah said in agreement. Crystal thought he was nice, the women who came into the bookstore thought he was nice, and she knew he was nice. Her feelings for him were growing stronger with each passing day. What she didn't want was to rely on him for her emotional well-being because she would have him for a very short amount of time.

Deborah didn't want to think of his pending departure as she invited everyone back into the kitchen for dessert. She brewed coffee for Asa and herself and filled glasses with ice-cold milk for Whitney and Crystal. Slices of pecan pie and sweet potato pie were topped with scoops of vanilla ice cream from De Fountain and dollops of fresh whipped cream.

Asa patted his flat belly. "I don't know how you guys stay so thin, but if I ate like this every Sunday I'd blow up like a blimp."

Crystal drained her glass. "I burn a lot of calories cheerleading, and Whitney is on the basketball team. And Mom won't let us eat fast food more than once a week."

Asa gave Deborah a surreptitious wink. "That's because fast foods are loaded with calories."

Crystal nodded. "That's what Mom says."

"What position do you play?" Asa asked Whitney.

"Small forward."

"How many points do you average per game?"

"Fifteen."

Asa lifted his eyebrows. "Not bad."

"I stink, Mr. Monroe. There are guys on the team who hit twenty to thirty points every game."

Asa nodded, his expression serene. "Call me Asa. Those are the guys who, if they make it to Howard, will do so on an athletic scholarship. And who will have to be tutored in order to keep their scholarship. And if they're lucky enough to make it to the NBA, will mess up off the court during their first season and all the practicing and tutoring will be for naught. I went to high school with a couple of guys who did make it to the NBA, and wound up with six kids and four baby mamas between them before they were twenty-five. One couldn't stay away from the white powder and weed, and the other refused to go into alcohol rehab because he was in denial about his drinking problem." Asa shook his head. "It was tragic, Whitney. They had so much natural talent, but it was wasted because their actions had dire consequences."

Crystal stared at her brother. "I'm glad I'm not a boy."

"Don't start crowing, baby girl," Deborah crooned. "Girls are not exempt from drugs, alcohol, and stair-step babies from a bunch of different baby daddies."

"Like Doreena," the teenagers said in unison.

"Let's not repeat gossip." Deborah chastised.

Crystal rolled her head. "It's not gossip, Mom. Everyone in Charleston knows that she had babies from two brothers and their cousin. Kids call her Chuck Town Ho."

"Crystal!"

"It's true, Mom."

Leaning back, Asa crossed one leg over the opposite knee. "Don't mind me. I've heard worse."

Deborah held her forehead. What was she going to do with her daughter other than love her? And Asa appeared to enjoy her kids' antics. Reaching across the table, she removed plates, forks, and glasses, stacking them in the dishwasher. She turned it on.

"Asa, do you want me to pack up some leftovers for you?"

"But of course. I'll take a little of everything."

Whitney and Crystal stood up, Asa rising with them. They thanked him for coming for dinner. Whitney, after extracting a promise from Asa that he would come back again, dropped an arm over his sister's shoulder and led her out of the kitchen.

"Mom, we're going to Angels Landing to hang out at Simeon's house for a while," Whitney called out.

"Don't come home too late."

"We won't," they chorused.

"You have great kids," Asa said when he and Deborah were alone.

"Even with my daughter going off on you?"

Asa walked over, stood behind Deborah and rested his hands on her shoulders. "It was understandable."

Deborah looked up at him over her shoulder. "Why didn't you tell me you'd lost your wife and son?"

"You didn't ask." Lowering his head, he pressed a kiss to the column of her scented neck. "How can I thank you for the best day I've had in more than a year?"

"Just say thank you."

He chuckled. "That's not enough."

Deborah turned until they were facing each other. "What else is there?"

Asa angled his head, his mouth covering hers in an explosive joining that weakened her knees, forcing her to hold on to him to keep her balance. Her fingers caught the front of his shirt, tightening as her lips parted.

Anchoring her arms under his shoulders, she went on tiptoe to get even closer. Her breathing quickened, her breasts grew heavy, and the area between her thighs was moist and throbbing, reminding her how long it had been since she'd had sex.

Deborah wanted Asa. She wanted to be in his bed and with him inside her. But somewhere between sanity and insanity, she surfaced from the sensual fog clouding her brain and regained her common sense.

"No, Asa." The protest came out weak.

"Come home with me, baby. I need to hold you, taste you. I have protection."

She shook her head. "I can't."

"I'll bring you back before your children return."

Breathing through parted lips, Deborah felt slightly lightheaded. "It's not about them."

Asa pressed his mouth to the side of her neck again as if he wanted to sink his teeth into her skin. There were other places on her body on which he could feast that would remain hidden to everyone except her. The thought made her blush.

"What is it about, then?" he asked, rousing Deborah from her thoughts.

"Asa, when we make love I want to savor the moment. I want to give you my undivided attention without having to rush."

He smiled. "When?"

"Tomorrow. I'll come before noon and stay until it's time for me to pick up Crystal from school. I'd promised to take her shopping for the school's Valentine's Day dance."

Asa's hand caressed her back in a circular motion as he stared at her mouth. Her thoroughly kissed lips felt fuller. He nodded his approval, then watched as she packed plastic containers with food, then stacked them neatly in a shopping bag.

He took the bag, his eyes seemingly searching her face.

She'd pulled her hair back in a chignon; giving him an unobstructed view, highlighting her sprinkling of freckles and high cheekbones.

"I'll walk you out," Deborah said with a mysterious smile. They left the brick-walled kitchen and walked down the narrow hall that led past the dining room and into the living room. She stood on the porch, watching as Asa got into the Range Rover and slowly backed out of her driveway. Lifting her hand, she waved to him. She wasn't disappointed when he put his hand out the window and returned her wave. She stood there a long time, staring at the space where his truck had been, then turned and went back into the house.

"I'm falling in love with him," she whispered. She was falling in love with a man she'd known a month—with whom she shared a similar fate. Both had loved and lost, but with Asa the loss was more complete.

Deborah, although knowing he was going to leave Sanctuary Cove, had agreed to sleep with him. She was a thirty-eight-year-old widow with two teenaged children and she was about to embark on a short-lived affair with a transient widower. Neither of them were kids, so there wouldn't be any promises of a commitment or declarations of love. They would enjoy their time together and when it ended they would be left with memories of the time they shared.

Chapter Eighteen

⁓

Deborah got out of the car, carrying her handbag and another larger bag filled with several changes of clothes and toiletries. She'd managed to finish cleaning her house by the time Whitney and Crystal left for school. Dusting, vacuuming, and changing beds had kept her busy so she wouldn't have to think about what would happen once she arrived at the bookstore. She was filled with nervous energy as she stopped to deposit her weekly receipts, before driving the short distance to the lot behind the store.

The back door opened and Asa smiled down at her. "Hey, beautiful."

Deborah returned his smile and, rising on tiptoe, brushed her mouth over his. "Hey yourself."

He took the bags, then closed and locked the door behind her. Wrapping an arm around her waist, Asa pulled Deborah close. "Let me escort you up to the penthouse."

Deborah giggled like a schoolgirl. "How are the views?"

"They're all right."

"Just all right, Asa?"

His hand moved from her waist to her backside. "This view is a lot better," he crooned in her ear.

Her free hand went to his tight butt in a pair of relaxed jeans. "And this one isn't too bad either."

"You haven't even seen it."

Deborah laughed again. "My hands have special powers."

"Ah-h! So, my girl is a superhero."

"Super heroine, thank you very much."

Asa set the bag on the floor, then bending at the knees scooped Deborah up in his arms and carried her up the staircase and over to the bed. He placed her gently on the mattress, his body following hers down. Supporting his weight on his elbows, he covered her like a warm blanket. "Are you okay?"

"I'm wonderful. You know, you're good for me."

"Why is that, baby?"

"Because you make me laugh. I've laughed more with you in the past couple of weeks than I have in months. And you make me feel like a woman. It's been a very long time since I've felt that way."

No more words followed; only the sound of measured breathing could be heard in the room. The lowered blinds only allowed for slivers of light to slip through the slats covering the windows.

Deborah turned on her side to face Asa. "I can't promise—"

"Don't," he interrupted, placing a finger on her lips. "Please don't say what I think you're about to say. I don't want any promises."

"What do you want, Asa?"

"I don't want yesterday or tomorrow. I want right now. I'm sorry but that is all I can offer you."

"Why are you always apologizing?" she asked him.

Asa sat up and straddled her. "I find myself doing that a lot with you."

Deborah closed her eyes when she felt his hands brush her breasts, and then slowly unbutton her blouse. She heard his intake of breath when he stared at her breasts in her sheer bra, the color of *café con leche*. It seemed like an eternity before he removed each article of her clothing, until she lay completely naked.

She watched him undress, removing his shirt, jeans, and briefs and throwing them in a pile with hers at the foot of the bed. Asa's clothes had concealed a lean, hard body that belied his age. A light dusting of hair covered his broad chest, and her gaze travelled downward to his flat belly, on to the inverted triangle where his semi-erect penis hung heavily between his thighs. The side of the mattress dipped as he slid in beside her, his hand going under the pillow to retrieve a condom. He quickly opened the packet and slipped on the latex sheath.

Asa gave her breasts his undivided attention, suckling one breast, then the other. Waves of pleasure raced through her body, and her hips bucked upward to meet him. Deborah's fingers dug into his biceps, trembling uncontrollably as a rush of moisture flowed down her inner thighs onto the sheets. He reached down, stroking her clitoris as he continued feasting on her nipples.

Deborah was losing control and didn't want to come without him inside her.

"Please," she pleaded shamelessly, her body on fire.

Heat, followed by chills, then more heat singed her

sensitive flesh. Asa kissed her mouth, the hollow in her throat, his lips charting a course down her body. He kissed her breasts, her belly, the inside of her thighs, retracing his path as he explored every inch of her. She didn't want him to stop. He'd discovered erogenous zones on her body she hadn't known existed. Her heart pumped so hard she was certain it could be seen through her chest.

Holding his hard length in one hand, Asa parted her legs with his knees and positioned his erection at the entrance to her sex. He pressed into her body, watching as his hardened flesh finally slipped inside her. She was so tight but managed to take all of him. They'd become a perfect fit.

Deborah gloried in the hard body atop hers, his swollen member sliding in and out of her wetness. A shiver of delight washed over her, a moan slipping past her lips as she felt ready to climax. Finally letting go, her first orgasm took over, holding Deborah captive for mere seconds before another earth-shattering release rocked through her core, taking her straight to heaven.

"You are incredibly beautiful," Asa whispered in Deborah's ear as her body calmed from release. What he wanted to tell her was that he loved her passion, her strength and loyalty to those she loved. Actually, he was beginning to love everything about her and had come to depend on her emotionally. He went to bed thinking of her. Woke looking for her. The moment she walked into the bookstore his day brightened, and when she left he found himself waiting for her to return. He felt like a mouse on a tread wheel, going around and around and not being able to stop.

Again, he grew hard for her, the blood rushing so quickly to his penis that for a moment he felt lightheaded. Asa took a deep breath, held it, and then let it out slowly. He wanted to savor this moment before taking her again. All of his senses were heightened: the soft sounds of Deborah's moans, his own groans, the silken feel of her body against his, and the smell of her perfume mingling with the tantalizing aroma from their lovemaking. It had become an aphrodisiac.

Reaching for Deborah's hand, he cradled it gently, his thumb making tiny circles on her inner wrist. Making love with Deborah was more than he'd hoped for, and he did what he hadn't done in some time. He prayed. He prayed he would be able to leave when the time came for him to join Doctors Without Borders.

"Are you all right, darling?"

Deborah sighed softly, then suddenly tensed beside him. "Yes."

"I didn't hurt you, did I?" he asked, now concerned by the change in her mood.

"No," she said after a long silence.

Asa knew something was bothering Deborah. He wondered if she was conflicted because they'd slept together. Had she felt as if she'd dishonored her husband's memory?

"I want you to tell me about him, Deborah."

She glanced up at him, tears in her eyes.

"How did he die?"

Deborah knew eventually she would have to tell Asa about Louis. Taking a deep breath, she willed herself to begin. "Louis taught high school math," she said in a soft voice. "He'd go in early to work with students that needed extra help. Louis was aware of the school policy that required the door to remain open whenever he had a student in his office, so I don't know why he'd chosen to ignore the rule when a female student came to his office early one morning. I suppose it was because she was crying and told him she didn't want anyone to overhear what she wanted to tell him.

"She was a sixteen-year-old junior who'd found herself pregnant after she got involved with a much older man she'd met on the Internet. Louis asked if she'd told her parents and she claimed she couldn't because they were ultra-religious. When she told her boyfriend about her dilemma he'd suggested she have the baby and sell it to a childless couple willing to pay thousands of dollars for a newborn. The poor girl didn't know what to do, because to her abortion was not an option.

"Louis told me she started to cry. He put his arms around her in an attempt to comfort her, and that was when the principal walked in on them. Louis was suspended without pay pending a school board hearing, and the news spread that Louis Robinson had been caught in a compromising position with a female student."

"Didn't the girl set the record straight?"

"No. If she'd told why she was in her math teacher's office, then she would have had to recount their conversation. It was the first time in eighteen years that I saw my husband depressed. He stopped eating and would sit in the dark regardless of the time of day. I kept begging him to tell the principal why Melissa was in his office, but he refused. Meanwhile, my own kids were catching hell from other students who were as cruel as their parents, who were divided into pro- and anti–Louis Robinson factions. People whom I'd believed were my friends turned on me. Even the woman who worked for me in the bookstore quit. Then one day he told me he was tired of hiding and left the house."

"Did you know where he was going?"

She nodded, then said, "Yes. Louis loved the beach. He would spend hours sitting on the sand staring at the water.

"The weather was cool that day, the water choppy, and there were marine warnings about riptides and dangerous undertows. A group of high school students who'd cut classes were fooling around in the water. Several of them swam out too far and were caught in an undertow. Witnesses said Louis didn't hesitate when he jumped in in an attempt to save the drowning boys. He pulled two back to the beach and went back into the water for the third one. But he was larger and much stronger than Louis. He panicked, pulling them both under. By the time the police got to the scene Louis and the kid had disappeared. Divers managed to recover the boy's body but Louis was listed as missing and presumed dead."

Asa buried his face in Deborah's moist curls that smelled like fresh coconut. "Did they ever find his body?"

"Yes. Days later his body washed up on the beach a mile from the accident. Once the news got out that Louis had sacrificed his life in order to save three boys everything changed. The ones who were ready to lynch him became remorseful. And those who'd believed Louis would never harm a child pointed fingers at the hypocrites. I had a private ceremony with my family and closest friends, followed by a cremation. I sprinkled his ashes in the very waters that had taken his life.

"Overwhelmed with grief, Melissa told her parents

about her pregnancy. They pressured her to tell the principal why she'd come to Mr. Robinson's office that morning.
Eventually the board voted unanimously to reinstate Louis's salary and that made me eligible for his pension and
life insurance. The people who were quick to condemn
Louis made a complete one-eighty and they sent flowers
and condolence cards, and my neighbor became a buffer,
answering my phone and the door. But once my parents
returned to Florida I realized I could no longer live in
Charleston. I sat down with Crystal and Whitney, asking
whether they would be opposed to living here. They were
ecstatic. Though living here put distance between them
and the kids who *had* been their friends, they were okay
with it because they would continue to attend the same
school."

"What happened to Melissa?"

"Her parents sent her to California to live with an older
married sister. Before she left she called to tell me she'd
planned to have the baby, and then give it up for adoption.
I don't blame Melissa as much as I do the principal. She
was a frightened girl, but Francis is a mean-spirited SOB
who was jealous of Louis's relationship with the students.
He didn't have to suspend Louis. He could've pulled him
out of the classroom and put him on administrative desk
duty, but he just had to get him out of *his school*."

"I can understand your animosity, Deborah, but you
can't blame anyone for your husband's death. It was an
accident. A very tragic accident where he'd made the ultimate sacrifice to give up his life to save someone else's. I
know it hurts, and the pain is like a deep hole you believe
will never be filled, but you will heal."

"Have you healed, Asa?"

"Not completely."

"I suppose it's going to take time—for both of us. However, living here has changed me," Deborah admitted, "and I don't think that would've happened if I'd stayed in Charleston. I've let go of the anger and resentment that gnawed at me like a malignancy, because if I hadn't I'm certain it would have eventually destroyed me. I don't live for myself. I live for my children. I'm all they have, and the way Louis gave up his life to save that boy I would do the same for Crystal and Whitney."

Deborah sat in her car in the visitor's parking waiting for Crystal to come out of school. Each time she moved she was reminded of what she had shared with Asa earlier that morning. They'd made love twice. Once in bed and again when they'd shared a shower. This second coupling had been more uninhibited, when she went to her knees and took him in her mouth and suckled him until he bellowed for her to stop. Then it was his turn, when he carried her out of the bathroom and to the bed, and his teeth and tongue worked their magic as they climaxed simultaneously. It wasn't until she was slipping on her panties that she felt the slight ache from muscles she hadn't used in a while.

During the ferry ride she'd stood at the railing thinking about what had happened between her and Asa, realizing she was confused. Asa made her feel very feminine and desirable, but sleeping with him reminded her of what she'd shared with Louis.

A tapping on the window caught her attention and she smiled at Crystal. Pushing a button, she unlocked the car. Leaning over, Deborah offered her cheek for a kiss and was happy when Crystal kissed her.

"How was your day?"

Crystal tossed her tote onto the rear seat. "Good. How was your day?"

Deborah smiled. "It was very good." She started up the car and drove slowly out of the parking lot. Students were pouring out of the building and strolling across the street to student parking. "Did you tell Whitney that you were going with me?"

"He knows. He's staying late to work on the paper."

"What do you do when he stays late?"

"I either hang out in the library and do my homework, or I go to the newspaper office and take a nap on one of the sofas."

"What color is the dress you want?"

"Red."

Deborah gave Crystal a quick glance before returning her attention to the traffic in front of her. "Do you also want red shoes?"

"Nope. I want them in black; that way I can wear them with other outfits," she said decisively. "Whitney told me Nate gave him two invitations for Janelle's party."

"You're going to be doing a lot of partying that night. First the dance and then the sleepover."

Crystal snapped her fingers. "That's how we Robbies roll."

"Robbies?"

"That's what the girls call Whitney. 'Robbie' is short for Robinson."

"Interesting," Deborah drawled. She tapped her horn to get the attention of a driver drifting into her lane. "I really don't miss this."

"When are you going to let me drive?"

"When you get your license."

"I plan to take the road test this summer."

"As soon as you take the test and get your license, then you can drive me around."

Crystal gave her mother a puzzled look. "You don't like driving?"

"Not really. I drive because I have to, not because I want to."

"If that's the case, then I'll be your driver."

Deborah wanted to tell Crystal that when she did get her license the last thing she'd want to do was chauffeur her mother around, but decided not to. She turned and drove down King Street. "Where do you want to go first?"

"Finicky Filly."

Within minutes of entering the elegant boutique Crystal found the dress she wanted. It was red with spaghetti straps, a fitted bodice, and a skirt with four tiers of ruffles that ended at the knee. It was a perfect fit. Finding shoes proved a bit more challenging. The pair that Crystal wanted was in stock but they didn't have her size. After trying on half a dozen pairs, she finally selected a black silk pump with a three-inch heel that flattered her long, slender legs.

When Deborah suggested they eat out, Crystal said she wanted to go home because she had a history test the next day. During the return trip to the island Deborah did something she'd never done before: she took the causeway. She thought she'd imagined it, but the hair stood up on the back of her neck when she passed the marker for Angels Landing. People had talked about the town being haunted and now she believed it. She wasn't able to relax until they were back in the Cove.

Once there, Deborah prepared a quick dinner for herself

and Crystal, using leftovers from Sunday's dinner. After cleaning up the kitchen, she retreated to her bedroom and closed the door. Walking into the bathroom Deborah stripped off her clothes and stared at her naked body in the full-length mirror on the back of the door. Evidence of the time she'd spent with Asa showed on her breasts and thighs. There was no way she would have been able to explain to her children how she'd gotten the red splotches if he'd bitten her neck.

She smiled at her reflection. It had been years since she'd gotten a hickey. "Shame on you, Dr. Monroe." Her smiled faded when she said his title aloud. She couldn't believe he'd spent so many years studying to become a doctor, only to give it up when his wife and son died. At forty-six he was too young to retire, and she wondered what he intended to do once he left the Cove.

Deborah washed her face and brushed her teeth before pulling a nightgown over her head. She got into bed and reached for her journal. What she was feeling, what she had done earlier was still so intense that she had to write it down on paper.

February 12th—Asa and I made love for the first, second, *and* third time. It was as if I'd been dying of thirst and he was an oasis. I just couldn't get enough of him.

Making love with him was very different from what I had ever experienced, because Asa is totally uninhibited. I love it and I'm in love with him.

It was Thursday, The Parlor's late night, and as announced, the night of the raffle drawing. This was the first Thursday Deborah had worked since the bookstore opened. Usually on Thursdays Asa worked until eight, assuming responsibility for closing up. The bookstore was crowded and the excitement palpable; three gaily wrapped sweet-grass baskets were on display for those who'd dropped their tickets into the fishbowl.

Deborah signaled for silence. "I'd like to thank everyone who came out tonight for our first Valentine's Day raffle drawing. There will be other drawings for Easter, Mother's, and Father's Days."

"How about Grandparents' Day?" someone called out.

"That, too," she said, smiling. "How could I forget that day?" She picked up the fishbowl and stirred up the red tickets. "The first drawing will be for the basket with fruit, cheese, and sparkling cider. All of the baskets were made by our own Rachel Dukes-Walker." A smattering of applause followed this announcement. "Asa, will you please pick the first ticket?"

A murmur of approval rippled through the assembly when he came over and put his hand into the bowl and took out a ticket. He read the name and a scream went up as a young woman ran over to retrieve her basket. At the last possible moment, she put her arms around Asa's neck and kissed his cheek.

"Why she got to be so shameless?" whispered an elderly woman standing next to Deborah, who wanted to agree with her.

"The next basket is also a sweet-grass basket from A Tisket A Basket. This one contains bottles of red and white wine, cheese, crackers, Baci, and nuts." Asa pulled a ticket, but the person wasn't present. He pulled two more before they finally got a winner.

"The third and certainly not the least basket contains a bottle of Möet champagne, Godiva chocolate, and an assortment of gourmet cookies. And before we pull a ticket for this basket I'd like to tell the winners there is a bookstore gift certificate in each of the baskets." She nodded to Asa. He pulled the last ticket.

"The grand prize winner is Mabel Kelly."

Mabel ran over to claim her prize. "That's what I'm talking about!" she shouted. "Oh, damn! It's heavy." Everyone laughed.

"I'll carry it for you," Asa volunteered.

Mabel fluttered her lashes at him. "Thank you so much."

Deborah placed the bowl on the table. "I'd like to thank everyone for participating and for coming out tonight. And don't forget to be nice to your valentine."

She waited until the store had emptied, then lowered and closed the blinds, locked the front door, and went through the ritual of turning off lights and lamps, leaving one on at the back of the store. Punching in the PIN for the cash register, she counted the cash, leaving enough in the drawer to make change for the early morning customers.

The Parlor was thriving. The response to the book club discussions had generated a waiting list to join, and the same women attended afternoon teas. Asa alternated playing the piano with pre-recorded music, and customers seemed to sense whenever he was in the store because they came in droves.

She and Asa spent siestas upstairs in his apartment where they shared lunch *and* the bed, and when Deborah reopened at two she couldn't stop blushing or smiling. Making love in the afternoon had become a thrilling experience.

The back door opened and Asa entered. "It's beginning to rain."

Deborah closed the distance between them. "I'd better get home before it comes down too hard."

Cradling her face, Asa brushed his mouth over hers. "Can't you stay a little longer?"

She deepened the kiss, and then forced herself to pull away. "I would love to, but I have to make certain Crystal packs everything she needs for her sleepover."

Resting his hand on her hip, he pulled her closer. "When are we going to have a sleepover?"

"Tomorrow night. The kids are staying over in Charleston. I'll call you after they leave and you can come and get me. If my car is parked out back all night I think it would raise a lot of suspicion as to why I'm hanging out here after closing." Ironically the gossip Hannah had spread about her sleeping with Asa had died, when in reality they were *now* actually sleeping together.

"Tell them you're celebrating Valentine's Day with your man."

Deborah's eyebrows shot up. "Are you really my man, Asa? I didn't think so," she said when he didn't answer. "We're two ships passing in the night. And when it's over I'm certain I won't have any regrets and neither should you. Good night."

Asa stood there, amazed and very shaken that Deborah could be that disconnected when it came to their relationship. Yes, they were friends, but they had become much more. They were now lovers and every time he made love to her he found it more and more difficult not to blurt out what lay in his heart. He didn't want to leave her or

Sanctuary Cove, but knew his leaving was inevitable. The last time he'd checked his e-mail the reply was that he would receive a determination as to his status within three weeks. He'd looked at the calendar and had begun counting the days. Between now and March fourth he would know his fate.

Asa was suddenly attacked by a gamut of emotions. He was in love with Deborah, wanted to marry her, but he also wanted to fulfill his dream of working for DWB. Long ago, he'd talked to his son, telling Isaac that once he became a doctor and took over his father's practice Asa would become a humanitarian physician, offering free medical care to those in need and in war zones. But now, instead of joining Doctors Without Borders at sixty-five, it would become a reality at forty-six.

Chapter Nineteen

❧

This isn't the way to the bookstore, Asa."

"I know."

"You're driving toward the causeway. Where are we going?"

"Out."

"Out where?"

"I'm taking you to a place where we can have a proper Valentine's Day celebration."

She glanced down at her peach-colored twinset and chocolate-brown slacks. "I'm not dressed."

Asa gave her a quick glance. "You look okay."

"I don't want to look just okay, Asa. You could've told me beforehand and I would have at least put on some makeup."

"You look beautiful without it."

"If you don't tell me where we're going I'll—"

"You'll what?" he smiled. "You're not going to do anything but sit back and enjoy the ride *and* the night."

Pouting, she folded her arms under her breasts. "This

will be the first and the very last time I'll agree to a sleep-over with you," she said, trying to hide her excitement.

They rode in silence and Asa wanted to tell Deborah she was probably right; that was why he wanted this night for lovers to be a special one for them. He touched a button on the wheel and music flowed around them. Traffic was heavier than usual heading toward Charleston. Following the GPS, once they were on the mainland, he turned down a street and maneuvered into the drive leading to a small boutique hotel. "Don't move," he told Deborah as he parked, then got out and retrieved their bags from behind the front seats. Setting them on the ground, he opened the passenger-side door and extended his hand to help her out.

As Deborah looked around, Asa could see the realization in her eyes. "No, you didn't," she said softly.

He smiled and winked at her. "Yes, I did. See, I planned something special for us, and you caught a major attitude."

"I wouldn't have had an attitude if you'd told me where we were going."

"If I did, then it wouldn't have been a surprise."

A bellman came out to greet them. "Dr. and Mrs. Monroe?"

"Yes," Asa replied.

"Welcome, sir. I'll take these to your room while you check in."

Reaching into the pocket of his slacks, he handed the man a bill. "Thank you."

The bellman nodded. "Thank you, sir."

Asa rested his hand at the small of Deborah's back. "Come, darling. Let's check in, and then we can relax."

"When you made the reservation did you put me down as Mrs. Monroe?"

"No. He probably assumed you're my wife."

They walked into the converted mansion. Chandeliers, marble flooring, stately antiques, and reproductions of oil paintings of bewigged men graced the ornate lobby. She stood beside Asa as he gave the clerk a credit card and his driver's license.

The woman, with a peaches-and-cream complexion and friendly light-brown eyes, gave him a smile. "Your suite is ready. Go down the hall on your right. Suite 147 is at the end of the hall." She gave him two cardkeys. "Enjoy your stay."

Deborah looped her arm over Asa's as they walked down the carpeted hallway. "You are chock-full of surprises."

"I aim to please," he drawled.

"I'm pleased."

"Good."

Asa patted the hand on his arm. He slipped the key in the slot, waiting for the green signal, then pushed it open. Dozens of candles flickered in the semi-dark suite. When he'd called to make the reservation he had requested the special Valentine's package with candles, flowers, chocolate, and dinner with wine and champagne. He'd ordered wine because he remembered Deborah had little or no tolerance for bubbly.

He closed the door and caught her hand. "Let's see what the bedroom looks like." There were more candles in the bedroom, and there was enough illumination to see the California-king four-poster bed. Rose petals littered the sheets and pile of pillows.

They walked through the bedroom and into the bath. More candles lined a garden tub and the ledge of twin marble sinks. Porcelain dishes were filled with chocolate and flower petals. She returned to the bedroom to find their bags on luggage racks, and thick bathrobes spread over the foot of the bed.

"I love it, Asa. Thank you."

He walked over to her, took her face in his hands and nibbled her lip. "I'm the one who should be thanking you. Come over here. I ordered a little something to eat before we begin our sleepover."

They sat at the table in the dining area, eating steak frites, an Asian slaw, and a fruit salad with fresh pineapple, pears, strawberries, and shredded coconut. Asa drank two glasses of rosé to her one, and she didn't protest when he carried her into the bathroom and undressed her and then himself while the tub filled with water. She settled into the warm water, resting her head on a bath pillow. Asa stepped in and sat behind her and started up the Jacuzzi.

"Are you falling asleep on me?" he whispered in her ear.

"No. I'm just relaxing my eyes. Do you know what?" she asked, after a pregnant pause.

"What, baby?"

"I'll always remember this Valentine's Day."

Asa kissed her hair. "And I'll always remember you."

Deborah took a deep breath, trying to will away the negative thoughts that threatened the magic. She didn't know why she felt like crying. Maybe it was because something told her this would be their last time together even though Asa planned to stay until spring. But if he was going to leave, then she told herself she preferred now rather than later, before she found herself in too deep.

Did she know what she wanted from Asa aside from their lovemaking? Did she want him to be a part of her future? Or could she hope to become a part of his?

"What's frightened you, Debs? Your heart is beating so fast."

Deborah stared at the hand cradling her left breast. How had she forgotten he was a doctor and no doubt tuned into subtle changes in her body? "I was thinking about making love with you," she lied smoothly.

"That makes two of us. There are very few times when I'm *not* thinking about making love to you. If you were a drug, then you would be an opiate. Every time I hear the word 'siesta' it will remind me of making love with you."

"I'm that addictive?"

"Crazy addictive."

"That sounds serious, Dr. Monroe."

"You just don't know how serious I am."

Deborah reclined against Asa's chest while bubbles eddied over her body; moisture beaded her face and curled her hair. Her apprehension was slowly replaced by an inner peace that swept away her fear, uneasiness, and confusion. She was resigned to let Asa go.

"Are you ready to go to bed?"

She exhaled a lingering sigh. "I think so."

Asa stood up and stepped out of the tub. Reaching for a towel from a stack on a chair, he dried his body. He helped her from the tub, blotting the moisture from her body.

Deborah lay on her side, waiting for Asa to join her in bed. The suite was exquisite, the food and wine delicious, and her date generous, attentive, and sexy. *He* was the addictive drug—she never got enough of him. Whenever they made love during siesta, it was never enough for her, because she wanted seconds and thirds. Despite his asking her to delay going home after closing, she never did; she and Asa were consenting adults but she didn't want to flaunt her affair, risking that her children might become fodder for gossip.

A soft gasp escaped her when his hand slipped between her thighs. Deborah managed to turn until she was facing him. Her hand closed on his flaccid flesh, stroking gently until he grew hard and heavy against her palm. They had time to explore, arouse, and offer each other ultimate pleasure. Her fingers moved over the hard planes of his body like a sculptor admiring her design.

She snuggled against him, their limbs entwined. Her hand reached lower. Her fingers tightened until he gasped before she eased her grip. She repeated the touch over and over until Deborah found herself on her back with Asa inside her. The ferocity of his penetration sent her libido into overdrive. Grunts, groans, moans, arching, and thrusting punctuated the coupling—not lovemaking this time, but mating. They strained to get closer and together they found a tempo where their bodies were in perfect harmony. Waves of ecstasy held them captive until the dam broke, and they surrendered to a passion that left them shuddering from release.

It wasn't long after his heart rate slowed and erection had gone down that Asa realized the enormity of what had happened. He hadn't used a condom. Even when he'd been a randy teenage boy he'd never not used protection when sleeping with a woman. The only exception had been his wife. "Forgive me," he whispered hoarsely. "Please forgive me," he repeated over and over, his voice breaking.

Deborah cradled Asa's head to her chest. "Don't, Asa. I'm safe."

His head came up. "Are you sure?"

"Ninety percent sure."

Asa's eyes searched Deborah's. They were calm. "It won't happen again."

He pulled away from Deborah and lay on his back. Asa knew he had to tell her about what he'd planned for the next year. She had to know he wasn't some nomad wandering about the country, stopping only when he was too mentally and physically exhausted to go further.

"Deborah." Reaching over, he pulled her close to his body. "I need to tell you something."

"You're leaving."

"How did you know?"

"I feel it. Here in my heart," she whispered. "When?"

"As soon as I'm notified that I've been accepted by Doctors Without Borders."

Asa felt Deborah's heart skip a beat. "Doctors Without Borders?"

"Yes. I'd always planned to work as a humanitarian doctor when I retired, but after Claire and Isaac died I filled out an application. I'll know within three weeks whether I'll be going."

Deborah wanted to cry. But she didn't.

She wanted to scream and throw things. But she wouldn't.

"How . . . long have you been planning this, Asa?"

"I just told you..."

"No. How long did you plan to sleep with me before you leave town?" Jerking away from Asa, she sat up. "Why didn't you tell me your hopes before we started sleeping together?"

Asa pushed into a sitting position. "I never deceived you. You knew I wasn't going to stay."

She extended her hand, caressing his face gently. "You know, you're right, Asa," she said with a sad smile. "This is my mistake. It's just...when you announced at the town council meeting you were a snowbird I thought you would probably stay for the winter. And then when you came into the bookstore for a job, I was more than aware you were transient and temporary, but I guess I thought I meant enough for you to stay."

"You're wrong. It wasn't like that."

"I know, Asa, because it isn't like that." She turned to gaze into his eyes as she caressed his cheek. "You are a very special man, Asa Monroe. What kind of monster would I be to deny you the chance to help people who need you?"

"Deborah, I—"

"But I can't pretend this doesn't change things." A gentle kiss on the lips silenced him. "Good night, Asa."

Asa drove back to Sanctuary Cove and dropped Deborah at her house, then headed for the bookstore. Everything had changed when he decided to tell her about DWB last night. He knew she had a reason to be angry. She was right. He should've told her about his dream of practicing abroad even before he'd blurted out that he was a widower.

He hadn't told Deborah about Claire and Isaac; he'd told her children. He'd wanted to tell her that he loved her, but he thought she probably wouldn't believe that. What Asa hadn't wanted to acknowledge was his fear of losing her if he told her about DWB. He knew she was comfortable with his disclosure that he was a snowbird, because that left open the possibility that he would return the following winter. But once he was assigned to work in Africa he doubted whether he would ever return to Sanctuary Cove—or even the States, for that matter.

The thought pained Asa. He realized how much he was going to miss Deborah *and* her children. He wanted to get to know them better—form a relationship with them, especially after Crystal's heartfelt outburst at Sunday's dinner. She'd resented him for taking her father's position at the table, but he had been able to ease her fears. That made him feel good and had also helped him to deal with his own grief.

However, he hadn't been completely honest. When he'd returned to his apartment he realized that he did want to occupy that place at Deborah's table and in their lives, not just on Sundays but every day. Asa wanted to fill the void that Louis had left.

Asa had reminded Deborah over and over that despite losing her husband she still had her children, and now him, while all he had were memories. Painfully, he knew what he had to do. He had to make a clean break and leave Sanctuary Cove. The bookstore was doing well and it could practically run itself. And one thing he knew about Deborah Robinson: she was a survivor. She'd survived a scandal to protect her children. And she would survive what she viewed as his duplicity.

• • •

Deborah entered through the rear door of The Parlor, expecting to see Asa, and she wasn't disappointed to find him standing there waiting for her. "You're leaving today." The query was a statement.

"Tomorrow."

"You're welcome to stay until you hear from DWB."

Asa angled his head. "That would complicate everything. It doesn't matter what you think or believe, because this, what we have, isn't about sex. It was never about sex."

"What was it about, Asa?"

"You. Me. Friendship and feelings that go so deep they are impossible to explain. That's what it *is* all about. I'll write you. Every day. And that's a promise."

Placing a hand over her mouth, Deborah willed the tears filling her eyes not to fall. Not now, or she would blurt out how much she loved him. She sniffled. "I'll accept your promise, but never an apology."

He winked at her. "That's a promise. Now, close the door and give me a hug."

Deborah pushed the door closed and stepped into Asa's outstretched arms. She inhaled his familiar scent, committing it to memory. "Thanks for everything, friend."

Asa dropped a kiss on her curls. "You're welcome, friend."

Chapter Twenty

It was April and spring had come to the Lowcountry, bringing a foreshadowing of the intense summer heat that would make it impossible to remain outdoors for long periods of time.

Asa kept his promise to write every day. The postcards had stamps from Myrtle Beach, Brunswick, Savannah, Jacksonville, and Miami. Then they stopped for three weeks before they started up again, this time from South Africa.

She read the latest one:

Hi Debs,
Arrived in South Africa yesterday.
It's beautiful and hot. For the first time in my life I own a firearm. It's not to protect me from criminals, but from the wildlife.
I love my work and the people—especially the children. When I get a chance to go shopping I'll send you something for the bookstore.
Give Whitney and Crystal my best.

Love, Asa

"Mrs. Robinson, you're next."

Deborah put the postcard in her handbag and stood up. She'd made an appointment to see her doctor because she hadn't been feeling well. She woke up tired and went to bed tired. Maybe she needed vitamins or iron pills.

Forty-five minutes later she knew why she'd been so tired. She was pregnant! Deborah had told Asa she was ninety percent certain she wouldn't get pregnant, but she was wrong. The only reason she'd been so adamant was because she thought she knew her body. For years she and Louis had used the rhythm method and she'd never gotten pregnant, but apparently it hadn't worked with Asa. After all her preaching to Crystal about teenage pregnancy, safe sex, and marriage, she was going to be an unwed mother.

She drove back to Sanctuary Cove instead of taking the ferry, which would have made her nauseous. Deborah didn't want to believe that as a thirty-eight-year-old widowed mother of two teens she was going to start all over again with an infant. When her doctor mentioned she had options, her comeback was that her only option was to give birth to a healthy baby.

Deborah climbed the stairs to the porch and opened the door. She wanted to get into bed and sleep. When her children came in from school she would tell them that come Thanksgiving they could look forward to a new baby brother or sister.

Deborah sat on the living room sofa. Whitney was on one side of her, Crystal on the other. "I need to tell you guys something that will change your lives," she said quietly as she took their hands.

"Mama, you're scaring me." Crystal's eyes searched hers.

She squeezed Crystal's hand. "I don't mean to frighten you, honey, but you have to know."

"Know what, Mom?" Whitney asked.

"I'm pregnant." There, she'd said it. The two words Deborah were certain would rock her children's world.

"You can't be," Whitney retorted.

"But you're too old," Crystal cried.

"I am and I'm not too old," Deborah argued softly.

Crystal eased her hand out her mother's loose grip. "It's not Dad's."

"No!" Whitney shouted. "It's not Dad's. If it was she wouldn't have waited this long to tell us."

"Then, whose is it, Mom?"

Deborah sat up straight. "Asa Monroe's."

"Shit!"

"Whitney!"

"Where's your baby daddy?" he sneered.

"You're forgetting who you are talking to." She closed her eyes and squeezed the bridge of her nose, trying to relax. "I understand how you two must feel right now, but please adjust your attitude and watch your language."

Whitney didn't say anything further and neither did Crystal, although she rolled her eyes.

"I wanted to be honest with you both because this baby will be, is, your brother or sister, and I really need your support on this. You're my family and I love you." She smiled. "Besides, I won't ask you to babysit too often."

Whitney managed to look contrite. "I didn't mean for it to come out like that, Mom, but it's April and in four months I'll be leaving for D.C. You're going to need some-one to look after you."

Deborah patted his cheek. "I want you to stop wor-rying about me, Whit, and take care of yourself. You're going to live away from home for the first time, and trust me when I say it's not easy adjusting to living with strangers."

Placing a hand over her mother's flat belly, Crystal leaned into her. "Don't worry, Mama. You still have me. I'll help with the cooking and housework."

Wrapping an arm around Crystal's shoulders, Deborah kissed her daughter's hair. She'd taken her advice and was letting it grow out. "I'm going to pay someone to clean the house and the bookstore. We can take turns cooking." She kissed her again. "Okay, baby girl?"

"If you have a girl, then she'll be baby girl."

"No, Chrissie. You will *always* be my baby girl."

"Does Mr. Monroe know about the baby, Mom?" Whitney asked.

"No."

Deborah caught the look Crystal gave her brother as their eyes met. "Are you going to tell him, Mama?"

"No."

Crystal opened her mouth to ask why not when Whit-ney shook his head, warning her to let it go. "How are you feeling?" she asked instead.

"I tire easily. That's why I take naps," Deborah admit-ted, smothering a yawn with her hand. "You guys are on your own tonight, because Mama is going upstairs to lie down."

Waiting until their mother was seemingly out of ear-shot, Crystal pulled her legs up under her body and leaned closer to Whitney. "Why won't she tell him that he's going to be a dad?"

"I don't know, Chrissie. Maybe they had a fight before he left."

"Fight or no fight, Mr. Monroe should know about the baby. And it's up to us to find him."

Whitney scratched his chin. "We have his name, he's a doctor, and his car had a Delaware plate. I'll go online and see what I can come up with." He lowered his hand. "If he was Mom's employee, then she had to have some paperwork on him. Maybe you can go to the bookstore and see if you can find anything."

"The store is closed today," Crystal whispered. "Maybe if I get the key you can drop me off and we can check out her desk."

"I have a set of keys to the shop." Whitney rose, pulling Crystal up with him. "Let's go."

"Wait, Whitney. I'm going to leave a note for Mom to let her know we're going downtown. She doesn't have to know exactly where downtown."

"Okay, Sherlock. I'll be outside in the car."

Chapter Twenty-one

Lilongwe, Malawi

Dr. Asa Monroe's step was slow and heavy as his booted feet echoed on the rickety staircase leading to his quarters. He didn't think he would ever get used to triple-digit heat, the odor of sickness, and the smell of death.

He'd spent the past two weeks working at a remote village delivering babies, inoculating adults and children, and treating patients with diseases that had been eradicated in the States more than fifty years ago. And he still didn't have enough anti-venom to treat the snake-bite victims.

He unlocked the door and the exiting buildup of heat from within caused him to step back as if someone had opened the door to a blast oven. Setting his medical bag and rucksack on the floor, he flipped the switch for the ceiling fans. When he'd moved in there had been only one fan in the one-bedroom apartment, and that was in the bedroom. The next day he'd gone out and bought fans for the living/dining area and the kitchen.

Asa paid a woman to come and clean the apartment twice a week, although he was rarely there. It was simply his home base, where he picked up his mail and where he'd unwind while waiting for his next assignment. Sitting on a stool, he unlaced his boots, leaving them on the rush mat. Thick cotton socks followed. Within minutes he'd stripped off all his clothes and walked into the bathroom to shower away nearly three weeks of dirt, dust, and grime.

He brushed his teeth, and then opened the door to the stall, turned on the water, and stood under the spray of tepid water that was akin to rain soaking the dry, parched earth after a prolonged drought.

It wasn't until he'd returned to the apartment that Asa realized how bone-tired he was. Sleeping thirty-six consecutive hours still wasn't going to be enough. He felt every one of his forty-six years of living. Sleeping in a tent, with his hand grasping a high-powered automatic pistol in the event a wild animal would find its way inside, had disrupted his sleep pattern.

It was ironic how quickly he'd come to think of the apartment as home when home had once been a stately Colonial in a Dover suburb, or the space above the bookstore where he'd made love to Deborah. He'd continued to write her—every day—but had yet to receive a response. Asa had decided to give her until the end of the year and if she didn't write back then he would let her go—in his head and in his heart.

Asa never would've imagined having to grieve twice in just a year because he'd fallen in love for only the second time in his life.

Once the water ran clear, he picked up a bar of soap

and began lathering his body from head to toe. Although he'd been given a battery of inoculations he still feared succumbing to a parasitic infection.

He rinsed off, then repeated the ritual until he felt clean. A loud buzzing sound caught his attention, and Asa glanced up to find a large bug against the window screen. The bathroom had been a breeding ground for insects and reptiles before he'd requested the owner of the building replace all the damaged screens. Turning off the water, he stepped out of the stall, slipping his feet into a pair of rubber shower shoes. He smiled. The cleaning woman had remembered to leave the shoes where he'd instructed.

It was still so hot that he didn't need a towel to blot the water from his body. Walking into the bedroom, he sat on the side of the bed and picked up the letters that had been left there. Fanning the envelopes he looked for one with a Sanctuary Cove return address. His heart sank. Deborah still hadn't written. Falling back on the clean sheets, he supported his head on folded arms and fell asleep.

Suddenly, Asa jolted awake, totally disoriented. He didn't know whether it was night or day, or how long he'd slept. Swinging his legs over the side of the bed, he turned on the lamp, opened the drawer in the bedside table and took out his Netbook. He was thirsty and hungry but he needed to go online and connect with a world beyond the one into which he'd been assigned.

One of the reasons he'd accepted an apartment in this building was because it was wired for the Internet, and he had excellent cell phone reception. The tiny computer booted up and he was online in no time. There were ten new e-mails. A slight frown furrowed his forehead when he saw one with an e-mail address he didn't recognize, with the subject line: Urgent.

He opened it, his gaze scanning it quickly. Asa read it once, twice, and then a third time.

Dr. Monroe,

   Please call my mother because there is something she needs to tell you.

Respectfully,
Whitney L. Robinson

He glanced at the date of the e-mail. It was almost three weeks old. Rubbing his hands over his bearded face, Asa did something he hadn't done in more than six months: he prayed.

Slipping off the bed, he opened a drawer to the dresser and took out a pair of boxers and pulled them on. Retrieving his rucksack, he took out his cell phone and turned it on. It was of no use to him in the bush, but he'd tried to keep it charged.

The time on his computer indicated it was eight o'clock at night. That meant it was one o'clock in the afternoon in South Carolina. Asa scrolled through the phone's directory and dialed the number to the bookstore. If Deborah was in the store, then she would be alone because it was siesta. It rang three times before there was a connection.

"The Parlor Bookstore. This is Deborah. How may I help you?"

"Debs? Asa."

"Asa! How are you?"

"I'm good, but you already know that from my post-cards. You did get my postcards, right?"

"I did, Asa. Every one."

"Is... there something you need to tell me, Debs?"

"Yes, there is something I need to tell you," she replied quietly.

"Debs... hello?..."

"Are you sitting, Asa?"

"Should I?"

"Yes."

He moved over to a rattan chair with a distinctive kente cloth pattern and sat down. "I'm sitting."

"I'm pregnant. With your baby."

His eyes narrowed. "I thought you said you—"

"I know, Asa. Clearly I was wrong."

He was glad Deborah couldn't see him because his hands *and* knees were shaking. "Were you going to have my child and not tell me?"

"Yes."

"Why?"

"Why, Asa? Because I didn't want to use this baby to get you to come back to me."

Counting slowly to ten, he tried to compose himself. "I'm sorry."

"Don't you dare apologize. Just don't do it."

"What do you want, Deborah?"

He heard her breathing through the earpiece. "I want to carry to term and give birth to a healthy baby."

Asa smiled for the first time since hearing her voice. "I want that, too. What about your baby's father?"

"What... what about you?"

"Will you allow me to be in your life?"

"I won't keep you from the child, if that's what you're worried about."

"My God, Debs. How can you say that? This isn't only about the baby, Debs. It's about us. I love you. I love you with or without a baby, and if we're going to be together, then it has to be for each other."

"You love me and I love you, but we can't be together, Asa. You're so far away. You're on the other side of the world."

"I can apply for a hardship waiver. I'll probably have to wait for a replacement before I'm able to return to the States, but...I want to marry you, Deborah. I want to try to be a father to Whitney and Crystal and to that precious gift inside you."

"Can I give you my answer when you get back?"

"Of course, but..."

"We have so much to talk about...nothing to do with the baby...trust, and commitment, and..."

Asa clutched his chest. "You're not going to make this easy for me, are you?"

"I'm not trying to give you a hard time, Asa. I've decided to take a chance on love, and I don't want to go through what I did with Louis."

"And what's that?"

"He left me with his children."

"Okay." The single word was whispered.

"Can you answer one question for me?" Deborah asked.

"Sure. Anything."

"Why did you call me?"

"One of the kids e-mailed me."

"Please don't tell me it was Whitney?"

Asa laughed when he heard her incredulous tone. "Yes, Whitney."

"I told him about—"

"Leave the boy alone, Deborah. He's only trying to protect you. He won't have to do that much longer because once I get back that will be my responsibility."

"When do you think you're coming home?"

"I don't know, but I hope it's soon."

"Asa?"

"Yes, baby?"

"I love you."

Asa pulled his lip between his teeth, biting until it throbbed like a pulse. "I love you more." When he finally ended the call he knew he had been given a second chance.

A second chance at love.

A second chance to be a husband.

And a second chance at becoming a father.

Chapter Twenty-two

Three months later

Deborah tried to adjust the neckline of her dress in an attempt not to reveal too much cleavage. "I'm spilling out of this," she said when she saw Asa's reflection in the full-length mirror. She turned to face her fiancé. "Look at my breasts."

Asa angled his head. "They're like lush fruit."

She gave his shoulder a playful slap before staring at the man who, within the hour, would become her husband. He looked incredibly handsome in a tuxedo, white shirt, and Winsor-knotted pearl-gray silk tie. The African sun had darkened his skin to a rich sable-brown.

When she'd seen him come through the terminal at the airport Deborah had hardly recognized the man she'd fallen in love with. He was bearded and noticeably thinner. Instead of dropping him off at the bookstore, she'd brought him home where he'd showered and then closed the door to her bedroom and slept for twelve straight hours. It had taken almost a month for his appetite to return, and he'd regained six of the twenty pounds he'd lost.

Once he'd applied for a hardship waiver, it had taken nearly three months for DWB to get a doctor to replace him. But now he'd returned to Sanctuary Cove to live and set up a practice. It would be the first of its kind in the Cove, as residents had relied on midwives to deliver their children and on facilities in Charleston for all other medical emergencies.

A contractor had begun work to renovate the vacant storefront only doors from The Parlor where he would hang out his shingle for his family practice.

"The dress is scandalous, Asa. I'm going to faint if Reverend Crawford stares at my breasts instead of my face."

He chuckled then, easing her fears. They would marry at the Abundant Life Church, then host a reception under more than a dozen tents along the beach for everyone in the Cove. When Deborah had decided to come home she never would have imagined she'd love again while continuing the cycle of perpetuating the precious Gullah culture.

Cradling her to his chest, Asa kissed her forehead. Her hair, brushed off her face, was pinned into a chignon. Miniature roses and baby's breath had taken the place of a veil. The off-white, empire-waist dress with its seeded-pearl bodice artfully concealed her swollen belly.

She was in the last month of her second trimester and had only gained fifteen of the twenty pounds recommended by her obstetrician. Although high-risk, her pregnancy to date had been complication-free.

"Every man in Sanctuary Cove will be looking at you

this afternoon," Asa crooned. "You are just that beautiful. And the best part is, you'll be coming home with me." He rested a hand on her belly, feeling the baby's movements. A sonogram had revealed that he and Deborah were going to have a boy.

There came a knock on the door and Asa and Deborah found Herman and Pearl Williams outside the bedroom. Pearl's eyes filled with tears when she saw her daughter and soon-to-be son-in-law. "Oh, darling, you look beautiful." Pearl was stunning in a pale gray chiffon gown that flattered her tall, slender body. Her curly hair was more gray than red, and there were tiny lines around her eyes that had come from squinting in the brilliant Florida sunshine.

Deborah hugged her mother. "Oh, Mom, I am *so* happy!"

"Darling, you deserve it."

"I feel truly blessed, Mom," Deborah said as both of them brushed happy tears from their eyes.

Pearl placed a hand on Asa's arm, leaning in to press her cheek to his. "I know you'll take care of my precious babies," Deborah heard her mother whisper in his ear.

"That is something you'll never have to worry about, Pearl. I will take care of and cherish my family."

Whitney and Crystal walked into the room, stopping short when they saw their mother in her wedding dress. Whitney had flown in from Washington, D.C., for the weekend to stand in as best man at his mother's wedding.

"You look great, Mom. Wow!" Whitney complimented.

"You look kinda hot for a pregnant lady," Crystal quipped.

Herman Williams shook his head and smiled at his grandchildren. His features were Gullah and his speech still had a lingering trace of an accent that Gullahs recognized as their own. "Let's go, Crystal. The limo and the driver are waiting downstairs to take us to the church."

As Crystal headed for the staircase, Herman reached for his daughter's hand and gave it a squeeze before the two embraced.

"I'm so happy for you, sweetheart. You look gorgeous."

"Thanks, Dad," she said, gleaming.

"I'm looking forward to giving you away in marriage. I didn't have the privilege the first time, but I knew the moment I was introduced to Asa Monroe that you'd chosen a man who would not only take care of you, but my grandchildren, too."

"Oh, Dad," Deborah beamed.

They hugged again before Asa put an arm around her waist and led her out of the bedroom and down the staircase.

Soon, Deborah stood in the vestibule of the church with her father and Whitney, waiting for the familiar sound of the "Wedding March." Even as a little girl she'd fantasized about having a string quartet at her wedding and now it was finally happening. Whitney had shocked her when he'd announced he was doing double duty as Asa's best man, while sharing the honor of giving her away with his grandfather. She'd given her bouquet of miniature white roses and a delicate gardenia to Crystal when she realized she wouldn't have a free hand.

Whitney peered through the oval window in the door leading directly into the church. "There's standing room only, Mom."

Before she could reply, the opening of the "Wedding March" filled the church.

"I'm ready."

Those were the last two words she said before the ushers opened the door and Herman and Whitney led her down the white carpet to where Asa stood at the altar, smiling.

Her fingers tightened on her father's and son's arms as she saw familiar faces of the Cove residents in the pews. Her mother was dabbing her eyes, Barbara was grinning like a Cheshire cat, and Mabel gave her a thumbs-up.

Reverend Malcolm Crawford pulled back his shoulders under a flowing black robe. "Who gives this woman in marriage?" he asked, his sonorous voice carrying easily in the large church.

"We do," Herman and Whitney said in unison.

They took Deborah's hands, placing them in Asa's when he reached out for her. Whitney took his position on Asa's right, while Herman turned and sat down next to his wife.

Deborah smiled at Crystal, who looked ravishing in a rose-pink empire silk chiffon gown, before she turned her adoring gaze on the man who unknowingly had changed her and her life the instant their eyes had met in the Muffin Corner.

She felt as if she were a spectator instead of a participant in her wedding as she listened to Reverend Crawford talk about the significance of marriage as he recounted the story of the wedding at Cana. Her gaze never wavered when she and Asa repeated their vows. Whitney had given Asa the diamond eternity band to slip on her finger, and Crystal repeated the motion when Deborah slipped the wide gold band on Asa's hand.

"By the power vested in me by the state of South

Carolina, I now pronounce you husband and wife. Asa, you may kiss your bride."

Deborah didn't have time to catch her breath before she found herself in her husband's arms, his mouth covering hers in a passionate kiss that nearly sucked the breath from her lungs as the baby kicked vigorously in her womb.

Placing a hand over her belly, Deborah pressed closer to Asa. "I love you so much," she whispered.

Asa kissed her hair. "I love you, too, Mrs. Monroe."

Her chest swelled with love *and* happiness. She'd wept, mourned, and laughed. Now it was time to dance, and never stop dancing, with the man with whom she would share her love and her life.

Reverend Crawford raised his hands in a prayerful gesture. "My brothers and sisters, I'd like to present Dr. and Mrs. Asa Monroe."

There came a loud applause as Deborah hugged and kissed Crystal, then Whitney. Her eyes filled with happy tears when Asa hugged Whitney and patted his back. The two had grown close since Whitney had enrolled in Howard.

She and Asa proceeded down the aisle and out of the church, where they were showered with rice, bird seed, and flower petals. They stood long enough to pose for photographs before the wedding party went over to the fountain in the town square for official wedding photos.

Water flowed from the marble fountain as Asa wound one arm around his wife's expanding waist, the other around Crystal's lithe body. The realization that he was now a husband, a father to a teenaged son and daughter, and looking forward to becoming a father again when Deborah gave birth to their baby boy, was almost overwhelming.

He was going to open a family practice only doors from The Parlor, and when he closed up and went home for dinner it would be to share it with his family. "Is that your stomach growling?" he whispered in Deborah's ear.

Smiling, she nodded. "Mama's hungry and so is baby."

Asa raised his hand, signaling the photographer. "Let's finish up here, so we can go down to the beach. My wife needs to eat."

After a half dozen more frames, Herman, Pearl, Crystal, Whitney, Deborah, and Asa headed for the beach. There all of Sanctuary Cove, as well as the mayors and town council members from Haven Creek and Angels Landing, had gathered under tents to celebrate the traditional Cavanaugh Island wedding reception.

Once they'd arrived, Asa asked a member of the waitstaff to prepare a plate for Deborah, then sat beside her and fed her portions of broiled fish and steamed vegetables. "Please, no more," she pleaded quietly a little while later. "I can't eat another bite."

Leaning closer, he kissed her ear then gazed at her gorgeous face, unable to take his eyes off her as she rocked slowly to the music. A deejay had set up his equipment in a tent and was spinning tunes that had people singing, dancing, and swaying to the infectious music.

Reaching under the tablecloth, Deborah squeezed his hand. "I'm going to make mad, crazy love to you tonight."

Throwing back his head, Asa laughed loudly. "You won't get an argument from me, Sunshine. In fact, I'm looking forward to it."

Turn the page for a preview
of the newest book in the
Cavanaugh Island series,

Cherry Lane!

The brilliant afternoon sunlight shimmered off the numerous steeples and spires dotting Charleston's skyline. Despite the fatigue weighing her down from more than five hours of flight delays and layovers, Devon Gilmore found herself in awe of the sight that gave South Carolina town its Holy City nickname.

She grabbed her handbag and took out enough money for the fare and tip for the taxi ride from the airport to the city's historic district. She felt some of tension ease as the taxi drove down the broad tree-lined avenues and pulled up to the historic Francis Marion Hotel. When she'd complained to her friend Keaton Grace about the frigid, snowy New York City weather, he'd suggested she come to the Lowcountry for several weeks, and this visit was exactly what she needed right now. As much as she loved the bright lights and bustle of New York City, she was ready for a change. And going to Chicago to see her parents had been an utter disaster.

The taxi driver came to a complete stop at the same

time the bellhop rushed over to open the door for her. "I'll get your luggage, ma'am."

"Thank you." She'd brought her large, black quilted Vera Bradley spinner and matching roll-along duffel and stuffed them so full she could hardly lift it. The first order of business would be finding an outfit for the party Keaton had convinced her to attend this evening.

Devon placed a hand over her flat belly. She wasn't showing yet, but it wouldn't be long before her baby bump became visible. She took a deep breath. Even the air here smelled different—clean and sweet. Like a fresh start.

Devon wasn't particularly in the party-going mood, but she'd promised Keaton she'd go to his girlfriend's birthday party out on Cavanaugh Island. He'd reassured her that it was only going to be close family and friends. Maybe the distraction would do her good, especially the way her life was unraveling at the seams right now.

She slipped into the skirt to her suit and managed to zip and button it without too much difficulty. The waistband was tighter and tonight would probably be the last time she would be able to wear it for a while. Sitting on the chair at the table that also doubled for a desk, Devon reached the cosmetic bag. Flicking on the table lamp, she took out a small mirror with a built-in light. She stared at her reflection, noticing that although her face was fuller, there were dark circles under her eyes. Opening a tube of concealer, she squeezed a small dot on her finger and gently patted the liquid under each eyes and blended it to match her natural skin tone.

When she initially found herself facing an unplanned pregnancy, Devon realized she had two options: give up the baby for adoption, or do something no other woman in her family had ever done—become an unwed mother. It had taken a lot of soul-searching, but in the end she decided she would keep her baby. After all, she was already thirty-six. And her job as an entertainment attorney afforded her a comfortable lifestyle.

What she refused to dwell on was the man whose child she carried. They had slept together for more than a year, and at no time had he given her any indication that, not only was he involved with another woman, but he was also engaged to marry her. This revelation would have been so shocking to Devon if she were not pregnant. His cheating on her was bad enough, but how she'd uncovered his betrayal had affected her even more.

An hour later Devon stood in front of the Tanners' three-story Colonial. She walked up four steps to exquisitely carved double doors flanked by gaslight-inspired lanterns. A larger, matching fixture under the portico and strategically placed in-ground lighting illuminated the residence. She'd just raised her hand to ring the doorbell when she heard the low purr of another car pulling up.

Turning around, she saw a tall man get out of a late-model Lexus sedan. He paused to slip on a suit jacket and she couldn't help admiring the way the fine fabric fit his lean frame and broad shoulders. As he walked her way he deftly adjusted his emerald-green silk tie. Golden light spilled over his sculpted dark face and neatly barbered cropped hair.

"Are you here for the party?" he asked her.

The sound of his soft, drawling voice elicited a smile from Devon as she lifted her chin, staring up at him through a fringe of lashes. Not only did he have a wonderful voice, but he also smelled marvelous.

"Yes," she answered.

He smiled, drawing her gaze to linger on his firm mouth. "I had no idea Francine had such gorgeous friends."

Devon lowered her eyes as she bit back her own smile. The compliment had rolled off his tongue like watered silk. She wanted to tell him he was more than kind on the eyes but she'd never been that overtly flirtatious. "Thank you."

The tall, dark stranger inclined his head. "You're quite welcome." He rang the bell and then opened the door. Stepping aside, he let her precede him. "You must not be from around here because folks on the island usually don't lock their doors until it's time to go to bed."

"I'm a friend of Keaton Grace. I just got in from New York."

"Ah, well that explains it." He extended his hand. "David Sullivan."

A beat passed before Devon took his hand. "Devon Gilmore," she said in introduction. Truly, she was Devon Gilmore Collins, but just like her mother, she'd been raised to uphold the vaunted Gilmore tradition. And given her current state of being unwed and pregnant, her mother was no longer speaking to her.

"Well, it looks as if you two don't need an introduction."

David released Devon's hand. "Happy birthday, Red," he said to the tall, slender woman with a profusion of red curls framing her face. Angling his head, he kissed her cheek. Then he reached into the breast pocket of his suit jacket and handed her an envelope.

The redhead patted David's smooth cheek. "Thank you. Everyone's here," she said. Turning, she offered Devon her hand. "I'm Francine Tanner."

Devon shook her hand. "Devon Gilmore," she said, smiling. "Thank you for inviting me to your home."

Francine's green eyes crinkled as she returned Devon's smile. Her eyes matched the silk blouse she'd paired with black slacks. "Any friend of Keaton's is always welcome here. He had to go upstairs and should be back at any moment." She looped her arm through Devon's over the sleeve of her suit jacket. "Come with me. As soon as Keaton returns he can introduce you to everyone before we sit down to eat. And David, I want to warn you that my father is making Irish coffee again this year. If it were up to him, he would celebrate St. Patrick's Day every day."

Devon gave Francine a sidelong glance. "Is that good or bad?"

Francine laughed. "It all depends on your tolerance for alcohol. Yours truly learned a long time ago to pass, but most folks who've drunk Daddy's Irish coffee swear it's the best they've ever had."

Devon acknowledged each person with a smile and a nod when Francine introduced her to Jeffrey Hamilton and his wife, Kara, then Morgan Shaw and her husband, Nathaniel. Devon also met Francine's parents, Frank and Mavis.

"Next is David Sullivan, but it appears you two already know each other," Francine said with a wink.

Devon couldn't stop the rush of heat suffusing her face as everybody turned her way with questioning looks. She wanted to tell the others she'd just met him, but decided to let them draw their own conclusions.

"Does anyone need a refill before we sit down to eat?" Frank asked.

Mavis gave her husband a glance. "Sweetheart, it's

time we eat while we're still able to see how to pick up a fork."

The words were barely off Mavis's tongue when David extended his arm to Devon. She curled her hand into the bend of his elbow and could immediately feel the heat of his body against hers. She didn't want to read too much into the gesture, but it still felt good to be tucked against him.

Everything about David radiated breeding and class—qualities all Gilmore women looked for in a suitable partner. For a brief moment she wondered how her mother would react if she showed up on her doorstep with David on her arm. Would it make her condition more acceptable?

Devon's jaw dropped slightly when walking into the formal dining room, feeling as if she was watching an episode of an antebellum *Downton Abbey*. Prisms of light from two chandeliers shimmered on the silver and crystal place settings. The table was covered with a delicately crocheted cream-colored cloth and green liner, with seating for twelve. A hand-painted vase overflowing with white roses, tulips, and magnolias served as an elaborate centerpiece. A mahogany buffet server held a bevy of chafing dishes from which wafted the most delicious mouth-watering aromas. Keaton had introduced her to Lowcountry cuisine when she'd come to Sanctuary Cove to discuss the dissolution of his business relationship with his brother-in-law.

Devon found her place card, fortuitously right next to David's. She got a little thrill in her belly when he pulled out a chair for her. Whoever said chivalry was dead was definitely wrong, she mused. It may have been considered old-fashioned in other parts of the country, but the practice was alive on Cavanaugh Island. All the women sat, while their men lined up at the buffet table to fix them a plate.

She'd lost count of the number of times when men in New York lowered their heads and feigned sleep rather than get up on the bus or subway to give a woman their seats. And forget about holding open a door or helping a woman into or out of her coat.

"I'll bring you a plate," David offered. "Is there anything you can't eat or don't like?"

A slight shiver of awareness swept over Devon at his proximity. David was being so kind, but it wasn't the same as having someone who knew you inside and out bring a plate of food. Gregory, bastard that he was for cheating on her, would've known that she always took extra gravy and disliked rhubarb. Although an inner voice told her that her ex-lover wasn't worth her tears or angst, moving on wasn't easy. After all, he'd given life to the tiny baby growing inside her. A tentative smile trembled over her mouth.

"No allergies, and I'll eat just about anything. Thank you so much, David."

"No problem." He put a comforting hand on her shoulder and squeezed. Devon swore she could feel the heat right down to her toes.

Morgan caught her eye from across the table. "How long are you going to be here?" Morgan asked her.

"Probably for a month." She didn't tell the beautiful, tall dark-skinned woman with the dimpled smile that she wanted to stay until Northeast temperatures no longer hovered around the freezing mark. Although she'd grown up in Chicago and had managed to survive countless frigid winters in New York City, somehow this year was different. Despite wearing multiple layers, Devon still found herself chilled.

"Where are you staying?" Morgan asked.

"I have a suite at the Francis Marion, but I'm hoping to move to the Cove Inn by Wednesday so I can be closer to Keaton when we have to go over legal issues. I've always been a hands-on attorney when it comes to Keaton." Devon had shepherded his career from the time he wrote scripts for daytime soaps to his becoming an independent filmmaker.

"You can stay here with us," Francine chimed in. "I have an extra bedroom in my apartment."

Mavis shook her head. "She can stay down here with me and Frank. We have six bedrooms in this house, and that's not counting my mother-in-law's and Francine's apartments."

Devon was in a quandary. As tempting as the invitation was to sleep in the Tanners' historic home, she didn't really feel up to living with strangers. But she also didn't want to insult them by turning down their Southern hospitality. "I don't want to impose."

Mavis waved her hand. "Child, please. There's no imposition. We have the room, so you just move yourself out of that hotel tomorrow and come and stay with us. And I'm not going to take no for an answer."

Devon sat there, hands clasped together in her lap, as she attempted to bring her emotions under control. People she'd met for the first time had welcomed her into their home, while her own mother had slammed the door in her face.

Smiling, she blinked back tears. She couldn't believe she was going to start crying when she'd earned the reputation of being a no-nonsense, hard-nose, take-no-prisoners attorney. It had to be the hormones. "Please let me think about it. I promise to let you know after the weekend."

A slight frown appeared between Mavis's eyes. "I'm going to hold you to that promise."

Francine pressed her palms together as her eyes sparkled like polished emeralds. "Even if you decide not to stay with us, I still want you to join Kara, Morgan, and me for our Monday afternoon get-together at Jack's Fish House. It's the only time we can get to see one another, because I work at the salon Tuesday through Saturday, Kara just became a new mother, and Morgan is busy with her architectural and interior design company."

This was a proposition Devon could easily agree to, to connect with women her own age. "What time should I meet you?"

"Twelve noon," Kara said, smiling.

Devon returned the sheriff's wife's warm, open smile. She was scheduled to pick up a rental car the following morning, so she'd have the independence she needed to do some sightseeing on her own.

Five minutes later she looked down at the plate David set in front of her. He'd selected fried chicken, red rice and sausage, collard greens with cornmeal dumplings, and a slice of corn bread. "There are also sweet potatoes, ribs, Gullah fried shrimp, perlow rice, and barbecued trotters and turkey wings," he informed her.

"Thank you. This looks delicious. I'll make certain to save enough room for seconds," she said as she spread her napkin over her lap. Devon was amused that he'd referred to pig's feet as trotters. The Gilmores eschewed pig's feet, ears, chitterlings, cheeks, and other parts of the pig they deemed scraps. It wasn't until she moved to New York and visited several Harlem soul food restaurants and sampled sloppin' trotters and chitlins for the first time that she wanted to call her mother and let her know the scraps were to-die-for.

As David returned to the buffet, she wondered if he was always so buttoned up. Of all the men there, he was the only man wearing a suit. But then she was forced to look at herself, realizing she was the only woman wearing a skirt. Maybe it had something to do with their profession.

Devon turned down Frank's offer of a sparkling rosé and noticed that Kara and Morgan did the same. She thought Kara was a probably nursing, but was Morgan pregnant too? It would be so nice if she could talk to another woman going through the same thing.

At that moment, Dinah Tanner entered the dining room, and the men rose to their feet to greet her. The petite, slender woman had short, graying strawberry-blond hair and wore a leaf-green shirtwaist dress. "Everyone please sit down," she said, waving her hand in dismissal.

Frank pulled out a chair for his mother. "Do you want me to fix you a plate, Mama?"

Dinah smiled up at her son. "No thank you, Francis. I'll get it later."

Frank tapped his water glass with a knife. "I'd like to thank everyone for coming to help celebrate my baby's birthday." He ignored Francine when she pushed out her lips. "I know she doesn't like it when I refer to her as my baby, but that's who she'll always be to me. This birthday is very special, not only because I'm sitting here with the women who've made me the happiest man on Cavanaugh Island, but also because there's a man sitting at my table whom I'm honored to think of as a son." He raised his glass in Keaton's direction. "Keaton. Welcome to the family. Now, let's eat!"

Devon and the others sat down again, picked up their utensils and began eating. "I overheard Mavis inviting you to stay with her," David said in a quiet voice. "If you don't feel comfortable living in someone's home I can get you a room at the Cove Inn tonight."

She blinked once. "What are you going to do? Have management boot some elderly couple so I can get their room?"

Throwing back his head, David laughed. "Nothing that drastic," he said, sobering quickly. "My law firm reserves several suites for out-of-town clients. They seem to prefer the laid-back atmosphere of the island to some of the Charleston hotel chains."

Devon's eyebrows lifted slightly. Her internal antenna had just gone up. In the past, if a man did anything for her, he usually wanted something in return. It was either money or free legal advice or representation; however, it was never something for nothing. Now a man she'd met less than an hour ago had offered to put her up at the boardinghouse in his business-related suite.

What, she thought, did he want from her?

Kara Newell has been named the sole proprietor to a gorgeous estate in South Carolina. But the sudden change in her fortune has made her a target.

Will the charming sheriff sent to protect her keep her safe?

Angels Landing

Please turn this page for an excerpt.

Chapter One

"Good morning, ma'am. May I help you?"

Kara returned the receptionist's friendly smile with a bright one of her own. She'd recently celebrated her thirty-third birthday and it was the first time she'd ever been called "ma'am," but then she had to remind herself that she wasn't in New York but in the South. Here it was customary to greet people with "yes ma'am" and "sir," rather than "missy" or "yo, my man."

"I'm Kara Newell and I have a ten o'clock appointment with Mr. Sullivan," she said, introducing herself.

The receptionist's smile was still in place when she replied, "Please have a seat, Miss Newell. Mr. Sullivan will be with you shortly."

Kara sat in a plush armchair in the law firm's waiting area. The walls were covered with a wheat-like fabric and framed prints depicting fox hunting scenes. When she'd planned to take the much-needed vacation from her social worker position at a New York City agency for at-risk children, she never would've anticipated it would take her to Charleston, South Carolina, instead of Little Rock, Arkansas.

The certified letter from Sullivan, Webster, Matthews, and Sullivan requesting her attendance at the reading of a will had come as a complete shock. When she'd spoken to Mr. David Sullivan, Jr., to inform him that she didn't know a Taylor Patton, the attorney reassured her that his client had been more than familiar with her.

Kara had called her parents to let them know she wouldn't be coming to Little Rock as scheduled, because she had to take care of some business. She didn't tell her mother what that business was, because it was still a mystery as to her why she'd been summoned to the reading of a stranger's will.

She unbuttoned the jacket to her wool pantsuit. Although the temperatures had been below freezing when she'd boarded a flight in New York City, it was at least fifty degrees warmer in Charleston. One of the things she'd missed most about living in the South was the mild winter. By the time the jet touched down, Kara barely had time to hail a taxi, check into her downtown Charleston hotel room, shower, and grab a quick bite to eat before it was time to leave. She sat up straight when a tall, slender black man approached her.

"Miss Newell?"

Pushing off the chair, Kara smiled. "Yes."

"Good morning, Miss Newell. David Sullivan," he said in introduction, extending his hand.

His hand was soft, his grip firm, which took her by surprise. As she took in the sight of him, she realized he didn't quite fit the description she'd had. The one time she'd spoken to Mr. Sullivan there was something in his tone that made her think he was much older than he looked. Now, she doubted he was much older than she. Conservatively dressed in a navy-blue pinstriped suit, white shirt, blue-and-white dotted tie, and black wingtips, he released her hand.

"It's nice meeting you, Mr. Sullivan."

David Sullivan inclined his head. "Same here, Miss Newell. It's nice having a face to go along with the voice." Taking her elbow, he led her out of the waiting area and down a carpeted hallway to a set of double ornately carved oak doors at the end of the hallway. "I'd like to caution you before we go in. I don't want you to reply or react to anything directed toward you. Taylor Patton was my client, and that means indirectly you are also my client."

A shiver of uneasiness swept over Kara like a blast of frigid air. What, she mused, was she about to walk into? For the first time since she'd read the letter she'd chided herself for not revealing its contents to her mother.

"What are you talking about?" Kara asked.

"I can't explain now, Miss Newell. But I want you to trust me enough to know that I'm going make certain to protect your interests."

When the doors opened Kara suddenly felt as if she were about to go on trial. The room was filled with people sitting around a massive rosewood conference table. She heard a slight gasp from the man sitting nearest the door, but he recovered quickly when she stared at him. The resemblance between her and the man was remarkable. So much so that they could have been brother and sister. But Kara didn't have a brother—at least not one she was aware of. She was an only child. The hazel eyes staring at her were cold, angry.

David directed her to a chair at the opposite end of the room, seating her on his left while he took the place at the head of the table. He still hadn't revealed to Kara why he'd wanted her to attend the reading of the will of Taylor Patton, but his caution was enough to let her know she was involved in something that was about to change her life. The fact that she resembled several of those in the conference room led Kara to believe there was the possibility she just might have been related to the deceased.

Resting her hands in her lap, Kara listened as David informed everyone that a stenographer would record the proceedings, asking those present to introduce themselves for the record. Kara glanced at the stenographer sitting in a corner, fingers poised on the keys of the stenograph machine resting on a tripod.

David touched her hand, nodding. "Kara Elise Newell," she said, beginning the introductions. One by one the eleven others gave their names.

The men were Pattons, while the women were hyphenated Pattons, with one exception. Kara glanced at Analeigh Patton's hands. Unlike the others, her fingers were bare. A hint of a smile inched up the corners of Analeigh's mouth and a slow smile found its way to Kara's eyes.

Everyone's attention was directed toward David when he cleared his voice, slipped on a pair of black horn-rimmed glasses, and opened the folder in front of him. " 'I, Taylor Scott Patton of Palmetto Lane, Cavanaugh Island, South Carolina, do hereby make, publish, and declare this to be my Last Will and Testament, hereby expressly revoking all wills and codicils, heretofore made by me.' "

Kara felt her mind wandering when David mentioned

that as the executor he would judicially pay the deceased's enforceable debts and the administrative expenses of Taylor's estate as soon after his death as practicable. Taylor hadn't married; therefore there was no spouse to whom he could have bequeathed his belongings. All of the Pattons leaned forward as if the motion had been choreographed in advance when David paused briefly. Then he continued to read.

"'I do give and bequeath to my daughter, Kara Elise Newell, all my personal effects and all my tangible personal property, including automobiles owned by me and held for my personal use at the time of my death, cash on hand in bank accounts in my own name, securities, or other intangibles.'"

Kara went completely still, unable to utter a sound as pandemonium followed. The room was full of screams, tears, shouts of fraud, and threats to her person. Another two minutes passed before David was able to restore a modicum of civility. "Ladies, gentlemen, please restrain yourselves. Remember, this proceeding is being recorded, so please refrain from threatening my client. By the way, there is more."

The man who had glared at Kara stood up. "What's left? My uncle has given *this impostor* everything."

"Please sit down, Harlan. I can assure you that Ms. Newell is not an impostor."

Kara wanted to agree with the Pattons. Austin Newell, not Taylor Patton, was her father. She closed her eyes, her heart pounding a runaway rhythm as David outlined the conditions of what she'd inherited: She must restore Angels Landing to its original condition; make Angels Landing her legal residence for the next five years; and allow the groundskeeper and his wife, who would receive a lump sum of fifty thousand dollars, to continue to live out their natural lives in one of the two guesthouses. In addition, she could not sell any parcel of land to a non-family member without unanimous approval of all Cavanaugh Island Pattons; and the house and its contents could only be deeded to a Patton.

She opened her eyes and let out an inaudible sigh when David enumerated names and monies set aside in trust for three grand-nephews and two grand-nieces for their college education. This pronouncement satisfied some, but not all. There were yet more threats and promises to contest the will.

Twenty minutes after she'd entered the conference room, Kara found herself alone with Taylor Patton's attorney. Holding her head in her hands, she tried to grasp what had just happened. She hadn't risen with the others, because she wasn't certain whether her legs would've supported her body. David had warned her not to say anything and she hadn't, but only because she couldn't. Reaching for the glass of water that had been placed before her chair, she took a sip.

David removed his glasses and laced his fingers together. "So, Miss Newell, you are now the owner of a house listed on the National Register of Historic Places and two thousand acres of prime land on Cavanaugh Island."

Kara's eyelids fluttered as if she'd just surfaced from a trance. "I'm sorry to inform you, but Taylor Patton is not my father."

David's eyes narrowed. "Did your mother ever mention Taylor Patton's name?"

She shook her head. "No. The only father I know is Austin Newell."

"Well, I can assure you that you *are* Taylor's biological daughter. In fact, you are his only child."

Kara closed her eyes. When she opened them they were filled with fear and confusion. "How is that possible?" The query was a whisper.

"That is something you'll have to discuss with your mother. I, on the other hand, have legal proof I'll use if your cousins decide to contest the will. Meanwhile I suggest you talk to your mother about your paternity."

She would talk to her mother, but not over the phone. What she and Jeannette Newell needed to discuss had to be done face to face. Combing her fingers through her hair, Kara held it off her forehead. "Please tell me this is a dream."

David sat on the edge of the table, staring at Kara's bowed head, a look of compassion across his features. "Even if I did, it still wouldn't change anything." Reaching into the breast pocket of his suit jacket, he took out a small Kraft envelope, spilling its contents on the table in front of her. "These are keys to the house in Angels Landing, Taylor's car, and his safe deposit box in a bank in Sanctuary Cove."

Kara released her hair, the chin-length, chemically straightened strands falling into place. "Where's Sanctuary Cove?"

"It's on Cavanaugh Island, but southeast of Angels Landing. Do you have a rental?"

"No. I took a taxi from the airport to the hotel."

"Good."

"Good?" Kara repeated.

David smiled. "Yes. It means I don't have to get someone to drop it off for you. I'm going to have our driver take you back to the hotel so you can pick up your luggage, and then he'll take to you Angels Landing."

"I'm sorry, but I'm planning to leave for Little Rock tomorrow."

"Can you hold leaving off for a few days?"

"David. May I call you David?" He nodded. "When you wrote and asked me to come here I never could've imagined that the man I've believed was my father all these years, is not my father. Not to mention that I now have a bunch of cousins who can't wait to put out a hit on me so they can inherit my unforeseen assets, assets I don't need or want," Kara said.

"Are you saying you're going to walk away from your birthright?"

Fall in Love with Forever Romance

PASSIONATELY YOURS
by Cara Elliott

Secret passions are wont to lead a lady into trouble... The third rebellious Sloane sister gets her chance at true love in the next Hellions of High Street Regency romance from bestselling author Cara Elliott.

THIEF OF SHADOWS
by Elizabeth Hoyt

Only $5.00 for a limited time! A masked avenger dressed in a harlequin's motley protects the innocents of St. Giles at night. When a rescue mission leaves him wounded, the kind soul who comes to his rescue is the one woman he'd never have expected...

Fall in Love with Forever Romance

RESCUING THE BAD BOY
by Jessica Lemmon

Donovan Pate is coming back to Evergreen Cove a changed man . . . well, except for the fact that he still can't seem to keep his eyes—or hands—off the mind-blowingly gorgeous Sofie Martin. Sofie swore she was over bad boy Donovan Pate. But when he rolls back into town as gorgeous as ever and still making her traitorous heart skip a beat, she knows history is seriously in danger of repeating itself.

NO BETTER MAN
by Sara Richardson

In the *New York Times* best-selling tradition of Kristan Higgins and Jill Shalvis comes the first book in Sara Richardson's contemporary romance Heart of the Rockies series set in breathtaking Aspen, Colorado.

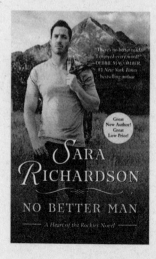

Fall in Love with Forever Romance

WEDDING BELLS IN CHRISTMAS
by Debbie Mason

Former lovers Vivian and Chance are back in Christmas, Colorado, for a wedding. To survive the week and the town's meddling matchmakers, they decide to play the part of an adoring couple—an irresistible charade that may give them a second chance at the real thing...

CHERRY LANE
by Rochelle Alers

When attorney Devon Gilmore finds herself with a surprise baby on the way, she knows she needs to begin a new life. Devon needs a place to settle down—a place like Cavanaugh Island, where the pace is slow, the weather is fine, and the men are even finer. But will David Sullivan, the most eligible bachelor in town, be ready for an instant family?

Fall in Love with Forever Romance

SANCTUARY COVE
by Rochelle Alers

Only $5.00 for a limited time! Still reeling from her husband's untimely death, Deborah Robinson returns to her grandmother's ancestral home on Cavanaugh Island. As friendship with gorgeous Dr. Asa Monroe blossoms into romance, Deborah and Asa discover they may have a second chance at love.

ANGELS LANDING
by Rochelle Alers

Only $5.00 for a limited time! When Kara Newell shockingly inherits a large estate on an island off the South Carolina coast, the charming town of Angels Landing awaits her...along with ex-marine Jeffrey Hamilton. As Kara and Jeffrey confront the town gossips together, they'll learn to forgive their pasts in order to find a future filled with happiness.